EMBER AND THE
ICE DRAGONS

Heather Fawcett

Balzer + Bray
An Imprint of HarperCollinsPublishers

For all the girl scientists,
whether human or dragon

PROLOGUE

Lionel St. George, aspiring Magician and Stormancer, was fed up.

For two days, he had been traveling through peat bog and prickly moorland. His exhausted horse had started to stumble, so Lionel had left it to wander its way back home at the edge of Muckross Fen, a particularly wild and desolate corner of Wales. Muckross Fen was exactly what you would expect from a place of that name—smelly; filthy; the air sharp with biting midges. There was also no sign of the magical storm, the sole reason he had come to the forsaken spot in the first place.

Lionel—just turned eighteen, with swirls of yellowish hair tumbling over his forehead and a series of pimples spread across his cheeks like indecisive punctuation marks—set his lightning bucket down in the heather and sat on it. He was tired, his feet were soaked, and it was a long hike back to the ramshackle tavern that his map optimistically labeled a village.

The sky began to drizzle. The storm he had been chasing through the Gwynedd Mountains had vanished.

Lionel decided he would hike to the nearest peak to survey the area before admitting defeat. And rather than trying to pick a path around the enormous fen, he simply plunged himself, clothes and all, into the murky water.

Green mountains loomed over him, clouds clustered at their peaks like frowning eyebrows. Lionel shook his storm compass, a small wooden box containing a moonstone and a single feather. How could the storm have dissipated so quickly?

Not all storms were sources of magic, but some were—that was why Stormancers chased them. If he had caught up to one that size, he could have drawn enough power from it to cast a dozen spells—or, perhaps, one very large spell.

Lionel's supply of magic was too low for the spell he wished to cast—a spell that, if it succeeded, would be the talk of the country, and surely that would be enough to change the minds of the professors who had rejected his application to London's Chesterfield University of Science and Magic.

He had scored highly on the written exam, but the practical test hadn't quite come off. He had cast an excellent firelighting spell—if only he had stopped there! But, wanting to impress the grim-faced professors, Lionel had shaped the fire into a giant floating orb. Unfortunately, a bee had chosen that moment to land on his shoulder, and Lionel—terrified of all insects—had lost his concentration in a spectacular fashion. By the time the fire had been put out, the professors were clothed in burned rags, and one had lost her eyebrows.

Lionel shuddered as a leech burrowed into his calf. The wind whispered past his ear. Wind had a language, like anything else, though no human could speak it—not even Lionel, who spoke to storms. But he thought he detected an undercurrent of anger.

Lionel hauled himself out of the muck on the opposite bank. He had lost a shoe somewhere, he noted absently, not particularly troubled. Lionel was rarely troubled by anything, not for lack of troubles (he had plenty), but because his thoughts were usually elsewhere. He wandered up the hill, heather prickling his bare foot and the leech gnawing away contentedly, its presence already forgotten. Then he stopped.

On the other side of the hill was a dead dragon.

Lionel's breath froze. Like most people, he had never seen a dragon, though the Natural History Museum had some remarkable skeletons—they were perhaps twice the size of a horse, with thinner, serpentine frames. Someone— hunters, no doubt—had removed the creature's scales, every last one. What remained was red and raw.

Though it was a dragon, a monster, Lionel felt a stab of sorrow. The sight of the fearsome creature sprawled awkwardly in the mud and stripped of its glorious scales felt wrong.

He found the second dragon—they usually lived in pairs—over the next rise. As he gazed at it, a tear opened in the clouds, and sunlight poured through. It tangled in the muddy grass, where something sparked. Lionel drew the object from the mud, brushing it clean with trembling fingertips.

It was a heartscale.

His mouth fell open. Everyone knew that the heartscale was the most important part of a dragon. An arrow through the heartscale, located at the back of the neck, would kill instantly. Most hunters preferred to avoid this, however, for the heartscale was exceptionally valuable. Half the size of Lionel's palm, it glittered with a color richer than rubies, deeper than amber, and threaded with veins like fired gold. The hunters wouldn't have left it behind knowingly—someone must have dropped it.

Pocketing the heartscale, Lionel stood, shivering in his wet clothes. This far north, the wind was woven with frost even at midsummer. He heard a faint sound.

Lionel brushed aside a clump of gorse. A baby dragon stared back at him.

He started back with an undignified yelp. The dragon blinked rapidly, but it showed no sign of fear. Its gaze was calm and unsettling, neither human nor animal, but simply *dragon*. It lay on its side, barely breathing, still half in its shell.

"All right there," Lionel found himself murmuring,

once he'd regained command of his voice. It clearly wasn't all right—the creature looked to have hatched within a day or two, perhaps just after its parents were killed. Now it was exhausted and likely starving. He removed the remnants of the shell, and the dragon stretched, though it made no move to get up.

Lionel worried his lip between his teeth. He couldn't simply leave the creature, though it was a beast that, fully grown, would think nothing of tearing him limb from limb. The best course, then, was to put it out of its misery.

The dragon made a faint sound in its throat. It was about the size and shape of a hairless cat, all sinuous lines, with scales the rich orange of molten lava. Lionel could have bought half of Chesterfield University with the profit from those scales, though the thought never occurred to him. He would bury the creature, scales and all, next to its mother.

At that moment, thunder exploded in the sky, and the clouds broke open like cracked eggs.

Lionel was instantly drenched. A small river ran past the dragon's snout, and it sneezed. Hesitantly at first, then eagerly, it began to drink.

The dragon wasn't as close to death as he'd thought—as it drank, its eyes lost their filmy quality. It fumbled around in the mud, as if to stand, and immediately fell over. It turned to Lionel and let out a surprisingly loud mewl, as if the entire situation was his fault.

Well, that settled it.

The young Magician stripped off his cloak and swaddled the dragon with it. The beast gave a satisfied snort and lay quiet in his arms, absorbing the heat from his chest. Lionel tried not to think about its proximity to his throat, but the dragon showed no interest in devouring him. It closed its eyes and slept.

After snatching up his knapsack and the lightning bucket from the muddy bank, Lionel hiked back in the direction he had come. He was covered in filth, and his clothes were so wet they made a strange *slop-swish-slop* sound as he moved, as if he were some mythic creature risen from the bog. He attempted to arrange his cloak around the dragon so that it would have the appearance of a human baby. A Magician wandering off into the moors and returning with an infant was certainly strange, but it was within the realm of eccentric Magician behavior, while dragons were not. Unfortunately, the creature's tail kept slipping free, ruining the disguise.

Lionel's thoughts churned. What was he to do with a dragon? He could feed it and restore it to health, but what then? He couldn't offer it to another dragon to raise—even if such a thing were possible, there were few fire dragons left. Only a handful remained here in Wales. The newborn could well be the last of its kind.

His thoughts circled and wheeled around the problem until, because he was Lionel St. George, they turned to magic again. How was he to impress the professors at Chesterfield now? He was beginning to doubt that his idea of an exceptionally powerful delousing spell would be enough. (Many of Lionel's spells involved eradicating insects.) If he wasn't admitted to Chesterfield, that was the end of everything he had ever longed for. Lionel was poor, and an orphan—his only living relative, his sister Myra, was in prison. Chesterfield was the sole school to offer free tuition to those of significant magical ability.

As the dragon began to snore, Lionel had the first inkling of an idea. It was stranger and more impractical than any idea he had ever had, and so it appealed to him immensely. The wind moaned and the rain pelted, and still the baby dragon slept on, oblivious to both the returning storm and the whirl of Lionel's thoughts. It burrowed its snout into the Magician's cloak, its tail twitching from some dream, as Lionel turned and walked back into the wind and thunder and hail, his cloak billowing and the storm compass flickering to life.

ONE

MAGICAE ET SCIENTIA

*The largest fire dragon ever documented inhabited the
Lithuanian marshes: it was twenty-four feet from nose to tail tip,
with three-foot horns and a fearsome set of teeth. . . .*

—*TAKAGI'S* COMPENDIUM OF EXOTIC CREATURES

Twelve years later

E mber St. George sat in the smoking ruin of what had
been her father's office, lost in thought.

"That wasn't very good, was it?" said the shadow in
the corner.

Ember shushed it. The shadow, used to her habits by
now, fell silent. This lasted about a minute.

"I don't care for these incidents." The shadow examined its sleeve, as if the fire might have scathed it. "Just
look at this place. The furniture is ruined."

"You don't use the furniture," Ember said icily. She
hated being interrupted when she was thinking.

"I look at it."

Ember didn't reply. Lionel St. George's office at Chesterfield University was cluttered with instruments—telescopes

and scales and sextants, both magical and scientific, and books piled upon books. She had spent many afternoons curled up in the chair by the window, lost in an encyclopedia or watching the globes spin. Her favorite was enchanted, orbited by a model of the moon that accurately waxed and waned. Now it was all ash. She picked up the tiny moon, and it drifted apart like the head of a dandelion. Tears welled in her eyes.

"I would prefer if you could warn me when you're going to catch fire." The shadow folded its arms. "It's most alarming."

"I'm sorry that it bothers you."

"It's not the sort of thing you see every day," continued the shadow, which had no concept of sarcasm. "A twelve-year-old girl bursting into flames—of course, you're not really a girl. How did it happen this time?"

Ember tried to sift through her guilt. She had been sitting by the window, reading a book on oceanography. She hadn't noticed the sun as it crept around the side of the building, spilling golden light across the page. Until her skin began to tingle in an awful, familiar way—

"The curtains," she said. "The servants must have left them open."

Ember didn't know why sunlight made her burst into flames. Nor did her father. It was a flaw in the spell that had transformed her from a dragon into a girl, a flaw he hadn't been able to fix. The episodes were random—some days, she could spend hours in the sun without incident. Other times, brushing against a sunbeam made her go up like dry tinder. What they did know was that she was far more volatile in summer. This made some sense, for fire dragons' powers were ruled by the sun—their flame burned fiercest on midsummer days, when the earth tilted toward its star. At night, or in winter when the sun hung wan and feeble in the sky, Ember was fine. Safe.

The shadow paced the room, on the lookout for left-over flames. But there were none—when Ember ignited, it was brief and white-hot. Next to the charred fireplace stood Lionel's favorite chair, a towering throne of oak and velvet, now a rickety skeleton. Ember picked at the remnants of her dress, which was missing a sleeve and half the skirt. Her hair had caught fire, too—it had been short before, from previous immolations, but now it clung to her scalp like the bristles of a brush, the blond hidden under all the soot.

"I don't want to leave," she whispered, so quietly that the shadow didn't hear. It was true that she'd been bursting into flames more often these days, and going somewhere with less summer would probably be wise. Her father would sometimes muse about moving them to Greenland or Svalbard—which, while no doubt interesting places, were not home.

The last few years had not been easy for Lionel St. George, and having to worry about Ember's sudden infernos surely didn't help. He was one of the most famous Stormancers in the country. After graduating from Chesterfield and being offered a professorship, he had rescued a duke from a group of bandits with a spell that made leaves sprout from the bandits' noses—which, while not particularly deadly, had been so disturbing that the bandits had run off. But he had also been arrested for an experiment that enlarged a frog to the size of the house. The sight of it hopping across the countryside had sparked a wave of terror and inspired horror stories that were still used to frighten naughty children. Chesterfield hadn't fired him for that. They *had* fired him for giving one of his students the ability to fly—unfortunately, that was all she could do, and so she was forced to walk around with her boots weighted with rocks to keep from floating away. That was the third time he had been fired, and Chesterfield had only grudgingly (after pressure from the rescued duke) taken him back last month.

"What about the lightning bucket?" the shadow asked fearfully. "Is it all right?"

Ember gasped. She raced over to the closet where Lionel St. George kept his extra magic. The door was scorched, the handle half melted. Fortunately, on the other side of the door, the bucket was unscathed. An unassuming thing of yew with a leather handle, it sat on its shelf, humming gently.

She patted it, relieved. No one was born with magic, but Stormancers were born with the ability to shape it.

They gathered it from thunderstorms, which theologians thought were created when the gods fought among themselves up in heaven, accidentally spilling their magic in the process. Lionel, who didn't believe in gods, thought that magical storms were a natural phenomenon as old as the earth. This was perhaps why he didn't treat magic as reverently—or carefully—as other Stormancers, keeping it in a simple bucket rather than a gilded chest or elaborate nesting trunks.

Ember shut the door. She had no idea what would have happened if she had burned the lightning bucket, releasing the magic from its protective spells. Perhaps it would have unleashed a magical storm upon her father's office, which was just about the last thing she needed right now.

Puff wandered into the room, nose twitching at the smoke. The unfriendly cat was fond of Ember (or perhaps cats preferred dragons to humans generally) and followed wherever she went. She was about the weight of an ordinary cat, but appeared almost perfectly round. Years ago, when Lionel St. George had been experimenting with language spells, he had given the cat the power to speak. Puff had been so startled that her white fur had stood on end. Somehow, all the magic in the air had made her stick that way.

"Now!" the cat said. This was her favorite word, which she applied to almost every situation. Cats had little interest in conversation and spoke mostly in commands.

"Now what?" Ember said.

Puff sniffed up to a teacup left on the desk. "Eat!" This was her second-favorite word. "Now now now now—"

Ember hushed her.

"I live here, you know," the shadow said, folding itself back into its corner. "If you could try to be less dramatic—"

"I'm not *dramatic*," Ember said. "If I could stop this, I would."

"It's almost summer." An ominous note entered the shadow's thread of a voice.

Ember swallowed. Her hand went to her ring. The setting held a fragment of red fireglass, which Lionel St. George had recovered from the place where her parents had been killed. It had likely come from her birth father.

She needed to get away from the shadow, to go somewhere she could think and plan and plot. Thinking her way out of bad situations was her special talent.

She was afraid, though, that there *wasn't* a way out of this.

"Lionel?" came a voice from the hall. "There's a dreadful smell. Are you at one of your experiments again?"

The voice was an elderly woman's—one of the other professors, no doubt—and it came from just beyond the door.

"Oh no!" Ember breathed. "What do I do?"

"How am I supposed to know?" The shadow sounded irritated. It was Lionel St. George's shadow, or had been at one time. Once shadows were detached, they were their own people, and nothing like their former owners. The shadow in the corner was fussy and uptight and occasionally menacing, though it liked Ember and her father well enough, in its curmudgeonly way. Ember often wished her father had never detached his shadow—he hadn't intended to do so, but as usual, one of his experiments had gone awry.

Fortunately, he had been able to trap it with magic before it could run away. Ember had no idea what would have happened if the shadow *had* run away—whenever she asked, her father gave a shudder and changed the subject.

"Lionel?" The door began to push open.

Ember jumped out the open window in one smooth motion, leaving the shadow staring after her.

She landed on a rosebush, which took its revenge by tearing her remaining sleeve. There came a scream from the office, but she was running again, into the twilight that enveloped Chesterfield's mossy stone buildings. She looked back and saw that the fire hadn't just burned her father's office. There was a blackened hole in the roof, and the statue on the green below the window—Beatrice August, discoverer of Stormancy—was completely scorched.

Ember ran faster. She didn't know where she was going. She just wanted to be far away.

Chesterfield sat atop an artificial hill in the heart of the city, on the Thames just west of the Tower of London.

The hill and the university had been built at the same time, more than five hundred years ago—the hill offered Chesterfield's Stormancers the perfect vantage from which to spot approaching storms. Ember fled through the rose garden and past the observatory, her feet silent against the flagstone path. Every stone had been painstakingly inscribed with Chesterfield's crest: *Magicae et Scientia*, it read in Latin, over an open book out of which reared a dark cloud. Magic and Science—the two forces that shaped the world.

Ember preferred Science. She could spend hours gazing at motes of dust under a microscope, or studying the formation of canyons or the strange creatures that lived in the deepest parts of the sea. She wanted to be a zoologist, in preparation for which she had begun memorizing a new species every week from Takagi's *Compendium of Exotic Creatures*. She tried not to think about how her flammability might affect her chances of keeping a job.

A group of students stood talking in the lantern light ahead. Normally, Ember would have gone around them, but today she simply pushed through, ignoring their mutters. One of her invisible wings brushed against a young man, and he batted at his arm, as if he'd felt an insect. For some reason, this made her tears flow faster.

Finally Ember stopped in the shadow of the ivy-veiled library. Then she spread her wings and leaped into the twilight.

The library had a steepled roof, and Ember liked to crouch at the very peak, one leg draped over either side as if the roof was a horse that might buck the earth and go soaring into the sky.

The night air was heavy with the smell of old stones and magic, which had a moist, purplish scent. Only Ember could smell it—humans and Stormancers, including her father, were all oblivious. She breathed it in—it was the smell of home. London stretched out below, halved by the silvery Thames and wreathed in tendrils of smoke. Kiteships drifted up and down the canals—though their decks were the size of an ordinary sailboat, each bore a half-dozen sails as tall as buildings, in bright colors that reminded Ember of butterflies. A row of glass-walled submarines waited to dock at Bankside Quay, ready to carry passengers to France or Ireland or beyond. The stars seemed so close she felt she could reach up and pluck them from the sky like berries.

She thought about the time her father had taken her to the mountains in Wales—the stars had been even brighter there. The two of them had made campfires and hunted for stoats and flown so high that a lacework of frost settled on Ember's skin. Her father didn't often bring her along when he traveled—chasing magical storms was a dangerous business—but when he did, they had a marvelous time.

She looked out over the university with a hungry sort of yearning, the spires and gabled roofs and cobbled streets shaded by ancient trees. Chesterfield had two colleges: Perseid College of Science and Owlworthy College of Magic. Between the two was a long promenade lined with statues of famous Magicians and Scientists. Her gaze roved over the professors' residences, a row of stately stone buildings where she lived with her father in a cozy flat. Next she found the Bridge of Moans, the botanical gardens, and the Reading Wood, a grove of horse-chestnut trees where students lounged and studied and engaged in regular chestnut fights. Ember had secretly instigated several of these herself. She liked to scamper up the trunks to launch her own missiles at unsuspecting students, who invariably blamed each other.

The wood was her favorite place, for it was also where you could find foxes and hares and slowworms and at least ten species of birds. She could sit for hours in the treetops, observing owls chasing mice, mice fighting over burrows, and all the other small dramas that were part of everyday life in the woods. She liked animals—there was something restful about them, unlike people.

When she wasn't in the wood, or curled up with her books, Ember spent much of her time gliding about the university like a sylph, taking advantage of its many nooks and groves and hidden passages—she preferred being unseen. It was safer to go unnoticed.

There came the sound of claws skittering over the eaves, then a strangled "Now!" as Puff sprang over a gargoyle and landed at Ember's side.

"I don't have any food," Ember said as the white cat sniffed her pockets. Puff placed her paws on Ember's leg.

"Warm!" she demanded.

Ember settled the cat on her lap. The breeze was cool, which was a relief, for Ember's skin still tingled. The fire didn't hurt her—apart from her hair—but that didn't mean it was pleasant to burst into flames like an inconvenient phoenix. Ember was just as nervous about the approaching summer as the shadow in the corner.

Minutes turned into hours, and still Ember didn't move. She gazed at the shadowy Tower of London, where her aunt Myra, Lionel St. George's younger and only sister, had once been imprisoned. Tiny lights flared along the streets as the lamplighters finished their work. She wondered how long she could stay up there. Perhaps she would never go down—she would remain on the roof until the wind and rain hardened her into a gargoyle. The birds would land on her wings—birds weren't fooled by magic—and make nests in her hair, and moss would creep slowly up her legs.

Her thoughts were interrupted by a strange flapping sound as her father floated into view. Lionel St. George was wearing his flying cloak, which was woven with raven feathers like a giant wing. His wavy hair was all over the place as usual, made worse by the wind he had summoned.

At thirty, Lionel looked much the same as he had at eighteen, pimples and all, apart from the dark circles under his eyes. It was a common trait of Stormancers, who spent many of their waking hours chasing storms from one corner of the country to another. Like all Stormancers, Lionel also glinted slightly, like a coin turned toward the sunlight, while his eyes shone in the dark like a forest creature's.

"There you are!" he exclaimed, settling beside Ember on the roof. Then his face fell, as he remembered he was supposed to discipline her for going up on the roof again. "Ember—ah, I don't think—"

"I'm sorry," Ember said quickly. "I shouldn't be up here. I won't do it again."

He looked relieved. "Yes, quite. That's it exactly. Good, good."

"You're back early," Ember said as dread settled over her. Normally when her father returned from a trip, it was an occasion to celebrate. Not this time.

His face lit. "Yes, I caught up with the storm sooner than expected. It was a very productive journey." Lionel St. George almost crackled with magic—it must have been a particularly powerful storm, perhaps one of those that lurked over the Atlantic. A moth circled his head, drawn by the energy. He eyed it suspiciously.

"I'm guessing you haven't seen your office," Ember said.

"I did stop by, yes." His tone was mild and not remotely

angry. For some reason, this caused Ember to burst into tears.

"There, there." Her father drew her into a hug, earning a hiss from Puff. "Think nothing of it, Ember. It's not your fault."

"Of course it was my fault." Ember wiped her hand across her face. "There weren't any other dragons in your office today. Now you'll get in trouble."

Lionel gave a vague shrug. "I'm used to trouble by now, my dear. Besides, I had been wishing for more time to work on my next book. . . ."

Ember froze. "They fired you again."

"Well . . . I believe that was the gist, though the rector didn't exactly use those words. I'm afraid I can't repeat the words he *did* use, but—"

"They fired you," Ember repeated. She felt as if she was falling head over heels toward the lamplit city. "Because of me."

"Because of the statue, specifically," he said. "The only surviving likeness of Beatrice August. Personally, I think a little charring is an improvement—gives her a bit of flair, doesn't it? Though the rector didn't take my view of things." He squeezed Ember's shoulder. "The statue doesn't matter, my dear. Nor does my job. They'll hire me back eventually—particularly if I can ever perfect that cockroach-to-chocolate spell! What matters is that you're all right."

Ember bit her lip. *She* was all right. But what if she had hurt someone? What if, instead of a statue, she had burned Puff? What if her father had been in his office? This time, she had gotten him fired—what if worse happened next time?

She couldn't let that happen. It was too terrible to think about.

"You were right," she said. "It's not safe for me here. Especially with summer coming. You should send me away. To Russia, or Greenland—I'll go anywhere, as long as it's cold."

Her father blinked. "Ember, I will not *send you away*. Now, if I was able to travel, we could go somewhere together—I've always wanted to visit Canada, haven't you? Polar bears! Northern lights! But as I'm not, at present, allowed to leave the country—a silly overreaction on the part of the police, of course—"

"We have to do something," Ember said. She pictured the blackened statue. What if that had been a student? "It's happening more often."

Her father looked away, but not before Ember had seen the shadow cross his face. Lionel St. George wasn't practical—that was the problem. She was going to have to be practical for both of them.

Ember gazed at the Tower in the distance. Lights flared in the battlement where her aunt had been imprisoned. She had an idea. "What if I went to stay with Aunt Myra?"

Her father blinked. "Myra?"

"Isn't she in charge of a Scientific research station?" Ember said.

"Ember," Lionel said, "your aunt Myra's research station is in *Antarctica*."

"But it would be perfect." Ember hurried on. "There's not much chance I'll catch fire there. And I'd like to learn about her research."

Her father winced. He did that whenever his sister came up, which was rarely. Ember had never met her—though she visited London occasionally, either she or Lionel always seemed to be too busy to see the other. While in prison, Myra St. George had earned multiple Scientific degrees by correspondence. Normally, a convicted thief would be an unusual choice to run a research station, but as Lionel had once said, there was a shortage of Scientists willing to spend months in the coldest, most remote part of the British Empire. "It wouldn't be appropriate. Your Aunt Myra is a thief."

"A reformed thief, according to her last letter," Ember said. Her father had left it lying around, as he did most things. "She promised she hasn't stolen a thing since she went to Antarctica." Privately, Ember had thought that this wasn't much of a promise, given that there was nothing to steal in Antarctica. But her aunt had sounded perfectly nice, even if she had used an odd amount of exclamation points.

"She isn't afraid of me, is she?" Ember asked.

"Not at all," her father assured her quickly. "She knows you aren't like the stories."

Ember chewed her lip. Dragons were said to be vicious killers—they hunted for sport, often tearing their victims apart. She was glad that she wasn't like that, even if she didn't understand why. The spell her father had cast had changed her form, not her *essence*. Her lack of interest in eating people or other dragonish qualities was as much a mystery to her as it was to her father, though as he often mused, no one really knew what dragons were like. Fire dragons were extinct. She was the last.

Ember felt a familiar pang, like an echo of a half-forgotten dream. She would have been terrified to meet a dragon. And yet something inside her always whispered, *Who were they?* And, *Who am I?*

She wrapped her arms around Puff. "Tail!" the cat yelped.

Her father squeezed her shoulder. "My dear, you don't have to go anywhere. I'm still working on a way to stop this. I'm certain I'm close."

Ember suppressed a sigh. Her father had been trying to stop her from bursting into flames for years, but no amount of magic had any effect. The flaw in the original spell was difficult to pinpoint. That spell had been imperfect in more ways than one, as evidenced by Ember's wings, which had, for some reason, refused to transform with the rest of her. For the first few days, she had been a winged baby, which hadn't gone over well with the midwife who had examined her. Finally, failing to find a way to correct the first spell, short of turning Ember back into a dragon (which he couldn't manage either), her father had simply cast a second, making her wings invisible. They were still there, which made it necessary to avoid both crowds and hugs from strangers—neither of which Ember cared for anyway.

"That's enough serious talk," her father said. "Let's get off this roof before the librarians raise a fuss."

Ember followed him to the ground, her thoughts whirling. A heavy sort of resolve settled in her stomach like a stone. If her father wouldn't take steps to protect himself from her, she would have to do it herself. One way or another, she was never going to burst into flames again.

TWO

THE ORPHEUS

*Fire dragons have given rise to many legendary stories. Among
these is the belief that these solitary beasts passed their lives
in the clouds that gather on mountaintops, and would immediately
perish upon contact with the earth.*

—*TAKAGI'S* COMPENDIUM OF EXOTIC CREATURES

Two weeks later, Ember gazed up at the demiship looming over the Thames. Half submarine and half ocean liner, its glass hull allowed its passengers to gaze out into the depths of the sea. Men and women jostled past the dock, off to work or to errands elsewhere in the city, part of its smoky, rippling fabric. Ember felt a pang of homesickness, which made little sense, for she hadn't left yet. She was even homesick for things she didn't like, such as the raucous parties of the first-year student Magicians, and the cantankerous raccoon who lived in the roof of the banquet hall, which everyone thought was the ghost of the cantankerous chef.

"Well!" her father said. He had been saying that a lot recently, in a falsely hearty voice. He looked down at her and muttered, "Ember, are you sure about this? There's still time to change your mind, my dear."

He looked so hopeful that Ember almost relented. But then she thought of Beatrice August, and her father's office, and the spring sunshine dancing on the Thames. "I'm sure."

He sighed. "Your aunt's letter caught me unawares, I admit. I haven't heard from her in months. Now here she is, out of the blue, inviting you to Antarctica. She's always expressed an interest in meeting you, of course, but I just thought we'd all go to a teahouse. . . ."

Ember said nothing. She had written to Aunt Myra herself, without her father's knowledge, explaining the situation as delicately as she could, leaving out phrases like "burst into flames" and "burned down my father's office." It had been a gamble, but it paid off—Aunt Myra had written her father immediately to invite her to stay, and had seemed quite excited by the prospect, judging by the abundance of exclamation points in the letter, some of which even leaped into the middle of sentences. Her father, huffing, had finally relented—after much pleading from Ember—and agreed to allow her to stay with her aunt until the end of the summer.

Lionel wrapped her in a hug. "At least you'll be back in time for the start-of-term banquet. Perhaps we'll have a celebration of our own! The shadow and I have a few ideas. . . ."

Ember smiled, though she couldn't meet his eyes. She

wouldn't return to London while she was still dangerous. She wouldn't risk her father's life, or Puff's. Or anyone else's.

Which meant, in all likelihood, that she would never return.

She didn't want to leave. Leaving felt like running away. But what else could she do? She felt a surge of helpless anger that was growing increasingly familiar. She didn't know who or what she was angry at, which somehow just made her angrier. Would London change while she was gone? Would Chesterfield? Would her father be all right without her? He sometimes became so obsessed with his experiments that he forgot to eat unless she reminded him.

"Your aunt seems to think you'd like Antarctica," her father said grudgingly. "She says it's a fierce place—and quiet. That sounds rather like you."

Ember smiled in spite of herself.

Her father's voice dropped. "I will sort this out, Ember. It was my fault in the first place. If I hadn't been so hasty in casting that spell—"

"That spell saved my life," Ember said. She hated it when her father talked like this. It made her feel like he had made a mistake in adopting her, though she knew he didn't mean that. "And it's not as if it had ever been done before. You did the best you could."

Lionel shook his head. "You shouldn't be comforting me, my daughter. I should have taken more care when I found you. But I promise that when you return, I will have a cure." His eyes sparked with excitement. "I think I've hit on something big."

He had said similar things before, and Ember wished she could believe him this time. Lately, though, she had begun to fear the opposite: that the spell would grow more and more threadbare until it fell apart entirely, returning her to her dragon form. She sometimes had dreams in which she was turned back into a dragon. In those dreams, she was lost and alone, soaring over gray countryside or chased by men with bows. She had no memory of being a dragon, and no desire to become one again. And what if she became something bad, something evil? Ember shuddered. Sometimes her own body felt like a cloak that could be shed or lost at any time—but what was beneath it, not even she knew.

"Ah, there's old Eli now," her father said, waving at a man approaching through the crowd. It was Professor Rosenberg, a Magician friend of her father's, and her appointed guardian for the trip. He was a heavily mustached man who wheezed alarmingly when he laughed, as if it was at risk of choking him. Ember liked him. Unlike most people, he was comfortable with mysteries—he knew there was something unusual about Ember, but he never pressed her father to explain it. "You'll be safe with him."

"Quite safe, my friend," Professor Rosenberg said. Like most Magicians, he wore an elaborate midnight cloak and walked with a divining stick, which detected storms, and cut an impressive figure on the grimy dock. He wasn't a Stormancer, though, someone who could wield magic—Magicians only studied it, as an astronomer studies stars. All Stormancers were Magicians too, but not all Magicians were Stormancers.

The crowd around the demiship was thinning. Ember tried to imagine that she was an intrepid Scientist heading off on an expedition of historical significance, and wondered if intrepid Scientists ever left home feeling as if they'd swallowed a stomachful of rocks. Her father gave her one last hug, and Ember breathed in the familiar smell of his cloak, a mixture of magic and ginger biscuits. Forcing a watery smile, she took Professor Rosenberg's hand and let him lead her up the gangway.

Ember squinted into the icy mist. The *Orpheus* had just passed through a storm—the ordinary kind—and the wind carried an echo of its fury. The ship's hull thunked gently against chunks of ice that speckled the sea. She wore a wool coat and hat, though she didn't need either. The coat was new, and like her dresses, had been enchanted to pass through her wings. In her pocket was a shard of broken flagstone from one of Chesterfield's paths (*Magicae et Scientia*), because she had thought leaving home might be easier to bear if she took a piece of it with her. She squeezed the flagstone against her palm until the letters made little indentations in her skin.

Before her, somewhere in the mist, was Antarctica.

Ember shivered, and not because of the cold. The frosty wind felt wonderful against her skin, though the burly sailors manning the deck of the HMS *Orpheus* were bundled in so many coats and scarves you could barely tell they were human.

Her three weeks aboard the *Orpheus* had passed slowly. She would have liked to go up to the deck on the days the demiship surfaced, but it was far too dangerous— particularly as they passed the equator and the sun grew even stronger. She was glad, at least, to be traveling aboard a demiship, one of the fastest and most advanced vessels in the British navy. She had fallen asleep each night watching sharks and seals and manta rays and fish of all description drift past the window of her undersea passenger cabin. She felt certain that she had discovered at least one new species of jellyfish, and made careful sketches, in the event that she became a famous zoologist one day and wrote a book about cnidarians. She tried to bury her sadness by reading, and memorized several new animals from Takagi's *Compendium*: the cheetah, the crenellated chimera, the alpine chipmunk, and three types of chickadee (black-capped, gray-collared, and African).

She wondered if there would be other children at the research station. She wasn't good with other children. She found them strange—loud and chaotic as a magical storm, shouting and darting around playing games without proper rules. She didn't have much experience with children, of course. Given the risk that she might set her classmates on fire, Ember had never attended school.

She pictured Chesterfield, perched on its lofty hilltop; her small bedroom with the windowsill she liked to curl up on. What was her father doing now? Was Puff napping in her favorite spot beneath Ember's bed?

Her homesickness swelled. It was like swallowing ice, cold and sharp.

"Eager to get your first look at it, are you?" said a voice behind her. First Officer Jack, a tall, bone-thin American with a permanent smile, stepped up to the railing.

"Yes," said Ember, who had often found that the best way to limit unwanted conversation was to agree with everything the other person said.

"Nervous?" First Officer Jack examined her. "Some get nervous, their first time here. Wouldn't think it'd bother you much, what with that famous pa of yours."

Ember didn't see the connection between having a famous father and being a nervous traveler, but then most people were awed by Lionel St. George and looked for ways to bring him up with Ember whenever they could. "I'm a little nervous," she agreed.

The man gave her back a thump—Ember only barely moved her wing in time. "It's all right. It's a strange place, make no mistake. Far side of the world, isn't it? I've been an officer of the empire my whole life, seen places you couldn't imagine, but I prefer to stay on deck when we stop here."

"Why?" Ember said. "It's just a lot of ice and snow, isn't it?"

First Officer Jack gave her a long look. "Ice and snow—yes, there's plenty of that. Too much, you might say. Enough to drive a man mad."

Ember's brow furrowed. She had little experience with snow—a few inches fell a year in London, enough to make the city look like a frosted cake for a few hours, until it grew sooty and hoof-beaten. She didn't see how it could drive someone mad.

"I expect you've been warned about the dragons," First Officer Jack said. "It's almost summer—which is to say, winter in these parts—and they're starting to roam again."

Ember shivered. The vast, icebound lands of Antarctica were home to the last known dragon colony in the world. Ice dragons were elusive and strange, breathers of frost rather than fire. Ember doubted she would get a glimpse of one—ice dragons avoided people as skillfully as leopards did—but the possibility filled her with dread and excitement. Would they recognize her? Would they see her as one of them, or as an enemy?

"Don't worry," First Officer Jack said. "The dragons don't go anywhere near the research station." He sighed.

"It's a shame the queen doesn't allow hunting here. I thought about trying my hand at dragon-catching in my youth. Would be an exciting way to make a living, don't you think?"

"No," Ember said.

First Officer Jack gave her a strange look. "What have you got there?"

Ember started. She had been absently toying with her fireglass ring. She tucked her hand back in her pocket. "Oh . . . that's just—"

"Don't need to play coy, girl." The sailor gave a laugh that sent up a cloud of breath. "I know fireglass when I see it. Not that I've ever owned a piece myself—cost me a year's wages! Little present from your parents, eh?"

Ember nodded silently.

"Well, just you keep it out of sight. Thieves, you know. Not that there's any among our crew, but you get some strange types at the station. Place like that attracts those as don't fit anywhere else, if you catch me. I remember the first time—"

"Ahoy there!" a voice shouted. "Approaching Great Bother Bay! All hands prepare to ground!"

Ember started. Sailors clomped past, calling to each other in their sea language, as incomprehensible as the language of birds. First Office Jack turned to the rigging, his smile replaced by a look of concentration. The mists were parting, and she laid eyes on it for the first time.

Antarctica.

Ember drew in her breath. It was a world of black and white, towering over the sea. The coastline was made of mountains of dark rock that folded into one another like crossed arms, steeped in snow and ice. It went on forever.

Ember had spent her life in London, where everything felt crowded—the winding streets, the messy skyline of rooftops and chimneys. Even the air was full of the jostling smells of horse and smoke and bakeries. Ember could hardly believe she was still in the same world—it was as if the ship had sailed through a door to Fairyland.

Ember sometimes had fanciful thoughts like this, and wished for someone to share them with. Her father traveled so much, and the shadow in the corner was too moody most days to carry on a proper conversation. She longed for a companion her own age. Not a human child, of course—Ember always pictured another dragon, also transformed into a boy or girl like her. If only her father had found two eggs that day in the Welsh mountains! She often wondered what that dragon child would have looked like, and whether they too would have invisible wings, or perhaps an invisible tail. You could go far in life with an invisible tail.

They sailed toward a bay with a small, snowy beach and a huddle of what looked like single-room huts. Then a figure stepped out of one, and Ember realized they were massive wooden warehouses. In this vast canvas of snow and ice, there were no trees, no streets lined with sooty houses, to help her eyes work out the distances.

An ice floe as large as a London city block scraped against the ship, prompting a flurry of shouts. The *Orpheus* was a huge vessel, its bow lined with mortars with enough firepower to sink a small navy, yet even it was vulnerable to Antarctica's fearsome seascape. Ember watched as Captain Llewelyn himself took the wheel and steered the demiship through the labyrinth of ice, his calm gray eyes narrowed in concentration.

"What's that?" Ember said to no one in particular. The mist was lifting to the east, revealing a row of towering sea cliffs. Atop one was a stone fortress clothed in shimmering frost.

"It's a castle," one of the sailors said.

"Oh, really?" Ember said. Unfortunately, the man seemed as impervious to sarcasm as the shadow in the corner. "I meant, what's it doing here?"

The man gave a short laugh. "You don't expect the prince to kip with the Scientists, do you? He had all them stones brought in from France. Took about ten years. More than one of those ships sank with all hands lost, even after they were magicked—not that he let it put him off."

Ember knew that the Prince of Antarctica was a man named Cronus, the fifth child of Queen Victoria, who was the true ruler of Antarctica and the rest of the British Empire. Cronus would likely never inherit the throne, and so had been sent to govern the farthest and, in the eyes of the nobility, most useless piece of the empire, being ill-suited for anything besides Scientific research. Antarctica had only been claimed by the British to prevent the Spanish or the Germans from having it, which seemed a silly reason to Ember. But she supposed that, being a dragon, she was unlikely to understand the thinking of human kings and queens.

"Is Prince Cronus there now?" Ember said.

"Doubt it. He's not around much. Prefers his country estate in Devon, he does, with his hunting dogs and fancy kiteships. But Prince Gideon's usually about."

"Prince Gideon?"

"Prince Cronus's young son," the sailor explained. "Future lord of Antarctica!" He swept his arm mockingly at the empty expanse of sea and ice in a way that made Ember wonder if he liked the princes much. "He's a bit of a bookworm, from what I hear."

The man said "bookworm" in a smirking way that instantly reduced Ember's estimation of him, while increasing her curiosity about the prince. She squinted at the castle. It was pretty and stern, completely out of place in that pale wilderness. Flags fluttered ambivalently from the turrets, startling splashes of blue and red.

She wondered what sort of boy Prince Gideon was. She pictured him at the window in his icy castle, surrounded by books, gazing at the ship as it passed. She felt a tug of connection—the prince would surely understand what it meant to be alone.

Ember shook herself. Prince Gideon had a legion of servants at his beck and call, and a home at Buckingham Palace that he could return to whenever he liked. They could have nothing in common.

The castle faded into the mist.

One of the sailors brushed against her wings, and Ember retreated to a safer spot in the bow. Then there was more shouting and hurrying, and Ember and her belongings were bundled into a rowboat, and then they had reached the shore of Antarctica.

THREE

THE FIREFLY AND THE DOORKNOB

The fire dragon's fierce temperament is well documented. Even when mortally wounded, the beasts have been reported to fight until the last breath leaves their body. Perhaps it was this that prompted William Shakespeare to write, "Come not between a dragon and his wrath."

—*TAKAGI'S* COMPENDIUM OF EXOTIC CREATURES

E mber's heart pounded as she treaded the narrow dock, which rolled under her feet. A big swell came in, and she grabbed at the railing. The sea was deepest, darkest gray, and the land was snow and shadow. Ember felt as if she had stepped into a daguerreotype of another planet. Then she was clambering onto a rocky beach, and taking her first step in Antarctica. The snow was hard-packed and slippery, and she nearly lost her balance.

She had little time to marvel, however, before Professor Rosenberg appeared behind her to hustle her along, his divining stick tapping smartly on the snow.

"Is that the research station?" Ember said, gazing at the dingy warehouses. She was relieved when Professor Rosenberg shook his head.

"This is Port Gloaming. Come along, and don't speak to anyone, child."

This surprised Ember, until she took a closer look at the people loitering about the warehouses. Some were rough and sailorish, which was expected, while others looked rough and *wealthy*, which in Ember's experience was a bad combination. They were all men, apart from a pair of women oddly clad in enormous white coats that, on closer inspection, turned out to be polar-bear skins, complete with heads. Fireglass flashed from necks and wrists and fingers, in all its shades: lemon yellow to sunset crimson. Several men had rifles or bows slung over their shoulders.

"Who are they?" Ember said to Professor Rosenberg.

"Seal hunters, I suspect. It's clear this is a rough place."

"Here to register, storm walker?" one of the men, lounging on a barrel, called to Professor Rosenberg. He had a mane of reddish hair and a pointed chin. He put Ember in mind of a well-fed fox. "Bit past your prime, don't you think?"

Several of the men laughed. Professor Rosenberg looked at the man, his face as impassive as an old log, and kept walking. His cold hand tightened around Ember's.

"What are they registering for?" Ember murmured.

"I don't know. I suggest we refrain from making conversation."

Ember looked into the face of each man she passed. She had never met a professional hunter before. Some leered;

others smiled kindly, seeming surprised by her presence. Even those who smiled sent a current of fear through her bones—many wore fireglass jewelry. One smile revealed a glittering red tooth.

Ember touched the back of her neck through her scarf. Her own heartscale was there, a scarlet diamond roughly the length of her thumb. It was the only other part of her that her father hadn't been able to transform. Oddly, he had also been unable to make it invisible like her wings; the heartscale seemed resistant to magic. As a result, Ember wore scarves at all times of the year, indoors and out.

Along the coast beyond the warehouses was a slope of rock, slippery with ice and seawater. At first Ember thought the rock was dotted with black-and-white lumps. Then she realized—

"Penguins!" she exclaimed.

So it was—hundreds of them, perched along the ridged stone. They were Adélies, which were much smaller than their cousins, emperor penguins, and would not have reached Ember's waist. As she watched, a parent led a chick toward the edge of the rock. The adult hopped into the water first, followed by its chittering offspring.

Ember was fascinated. Takagi's *Compendium* had drawings of penguins, but these didn't begin to capture the strangeness of them—the clumsy way they walked, like a child taking its first steps, or the honking sound they made, which was rather like a donkey imitating a crow.

She yearned for her notebook and sketch pencils.

She was just turning to ask Professor Rosenberg if they could stay awhile when a shot rang out.

Feathers exploded. The birds honked madly as they ran to and fro, a black and white pandemonium. Ember's heart dropped through her stomach. She couldn't see which bird had been struck—not until one of the hunters walked calm as a cat into the melee and lifted a motionless penguin by its foot. He turned to his two friends, who stood a little ways back, laughing.

It was the foxlike man from the dock, his orange hair stark against the snow. He strode across the beach as if he owned it, raising his hand in greeting to Ember and Professor Rosenberg.

Ember glared. She wished the professor was a Stormancer who could turn the red-haired man into an insect. One of the man's companions lifted his rifle and took aim at another penguin.

"*Stop,*" Ember said, startling herself. She shook off Professor Rosenberg's hand and marched into the chattering horde, stopping a few yards from the man. A young penguin, still covered in gray down, wandered up to her, peeping worriedly.

The man held up a hand. The other man lowered his rifle—as Ember had guessed, the redhead was their leader.

"I don't believe we've been introduced," he said politely, as if they were sitting down to tea. Ember couldn't stop staring at his hand—it was covered in blood, but that was not the only thing that drew her eye. The man wore a fire-glass ring on each finger, even his thumb. "Lord Norfell."

Ember's eyes narrowed. She doubted this man was a seal hunter—more likely, he was just a bored nobleman on a world tour. It was common for rich lords and ladies to go gallivanting about the British Empire, though most skipped its polar territories.

"Ember St. George," she said. Her left wing, often more attuned to danger than she was, gave a twitch as she met the man's gaze. "Why did you do that?"

Lord Norfell raised an eyebrow. He was graceful and handsome, and around the same age as Ember's father. But in his eyes was a glint of mischief that Ember found un-settling. His face was red from the cold, almost the color of his hair. "Oh, a bit of sport, you know. My men and I are in want of entertainment." He glanced at the dead bird at his feet. "Forgive me—you no doubt have a sensitive disposition. A gentleman should spare young ladies such sights."

"I wouldn't know what a gentleman should do," Ember said. "But I would like you to leave these penguins alone."

His eyes flashed—they were the murky green of algae or boiled vegetables. Then he smiled, as if he found Ember amusing, which she did not like at all.

"Where did you get all that fireglass?" she said. She had never seen so much worn by one person before, and much of it seemed rough-cut, nothing like what they sold at high-end London boutiques and canal markets.

The man touched one of the pendants around his neck. "These are trophies."

Ember felt cold. "Yours?"

"I was a prodigious dragon hunter in my day," the man said. "I slayed twenty-one beasts with my own hands."

Ember didn't trust herself to reply. Her heart thudded, slow and heavy.

"St. George," he murmured, staring at her. "Not Lord St. George's daughter?"

It was odd to hear her father referred to that way—he had been made a baron years ago by Queen Victoria, but he never used his title, and generally behaved as if he'd forgotten about it. "Yes," Ember said unwillingly, because she suspected he was the sort of man who would like her better if she had the word "lord" attached to her. She didn't want him to like her. She wanted to be his enemy.

"Lovely," Lord Norfell said, his smile growing. "Here to visit your aunt, are you?" He took her hand in his clean one, bowing over it. "Well, Miss St. George, you can rest assured that these penguins will be safe from me. After all, I am here for bigger quarry."

Ember pulled away. She hoped Lord Norfell hadn't felt the unnatural warmth of her hand through her glove. "Quarry?"

"Ember," Professor Rosenberg called. He stood a little

ways back, his expression dark. "Come along, child."

"Mustn't keep Auntie waiting." Lord Norfell tipped his hat, the gesture bringing out his slyness again. "Good day, Ember St. George."

As he walked away, Ember slowly relaxed her hands, which had been balled into fists in her pockets. She was taken aback by her own gumption. She generally avoided talking to people, let alone starting arguments, but Lord Norfell had made her so *angry*.

She turned up her coat collar, wishing she could make herself invisible the way she did at Chesterfield. There was no point in being angry—Lord Norfell was a nobleman, and a dragon hunter. He would do what he liked, even if that meant shooting penguins when he got bored again.

Nevertheless, from that moment on, she vowed that Lord Norfell was her sworn enemy, and if she could find a way, she would become his.

———

Ember and Professor Rosenberg continued along the path from the harbor, but before they could reach the station, they were accosted by a man with fogged-up glasses and wires of gray hair. It was clear that he was a Scientist, for he wore a spyglass on a chain around his neck, and also had the word "FIREFLY" stitched into his jacket, which was what the Scientists called the research station. He balked at the sight of Professor Rosenberg's divining stick, fixing the man with an indignant glare, and peered suspiciously into Ember's face when she introduced herself, as if she might be an imposter. Without a word, he hefted her suitcase and strode up the path. Ember had to say a hasty farewell to Professor Rosenberg. He touched her on the head and bid her goodbye in his grave voice.

"Hello?" Ember called after the man with her suitcase, who was traveling at a reckless pace over the beaten snow. "You haven't given me your name. And where is my aunt?"

"You're not supposed to be here," the man said. "Your ship was due on Saturday."

"That's not an answer," Ember said. It wasn't her fault that sea ice had delayed the Orpheus by four days.

The man twisted his head, swiping a finger over his glasses so that he could squint his blue eyes at Ember. "Name's Mac. That's it. Not Macdonald. Not Mackenzie. Not Macanythingelseyoucanthinkof. Just Mac. Em, eh, see. Got it?"

Ember couldn't help thinking back to what First Officer Jack had said about madness and too much snow. "Think so."

"I've no idea where Myra is. Thundering about somewhere, no doubt. She'll be mad as hops about this—she's gone down to the harbor every day to wait for you." He squinted at her. "Red sky this morning. Bad omen. Bad, bad omen."

"Oh," Ember said. She wished someone else had been there to greet her. She began to wonder if Mac was leading her to the station at all, or if they were just going to keep wandering over the ice forever, when finally they reached the crest of the hill, and there it was.

Ember's first impression was of a long metal caterpillar crouched over the snow. The station was composed of eleven joined-up hexagons, each mounted on four skinny stilts that bore an eerie resemblance to legs. A British flag had been painted onto the largest section, the one in the middle of the caterpillar, where there was a ramp leading down to the ground. Lights shone from several of the hexagons, which all seemed to be lined with windows.

"Beautiful, isn't it?" Mac murmured, swiping at his glasses again. His prickliness seemed to dissipate.

Ember wasn't sure she'd use that word. The station had no elegance whatsoever, and was, compared with the stately buildings of London, rather ugly. But it was absolutely unique, and possessed a certain charm, for somehow the station gave off the impression that it was aware of its ugliness, but too practical to care.

Mac turned to her. "What do you think?"

Ember bit her tongue. She had a natural inclination toward the truth—trying not to answer questions honestly was like suppressing a sneeze. She was also inconveniently incapable of lying. Perhaps it was a side effect of the spell that had turned her into a human girl, or perhaps it was that, as her father sometimes said, lying was a uniquely human power—a dark one, but useful. Ember often wished she could lie. Her honesty was always getting her in trouble.

Fortunately, Mac misinterpreted Ember's silence, as people tended to do. "Quite the sight, I know. I still find myself staring at it sometimes, and I've lived here for years. I wouldn't leave it. Not for a place on the Queen's Senate!"

Ember couldn't imagine Mac on the Queen's Senate, which was made up of six Magicians and six Scientists, including the prime minister. The Senate advised the queen, but they were elected, and almost as powerful as the queen herself. Ember's father had been asked to run for a spot on the Senate more than once, but he always said he wouldn't be able to stand being a member of such a stuffy group, particularly as it would take him away from his experiments.

Mac led her to the very last hexagon. Apparently the station had been designed in its piecemeal way so that the Scientists could take it apart and move it to another place if they wanted to. The windows, he said vaguely, had been magically strengthened through Stormancy. This immediately piqued Ember's interest.

"Are there any Stormancers at the station?" she said.

Mac snorted. "Stormancers, here? Why would we need them, girl?"

"But you just said—"

"This is a place of *Science*," Mac said.

"Even though there's a Stormancer stationed down at Port Gloaming to melt the sea ice?" Ember said. One of the sailors had told her that it would be impossible to have a proper dock in Antarctica without Stormancy—the ice would crush it.

Mac pretended not to hear this. "No magic is allowed at the station. So don't get any ideas."

"I'm not a Stormancer," Ember said.

Mac tossed a suspicious look over his shoulder. "Your father is. Quite the tales I hear about him."

"That doesn't have anything to do with me. Stormancy isn't inherited—it's random, and rare."

Mac made a skeptical noise. "All I can say is, if I see any books floating through the air, or catch a whiff of any strange potions . . ."

Ember sighed. She considered telling Mac that wasn't how magic worked—all magic was transformative in nature. Stormancers could change the shape of matter with a spell, but that was as far as their powers extended. They couldn't move things with their minds, or brew love potions, or do anything else equally silly. At the core, every spell simply transformed one thing into something else. Most Stormancers, in fact, could barely change a spoon into a fork. Only a few, like her father, could perform more complicated feats. The spell that made Ember's wings invisible changed how people *saw* her—or their ability to see her. Those were the trickiest spells of all, and the most dangerous. If miscast, they could drive a person mad, and were thus considered dark magic, which was illegal. Or, as Lionel St. George put it, technically illegal.

"As I was saying," Mac said, "each of the stilts is powered by hydraulics. . . ."

Ember followed him up the small ramp, which was painted bright yellow. She recognized the disdainful note in Mac's voice when he spoke of magic. It had been over a hundred years since the conflict that had pitted Magicians and Stormancers against Scientists, nearly tearing apart the empire in the process, but bitter feelings remained on both sides. It was why Chesterfield, which had once been a school dedicated solely to Stormancy, had begun teaching Science as well. Many Magicians and Scientists there now worked side by side in an attempt to reconcile the two disciplines, with little success. Science, so far, could not understand magic, while magic could not understand the value of Science.

Mac led her through two sets of doors into a hexagon that was little more than a hallway lined with more doors, all closed.

"Here we are," he said. "This is one of the sleeping sections—you're in number five, at the end of the hall."

Mac swung one of the doors open. "Told you it wasn't much."

Ember didn't reply—she was too busy staring. The room

was an odd triangular shape, being nestled into a corner of the hexagon, and quite small, only large enough for a bed and a wardrobe, and that was about it. But one of the three walls was glass, and beyond the glass were miles of snow and mountains and toothy rock, vast as the night sky.

"It's—" Ember paused. "It's beautiful."

"*Hmmph*," Mac said, but Ember could tell he was pleased.

"It's getting late," Ember said, surprised. The sky was darkening, and a single star hung in the violet blue.

"No, it isn't." Mac gave her a knowing look. "You'll have to get used to that, too. This close to the Pole, heading into winter, we only see a few hours of sunlight each day. In a couple weeks, even that will be gone, and we'll be left with the moon and the stars." He didn't sound at all displeased by this.

"Bathroom's that way," he said, pointing. "I'll see if I can find any trace of Myra."

Ember noticed again the odd way that he spoke of her aunt, as if she were some sort of wild creature that could be observed if one was lucky, but not predicted. He deposited Ember's suitcase by the bed and left, closing the door behind him.

Ember sat on the edge of her bed, which was squashy and piled with blankets. Then she burst into tears.

It was some time before she stopped. The horizon had become the color of crushed violets. The twilight felt clean and free here, not smothered between buildings or grimed with soot and gaslight. Though the view was breathtaking, she could not appreciate it. All she wanted was her little bedroom, with the sounds of Chesterfield coming in through the window, and Puff curled up on the bed, and her father muttering to his books in the drawing room.

Ember wiped her face. Dully, she took off her coat, first removing the flagstone from her pocket and arranging it on the bedside table so that the lettering was facing her. Then she set about unpacking her suitcase. But once she had put her clothes and books away, she discovered an odd lump at the very bottom. She pulled back the leather lining and found a small compartment, which held a folded piece of paper—and a doorknob.

The doorknob, to be sure, was unexpected, but Ember paid it little attention. She unfolded the paper at once, and immediately recognized her father's handwriting. *My dear Ember,* it said at the top, and then Ember could read no more, for she had burst into tears again.

When she stopped, she took up the letter and read.

My dear Ember,
I hope you had a safe journey, and that you have found the research station welcoming and comfortable. Your aunt has a unique manner, and as we know, an unusual history, and I ask that you inform me immediately if you experience anything concerning during your stay. As I write this, you are asleep in your bedroom and Puff is glowering at me from

the bookcase, as if convinced I am to blame for your looming departure. I wish I could tell her differently, but I confess I continue to feel guilty for this entire situation, my dear. I wish you to know that I have the beginnings of a plan, which I shall hopefully be able to tell you about by the time you read this. Speaking of which, please make use of the enclosed doorknob at your earliest convenience. You'll find that it will work on any door, though do ensure that you only turn it to the right.

With much love, as always, your father,
L. S.-G.

P.S. Please do not show the doorknob to anyone. Myra has informed me that some of the Scientists do not look kindly on the use of magic at the station.
P.P.S. Please excuse the doorknob's manners.

The letter smelled of Chesterfield. The university had, naturally, hired her father back—barely a week after firing him, a new record. Ember leaped up, seizing the doorknob. She considered the door leading to the hallway first, and had just taken a step toward it when the doorknob gave a strange jerk.

Ember almost dropped it. She exhaled slowly, reminding herself that she'd seen far stranger things at Chesterfield than irascible doorknobs.

"Not that one?" she said politely, trying to start things

off on the right foot. The doorknob made no reply. Ember next considered her wardrobe. It was finely carved and clearly expensive, and in that sense, it matched the door-knob, which was decorated with a delicate leafy pattern and gold filigree. The magical doorknob did not protest as Ember began to loosen the ordinary doorknob on the wardrobe—which was also inlaid with gold—nor when she lifted the magical doorknob to the screws. It twirled the screws into place, seeming rather pleased with itself.

Ember paused. Had the sun set back in London? It wasn't safe for her to go back during the day, when she was at risk of bursting into flames. She tried to calculate the hours, but her thoughts were a whirlwind. She supposed she could at least poke her head through to check.

She was just about to turn the knob when someone thundered alarmingly on her door. It was closer to an assault than a request for entry, and Ember was too startled to reply. After a moment of silence, the door flew open.

A young woman strode into the room, her expression so fierce that Ember fell back a step.

"Oh, I will strangle Mac this time, truly I will," Aunt Myra growled, and then she pulled Ember into a hug so strong it lifted her off her feet.

Ember was so surprised that she struggled, which made for an extremely awkward hug. Aunt Myra half dropped her, and when Ember's wings flapped automatically, the gust blew her aunt's shapeless hat into the hallway.

"Oh, I'm sorry, Ember," Myra said. "What a mess this is! I was down at the harbor all day yesterday, and the one before, and this morning, but then there was an incident with the soil samples, and I had to—"

"Yes, I know," Ember said abruptly, put off by the hug. "Mac told me. It's all right."

"No, it isn't. I was supposed to greet you, and instead, you got that surly old badger—oh, this is just my luck!"

Her voice was so despairing that Ember was perplexed. She gazed at her aunt properly for the first time. Myra, Ember knew, was two years younger than Lionel, and looked very much like him, with her ruddy complexion and mass of golden curls, though these were pulled back from her face in a severe bun. She was dressed in the sort of hideously respectable clothing—a shapeless gray skirt suit—that Ember only saw on the fustiest of Chesterfield's professors, who were, on the whole, a fusty sort. Her clothing was odd because it didn't seem to match anything else about her.

"It was a poor introduction, but we'll just have to make up for it as best we can," her aunt continued in the same voice. "How about I introduce you to the Scientists? Some of them have their children here. You'll like that—children your own age! And how about some hot chocolate? Winston makes the best you've ever tasted—"

Ember, who felt too homesick to enjoy hot chocolate and who never wanted to meet other children, made an involuntary noise of protest, which caused her aunt to stutter to a confused stop before launching off again in another direction like a spooked horse. She told Ember about the governess who worked at the station, and how Ember was certain to like her, as she had won several awards for her teaching methods back in Paris. Aunt Myra went on for some time about these awards. When Ember was able to get a word in edgewise, she asked her aunt when she might learn about her research, which she understood focused on Antarctic wildlife, including ice dragons. That set her aunt off again at a mile a minute, and she informed Ember of the many dangers of straying too far from the Firefly. Ember eventually understood that she would be spending most of her time inside, taking lessons from the award-winning governess, where she would be unlikely to learn anything about dragons.

"Well, how about a tour?" Aunt Myra said, seeming disturbed by Ember's silence when she finally paused for breath. "You must be curious about this place. We can have a good chat, just the two of us. It's such a pity that we've never known each other, though of course I have been in—ah, I've been unavailable during a large part of your life. . . ."

Ember didn't want to risk saying no again—her aunt made her feel unsettled, like a wind that kept changing direction. With a last glance over her shoulder at the doorknob, which preened from its place on the fancy wardrobe, Ember followed her aunt into the hall.

The research station was a strange place.

The hexagons were joined up like train cars, so you had to walk through one to get to the next. At one end were the two sleeping hexagons, then the lounge, which was filled with yet more shelves of books and enormous squashy armchairs that looked liable to swallow unwary occupants. Here Aunt Myra introduced Ember to several Scientists: a meteorologist, an entomologist, a climatologist, and two volcanologists. Ember thought the lounge would have been a nice place to relax, if only people didn't gawp at you as these Scientists were doing. She wondered if it was because she was the daughter of the famous Lionel St. George, or the niece of the infamous Myra St. George, or both.

The next two hexagons contained a dining room lined with banquet tables that smelled of yeast and gravy, and a kitchen with a large pantry. The main section of the station was a library, crowded haphazardly with shelves of books, Scientific instruments, and desks topped with oil lanterns. The floor was layered with expensive wool carpets. Ember gazed about wonderingly. On the outside, the station was a weird gray thing, but inside it resembled a manor house. It reminded Ember of the fine estate her father sometimes rented in the craggy wilderness of Ireland, where they went whenever he needed space to test out his new spells. The walls were made entirely of windows. She felt as if she was still among the snow and rocks of Antarctica, even while she stood surrounded by grandfather clocks and flickering lanterns.

"I expect you're hungry," Aunt Myra said. "How about some dinner?"

Ember ran her fingers along the bookshelves. The library was nothing compared to Chesterfield's, but at least all the books were about Science, not dull old Magical theory. "Do you have any books about ice dragons?"

Aunt Myra looked startled. "I—no. There *are* no books on ice dragons. No one has ever gotten close enough to study them properly."

"I know," Ember said. "Takagi's *Compendium* doesn't even mention ice dragons. But you're studying them. Can I see your research?"

"I . . . well, it's in the very early stages. Your father tells me you have an interest in zoology! You know, Dr. Wemmal is working on a fascinating study of blue whale migration; perhaps he could—"

"Do you ever go looking for dragons?" Ember said. "Could I come?"

Her aunt was looking more and more flustered. She ran a hand over her hair, and several curls sprang free, as if they had been on the lookout for an opportunity. "I'm afraid that would be too dangerous, Ember. Now, how about I show you around the observatory? Have you ever looked through a telescope the size of an elephant?"

"No," Ember said. Part of her wondered whether her

aunt meant an African or Asian elephant, but the rest of her noted that Myra seemed oddly intent on changing the subject from dragons.

"Really!" Her aunt seemed unnaturally surprised— Ember doubted that many people had experience with elephant-sized telescopes, Asian or African. "Well, come along, then. We'll see if we can't find a meteor or two!"

"But I—" But there was no interrupting Aunt Myra this time. She was off again at a mile a minute, recounting all the latest astronomical discoveries made at the Firefly. Ember, taciturn by nature, felt like a leaf overcome by a gale, and allowed Aunt Myra to lead her, silent, into the twilight.

FOUR

MONTGOMERY
TURNS TO THE LEFT

Some populations were migratory; Australian fire dragons, for instance,
were sighted as far from their native habitat as Mongolia. Most,
however, were unadventurous, preferring to spend their lives in the lands
where they were born.

—*TAKAGI'S* COMPENDIUM OF EXOTIC CREATURES

The next day, Ember went to school.

Her hands trembled as she brushed her hair. She
thought of how people said they had butterflies in their
stomach when they were nervous. Well, her stomach had
pigeons. Possibly an owl or two. She squeezed the Chesterfield flagstone, which she had tucked into her pocket, as
she walked to the classroom.

She had never attended school before. Her education had
mostly consisted of reading books on a patchwork of subjects. Sometimes her father gave her lessons on magic or
history, or asked one of the professors to tell her about their
research. But she had never had an actual teacher. She didn't
even know what children did in school—she assumed they

just sat quietly and read, like she did. She felt shivery with excitement at the thought of all the new animals and Scientific theories she would learn about, twinned with dread at the prospect of facing a roomful of children. Her pigeons cooed and flapped all the way to the classroom.

It turned out, though, that she had only three classmates—a twin girl and boy with blank, round faces and shiny black hair who reminded Ember of dolls on a shelf, and a girl a year older than her who wore a distracting number of ribbons in her hair—several dozen at least, in purple and green and blue, but especially purple. The children murmured their names at Ember, who promptly forgot them, being too uncomfortable under their curious gazes to pay attention. She was thoroughly tired of being stared at—she missed the ivy-shadowed paths of the Reading Wood and Chesterfield's many secret corridors, along which she could glide like a ghost.

Their governess was a tidy Frenchwoman with dark skin and close-cropped hair named Madame Rousseau, and her job was to stand at the front of the room and tell them things they could have read in books in half the time. Not everything she said was interesting, and you couldn't skip over the dull parts. Ember thought it an inefficient way to learn. After sitting for hours at a cramped desk, she yearned to stretch her wings, but if she did, they would brush against one of the twins.

Madame Rousseau tapped her pointer against a map of

the empire. British America, Greenland, and Antarctica, as well as the tip of Africa, which were all part of the empire, were painted red. The Spanish and German empires, which controlled Europe and most of South America, were in green and yellow. Australia was also red, which meant the map was old, for the Japanese Empire had taken it from Britain several decades ago. Part of British America, too, was a lighter shade of red, perhaps because the map had been drawn in the midst of the failed uprising of the 1770s. Ember didn't have much interest in geography, though her father had ensured she learned the basics. She tried to focus on what Madame Rousseau was saying, but her mind wandered back to last night, and her exhausting dinner with Aunt Myra.

Her aunt had kept up a steady stream of chatter about life at the Firefly and what the other scientists were studying (everything from supernovas to volcanoes to albatrosses). She said very little about her own work. Ember began to suspect that Aunt Myra found it awkward to discuss her research with an actual dragon. She imagined it would feel strange—like an ornithologist sitting down to tea with a robin. After eating, her aunt had hurried off to deal with another soil sample emergency, her heavy boots clomping like exclamation points. Aunt Myra seemed to spend much of her time "thundering about" the station, as Mac had put it, solving this problem or ordering that person about. She was a whirlwind of energy, enough to wear Ember out just looking at her. Ember had been too tired after dinner to try the magical doorknob, and had instead fallen onto her bed and slept.

Ember gazed out the classroom windows. The wind raced over the ice like a herd of ghostly horses, raising clouds of ice crystals. The white mountains were stark against the blue sky, and Ember yearned to explore them. The day was fading into twilight again—which, Ember had learned, lasted all night in Antarctica at this time of year: the sky maintained its purple glow until the sun rose again in the morning. This was because the earth was tilted, Madame Rousseau had explained that morning. During Antarctica's summer, the bottom of the earth leaned toward the sun, which meant that the sun never went below the horizon as the earth turned. At other times of the year, the sun dipped just under the horizon at night, and then came right back up again. Madame Rousseau demonstrated using a globe and a lantern to represent the sun.

Ember supposed there might be some value to school after all.

"So you live at Chesterfield?" a voice asked. "What's it like?"

Ember jumped. It seemed that school was over—Madame Rousseau was tucking her papers and books tidily into a smart briefcase. Her questioner was the girl with the ribbons in her hair—during a particularly tedious writing exercise, Ember had occupied herself with counting them. She had made it to sixty-eight.

"It's very old," Ember said. The girl's question hadn't

been specific, so Ember could only guess at the answer she expected. "It has twenty-two indoor toilets. The curtains smell of pipe tobacco. Two crow families live in the Reading Wood, and they have an alliance against the crows that live in the poplars by the driveway."

The girl's brow wrinkled. She was pretty, with brown skin and a veil of long black hair—less hair than ribbons, possibly. Ember was certain she had said something wrong, the way she always did when she spoke to other children, but then the girl said, "Twenty-two? How many in each building?"

Ember had to think about this. "I'm not sure."

"I'm Nisha," the girl said. "Would you like to play with us?"

"Us?"

"I don't mean them," Nisha said, shooting the Doll Twins a glare. "I mean me and Moss."

"Who's Moss?"

"Just a boy who lives here." For some reason, Nisha's face reddened.

"Why isn't he in school?"

"Oh, he doesn't like school."

Ember couldn't make sense of this. All human children attended school—that was just the way it was. "Don't his parents mind?"

"He doesn't have parents," Nisha said.

"Everyone has parents," Ember pointed out. "Do you mean they're dead?"

"No," Nisha said, calmly certain. "He doesn't have any."

Ember thought that perhaps Nisha had seen too much snow, too. "I'm sorry, but I can't—I have to speak with my father." The idea of spending time alone with two children filled her with a fluttery sort of terror. Besides, all day she had been distracted by thoughts of the doorknob, and she wanted nothing more than to test it out.

Nisha gave her a strange look. "Isn't your father in London?"

"Ah . . . yes," Ember said, realizing her mistake. The truth about the doorknob rose up inside her, but her father had said not to tell anyone. Being unable to tell the truth, and unable to lie, she could only be awkwardly silent. She and Nisha gazed at each other with mutual suspicion.

"Well, see you tomorrow," Ember said a bit too loudly. She hurried down the corridor.

Unfortunately, on her way past the storage room, she bumped into one of the Doll Twins. The girl had been hovering at the end of the shelves, peeping around the corner as if keeping a lookout.

"Move along, blondie," she said, giving Ember a shove.

"What are you doing?" Ember was less intimidated by the girl's rudeness than she had been by Nisha's friendliness. You didn't have to worry about saying the wrong thing to someone like that.

"Never you mind." The girl moved to the left to block Ember's view of whatever was going on behind her. This only increased Ember's curiosity, so she slipped around her in a movement quicker than the girl could follow.

She found the other half of the Doll Twins crouched behind a shelf, his knee pressed into the back of a boy whose face was turned away from her. He had a hand tangled cruelly in the boy's hair. As Ember watched, he opened a textbook at the midpoint—one of those textbooks that is so large and dull-covered it couldn't possibly be taken for anything else—and slammed it around the boy's head.

Ember didn't even think. She sprang forward and gave the doll twin a hard shove. It caught him by surprise, and he rolled across the floor and struck one of the shelves, his round, teacup-colored face screwed up in pain.

"Are you all right?" Ember said to the other boy. He sat up and gazed at her dazedly. His lip was cut, and blood trickled down his chin.

"I think so," he said in a very quiet voice. The boy's hair was silvery blond, and he was slender as a shadow. Ember thought he was probably her age, though he was shorter than she was.

"Moss?" It was Nisha. She hurried to Moss's side. She glared at the other boy, who had gathered himself to his feet. "Why don't you leave him alone? I'll tell Madame Rousseau this time, I really will!"

The Doll Twins glowered, and though they still emanated violence, they made no move to attack. Ember thought of the crows of the Reading Wood, who liked to gang up on the crows of the poplars and steal bits of their nests. The crows of the poplars couldn't do anything about it, because there were fewer of them. Right now, the Doll Twins were the crows of the poplars, and she, Nisha, and Moss were the crows of the Reading Wood.

The girl spat on the floor, and they strode off in a huff.

"You're bleeding," Nisha said to Moss. She touched his arm, flushed, then pulled back. Moss turned to Ember.

"Thank you," he said.

"Yes," Ember said, which wasn't right. Moss and Nisha were both looking at her, and Ember experienced a moment of pure panic. Already she had spent more time with other children in a day than she had in her entire life, and now she had rescued one of them, intervening in a battle that she sensed was part of a longer, entrenched war. She had no idea what to do.

"Goodbye!" Ember said, and ran away.

Back in her room with the door safely closed, she felt a stab of regret. Nisha and Moss seemed nice enough—or Nisha did, at least; she couldn't really assess Moss, for all he had done during their acquaintance was bleed. But she couldn't think what she would say if she went back to them—should she apologize for leaving so abruptly? But she had rescued Moss, so wouldn't it be wrong to apologize? Oh, children were so complicated!

And what had she been thinking, getting involved in their squabble with the twins? It wasn't like her at all. But as with Lord Norfell and the penguins, some instinct Ember hadn't known she possessed had taken over her.

She shook her head. Surely it was easiest—surely it was *best*—to keep to herself, as she had always done at Chesterfield, to stick to her books and stay out of everyone else's business. What if Nisha or Moss found out what she was?

Ember approached the wardrobe with trepidation. While she didn't think the doorknob would harm her, her father's magic hadn't grown any more predictable over the years, and she was half afraid she might step through the wardrobe into a jungle, or possibly an asteroid.

"Hello, Montgomery," Ember said to the doorknob, removing it from her coat pocket. "I would appreciate it if you could help me reach my father's study."

She had decided to treat the doorknob as if it were a person, including giving it a name. It had already tried to escape twice—yesterday, after she'd taken it out of the suitcase, and again in the night—both times rolling under the bed and tucking itself inside her fanciest scarf. Ember couldn't shake the impression that the doorknob didn't like her much, and felt it was cut out for better things.

The doorknob turned easily beneath her hand, and the door swung open.

Ember gasped. Beyond her coats and dresses was a room with a fire crackling in the hearth, and a candelabra, and an enormous desk piled with papers and books and quills. She was overwhelmed by the smell of home— woodsmoke, old books, and magic.

"Now?" said a familiar voice uncertainly.

Ember pushed past her sweaters and into her father's

office at Chesterfield. Puff was tangled in her feet in an instant, muttering and purring. Ember lifted her in her arms, and the white cat's purr swelled.

She gazed about, so happy her vision blurred. There was the familiar clock that her father had tried unsuccessfully to fix, which now told time backward and transformed, every few years, into an earlier style of clock. Currently, it was a spring-driven thing of oak and glass, topped with a mechanical globe, and would have been the height of fashion in the 1720s. There was the portrait of Lionel St. George's mother, a stern-faced woman who had died a year before Ember was born. There was the shadow in the corner, snoring. And there were Ember's favorite books in a pile on the window seat, just where she had left them. The burned half of the office had been mostly repaired—her father must have expended a good deal of magic to do so.

The university was quiet—the fire crackled, the clock tock-ticked, the nighttime wind rustled through the fruit trees in the courtyard. Puff nestled into her arms, her eyes closing blissfully.

Someone knocked quietly on the door. Ember froze. The knock came again, and she realized that it came not from her father's office, but from her room back in the Firefly, which she could still see through the door that normally led to a secondary hallway. Given the volume of the knock, she very much doubted it was her aunt. Ember wondered if she should close the wardrobe door. But if she did that, she wasn't sure if she would be able to get back.

In the end, it didn't matter, for the knock wasn't repeated. Her visitor must have given up.

The door to her father's office opened, and Lionel St. George marched in, clutching a stack of books that went up almost to his nose. He started, his books thudding to the floor. Then his face split in a massive grin, and Ember leaped into his arms.

"There, there," Lionel said. "All's well, my dear."

The noise had awakened the shadow in the corner. "Come back to the scene of the crime, have you?" it grumped. "Just when he got the smoke out of the curtains . . ."

"Go back to sleep, you old moaner," her father said. "Ah, I am glad the doorknob worked—one can never be certain when it comes to magical objects, particularly those that have been accidentally granted a sense of self. I'm not quite sure how it came about, in all honesty."

"How did you do it?" Ember said. "I didn't think it was possible to create a portal to somewhere so far away."

"Well, I had to put a crease in the fabric of the world," Lionel St. George said. "Which wasn't exactly difficult—the fabric, you see, is quite malleable. The real crux was connecting that crease to a specific place."

Ember marveled. She had never heard of a Stormancer transforming the shape of the world itself.

"I needn't have taken a ship to Antarctica," she said.

"Well, no—a portal requires two doors, one at each end. I suppose I could have mailed the doorknob to

Antarctica, though there is a law against leaving sentient objects unattended. Pesky, though not without merit, given the issues we had with feral wigs during the Magical Restoration of the 1740s. . . ."

He touched Ember on the chin. "Now, tell me how you're doing. Is your aunt treating you well?"

In a great rush, Ember told him everything that had happened since she left London. As she came to Lord Norfell, Lionel's face became grave.

"You must keep away from that man, Ember," he said.

Ember bit her lip, thinking of her vow to become Lord Norfell's enemy. But he had probably left Antarctica by now, sailing off to the Americas or back to Europe, where people would be sure to gawp admiringly at a dragon hunter as dashing and successful as he was. Her thoughts darkened.

Her father seemed to notice her expression and squeezed her hand. "I wonder if this might boost your spirits."

He strode to his desk and rummaged in a drawer. Then he handed Ember a torn piece of paper.

She was holding a sketch of a dragon. No—Ember squinted. *Several* dragons. The sketch was roughly done, as if the artist had been in a hurry, and not particularly graceful. The dragons appeared to be in some sort of underground room.

"When was this drawn?" she asked, taking a seat in her favorite chair.

"About ten days ago."

She stared at her father, who was smiling slightly. "Then these are ice dragons?"

"No. It's a group of eight fire dragons currently being held captive in a barge on the Thames. That sketch was drawn by a spy I sent in to investigate once I heard the rumors."

Ember's eyes widened. It wasn't possible. Fire dragons were extinct—she was the last. She had always been the last. She stared hungrily at the sketch, barely able to breathe.

"The owner of the barge is a wealthy merchant," Lionel said. "I believe he captured the dragons years ago, perhaps taking them from their parents, and raised them in captivity. Now he has been allowing rumors of their existence to surface in order to attract a bidding war among the country's wealthiest hunters. I'm sorry to say that there are a good many who would pay handsomely for the privilege of hunting a fire dragon again."

Ember touched the sketch. Fire dragons—real, live fire dragons! "Then you know where they are?"

"Yes. And what's more, I think I've figured out a way to fix the spell." His voice was low and earnest. "But I need the blood of a fire dragon to do it."

Ember's heart pounded. If her father was right, this could be the thing that stopped her from bursting into flames. She wouldn't have to stay in Antarctica forever; nor would she need to worry about hurting anyone. She could come home!

She looked back at the sketch and felt a pang. "Can you buy them?" she said.

Lionel's face fell. "I'm afraid not. Even if I had the funds, it wouldn't be fair to release them into a world where they would not long survive."

Ember bit her lip. Puff wove about her legs, purring in a demanding sort of way.

"The real difficulty was locating the barge," Lionel said. "It moves about, and the merchant has hired a Stormancer to alter its appearance every few days. A Russian Stormancer, by the feel of it . . . Russian magic has such a grassy aura; so many of their storms form over the Steppes . . ." Lionel brushed a hand through his hair, and a bolt of electricity sparked from his fingers.

"When can you take us to the dragons?" Ember said. She wanted—needed—to see them with her own eyes. "You can really do it?"

"Well . . ." Lionel smiled. "Technically, you can." His gaze drifted to the open door between Antarctica and London.

"Oh!" Ember exclaimed. She rose and went to her wardrobe, unscrewing the doorknob. She kept her foot in the jamb of her father's office door, afraid it would swing shut behind her. She returned with the doorknob and handed it to her father.

"I named it Montgomery," Ember said.

"Montgomery?"

"I think it's a bit of a snob," she explained.

Lionel held the doorknob out, allowing the magic that coursed through him to flicker through his palm and into Montgomery. It looked as if tiny lightning bolts, as delicate as spider silk, were wrapping themselves around the doorknob. Lionel murmured a spell in stormspeech, a rumbly sort of language that sounded nothing like any human tongue.

"There," he said, leaning back into the sofa once the light had faded. "Try the doorknob again."

Puzzled, she took it. Montgomery sparked, as if with static.

"Close the door to Antarctica first," Lionel said.

Ember did. Then, glancing back to her father for reassurance, she unscrewed the doorknob on the door that normally opened onto the secondary hallway. She replaced that doorknob with Montgomery, who seemed sluggish now, as if the magic had made it sleepy.

"My spy has already anchored a portal to the ship," her father said. "Turn the doorknob to the left this time, my dear."

"But you said—"

"Yes, I did. Before I cast the spell, the doorknob, if turned to the left, would have opened onto the Red Labyrinth between the worlds—an unpleasant place, I can assure you. But now I've linked it to the portal on the ship."

Nervously, Ember turned the doorknob, bracing herself in case her father was wrong and some beast from the Red Labyrinth decided to leap through.

She gasped. Her wardrobe and coats were gone. She was gazing down a narrow corridor. It was deserted and dingy, lit only by a sputtering lantern mounted on one wall, and ended in a strange metal door.

"It worked!" she whispered as her father came to peek through the door beside her.

"Probably," her father said. "There's only one way to be sure."

They exchanged serious looks, then stepped through the portal.

"They should be beyond that door," Lionel murmured, gesturing to the other end of the short corridor. "My spy told me that the first door—the one he used for the portal—was heavily enchanted, but Montgomery seems to have cut through all that, clever chap."

The floorboards in the little corridor creaked underfoot. They were underwater—Ember could sense it. Her left wing twitched. Lionel placed a hand on the metal door, which stretched all the way to the ceiling. In the dim light, his eyes were like a cat's.

"Yes, this is it," he said. "There's a spell on this door too, but it's a simple thing, cast only to strengthen the lock. They won't be worried about Stormancers getting this far." He murmured a few words, and the door creaked obligingly open. He had transformed the lock into dust, which drifted into the corridor.

Heat radiated through the gap. Lionel seemed to steel himself, and they pushed through the door.

It was like stepping into a forge—the room was smoky and dark, save for a faint glow at one end.

Ember felt as if she were in a dream. The dragons slumbered against the wall, steam rising from their nostrils. Four of them were small—only a little taller, perhaps, than Lionel St. George—but the rest were enormous, twice the height of a horse and several times as long. Their bodies were all serpentine curves, their claws enormous daggers. The males had antlerlike horns that were both graceful and terrifying. In the darkness, they glittered like a sea of rubies.

Ember gasped. One of the dragons lay curled on its side, its front foot bent at an odd angle. A bloody gash stretched across its left eye, which was missing. Ember noticed similar gashes on the other dragons—they looked like whip marks. The larger ones couldn't stand upright without hunching, and metal chains bolted into the floorboards prevented them from moving more than a few feet.

"How could anyone do this?" Ember breathed.

"I don't know." Lionel's expression was grim.

Ember couldn't bear it. "It's not fair," she whispered.

"No. I've often had reason to observe that there isn't much fairness in the world," her father said heavily. He squeezed her shoulder.

"Do we have to take their blood?" They were speaking in hushed voices, though the dragons had given no sign of noticing them. Some slept lying down, others standing upright like horses. "I don't want to hurt them."

Lionel frowned. He squinted into the darkness, then pointed.

Beside the cage was what looked like a puddle of water—but then one of the dragons shifted position, and the glow of its scales shone upon it. It was dark red, and reflected the light oddly. Dragon blood.

Lionel reached into his coat and withdrew a glass vial. "Stay behind me."

They slowly approached the dragons, who slept on, though one shifted slightly when a board creaked under Lionel's foot. They were close enough to feel their breath, which was hot and sour. Scorch marks covered the floor.

"Look," Ember murmured. Several of the dragons' chains were damaged—the metal was frayed in places, as if the creatures had been gnawing on it. "Do you think anyone noticed?"

"Doubtful. I don't think the owner of this ship is overly concerned about the safety of these dragons—or the men guarding them." Lionel knelt to collect the blood. As he did, Ember took a hesitant step closer to one of the dragons. She could scarcely believe it was real. She reached out a trembling hand and touched its brow, half expecting it to dissolve like a mirage.

The dragon's scales were warm, but not hot. This was all Ember had time to notice, for the dragon was blinking awake.

Ember froze. Her eyes watered as she returned the

dragon's gaze—it was so bright! Its eyes were like twin suns, glowing and pupilless.

"Hello," she whispered. She didn't know what response she hoped for—would the dragon recognize her immediately, or would it simply be confused? She stared, transfixed.

The dragon arched its neck and let out a terrible scream.

Ember stumbled back, her hands going to her ears. "Ember!" her father said, catching her by the shoulder. Other glowing eyes were opening in the darkness and fixing upon them. The young dragon strained against its chain, snapping and snarling. It caught the end of Ember's coat in its mouth.

If her father hadn't been there, Ember would have been wrenched into the range of the dragon's glistening teeth. But he held on to her, and the dragon came away with only a scrap of her coat. Another dragon roared, and another.

"Run!" her father shouted.

Ember ran. But when she looked back, her father had fallen behind. And one of the dragons was opening its fanged mouth, fire glowing at the back of its throat.

"No!" Ember cried. She turned back and flung herself between her father and the dragon. The burst of flame engulfed her, and she felt no pain—it was like being enveloped by a gust of wind.

She looked down and found that her clothing had been reduced to charred rags. Her hair, which she had been carefully growing out, was unevenly short—everything past the nape of her neck had been burned away.

Her father dragged her through the door. They slammed it behind them, and leaned heavily against it as the dragons roared in fury.

"I don't understand," Ember said between gasps. "They attacked me."

"I'm sorry, Ember." Her father's face was sheened with sweat. "I never should have brought you on this adventure. Those dragons, it's clear, have learned to despise humans—they saw us as enemies from the very start."

Ember felt as if someone had struck her. She had been so certain that the dragons would know her, welcome her—but then, why should they? She looked like an ordinary girl.

There came the sound of shouting from above, and the thunder of distant boots. The men on the ship must be coming to see what had set the dragons off. The door behind them creaked and groaned—the dragons were blasting it with their fire.

"We'd best be on our way," Lionel said. Together, they leaped through the portal, back to Chesterfield.

FIVE

THE BOY FROM NOWHERE

*Perhaps because of its beauty, the heartscale is a source of foolish
superstition. Some blame heartscales for the death of renowned
dragon hunter Sir Francis Tolemy II, who was driven to murderous
madness whilst wearing several around his neck. . . .*

—*TAKAGI'S* COMPENDIUM OF EXOTIC CREATURES

Ember and her father went for a walk around the
grounds of Chesterfield so that Ember could touch
her favorite trees and breathe in the smell of her favorite
library. When they got back to Lionel's office, the fire was
out, and there was a strange chill wind whistling through
the room.

"Oh my," Lionel said, gazing at a wet stain on the carpet. The wet seemed to be emanating from the open door,
which was the wardrobe door in Antarctica—from this
side, it looked like Lionel's ordinary office door, with several of Ember's coats hovering in midair in a ghostly way.
A snowflake fluttered past Ember's nose—a small drift had
accumulated on the carpet.

"What's happening?" Ember said. "Is it snowing in my room?"

"No—I believe it's Antarctica itself, seeping through the portal." Lionel sighed. "I'm afraid your time here must be limited—all sorts of nasty things can result from portals being left open too long. We will have to wait a week, at least, before your next visit, to allow the fabric of the world to unwrinkle itself."

Ember swallowed her tears and hugged her father goodbye. She stepped back through the wardrobe and closed the door behind her. Then she unscrewed the magical doorknob and replaced it with the ordinary one. When she opened the wardrobe again, she saw only her clothes.

Two days later, Madame Rousseau, sniffling from a cold, declared that a true professional did not risk passing germs to her pupils, and gave them the afternoon off school. Ember darted from the classroom just as Nisha opened her mouth to speak to her.

Ember didn't want to talk to anyone. Her encounter with the dragons had only fed the formless anger she had felt since leaving Chesterfield, which lurked like a hungry crocodile in a bayou. She had been so certain that somehow the dragons would *recognize* her. But they hadn't, and even if they had, it wouldn't matter. They were trapped, and there was nothing she could do about it.

The anger rose again. She wanted to run, to pull the shadows around her like a cloak as she did at Chesterfield. It seemed to her that the cozy research station, which was only a little bigger than her father's rooms at the university, grew smaller with each passing day.

A frigid breeze caressed her cheeks as she ran outside, past the greenhouse and the row of storage sheds. It was a pure blue sky that greeted her, though her shadow was longer than it should have been at midday. The sun didn't climb as high as it did in London.

The fresh, cold air made her feel light and bold. When she spotted Aunt Myra, she ran up to her.

"Ember!" her aunt said, starting. She stood by a sled with two other Scientists, all bundled in enormous coats and scarves. "What are you doing out here?"

"Madame Rousseau canceled school," Ember said. "Where are you going? Can I come?" She looked hungrily at the sled. She wondered if they were going all the way to the mountains, which loomed in the distance like slumbering giants.

Her aunt took her by the arm, drawing her back. "How many times have I told you that you are not to go outside unsupervised?"

"Twenty?" Ember guessed automatically.

Aunt Myra's mouth tightened. Ember hadn't been giving her cheek—it was just her honesty again, leaking out at the worst times. Before she could explain, though, Aunt

Myra said, "No, you're not going to come with me. It's far too dangerous. You're going to go back inside and do your homework."

Ember was surprised. "Why would I do that?"

Aunt Myra stared. "Haven't you been doing your homework?"

"No." Madame Rousseau had told them to read a chapter a day of a strange book about two children who had rhyming conversations with various animals that looked as if they'd been drawn by someone who'd never seen one. It was the most ghastly thing Ember had ever read. She had felt sorry for Madame Rousseau, who couldn't have seen many books if she thought something like that was worth reading. Ember hadn't been aware that this "homework" was mandatory. When she didn't like something her father gave her to read, she simply told him so, and they had a lively debate about it.

"Come along," her aunt said, taking her hand. Her mouth was a thin line.

"I know the way," Ember said, pulling her hand back. It was true enough, but it was also the wrong thing to say. Aunt Myra's expression darkened.

"Ember, when you are told to do something, you must do it," she said. "Now, please, go to your room and do your homework. We'll have a conversation when I get back."

Ember doubted very much it would be a conversation. Her anger rose again. She didn't want to go back to the station, but she knew Aunt Myra wouldn't listen if she argued, so she didn't bother. She waited in the library until she guessed that her aunt had left, then put her coat back on and went out again.

She wandered to the penguin beach, where she sat for a while, comforted by their squawks and honks. Two of the younger penguins came to sit at her side. They swiveled their heads, eyeing her from different angles.

For some strange reason, the penguins made Ember think of the dragons again. Perhaps it was the way they moved, so clumsy and helpless. She tore off a chunk of ice and hurled it into the water with all her strength.

It should have made her happy to learn that she wasn't the last fire dragon in the world. Instead, she had discovered that there was something worse than being the last of her kind. The fire dragons on the ship would never know freedom. Hunters would buy them, and then they would kill them, as they had killed her parents.

It's not fair.

She threw another piece of ice. "I've often had cause to observe that there isn't much fairness in the world," her father had remarked. Adults often said this sort of thing, as if noting the world's unfairness was supposed to be some sort of comfort. An excuse that let you ignore bad things. Well, it didn't comfort Ember—it made her wish she could turn those excuses to ash.

She was sick of unfairness. She had always darted through the world like an unseen ghost—she felt safe that way. But maybe she didn't want to feel safe anymore.

Still, that didn't mean she had any idea what she *should* do. She couldn't free the fire dragons. She couldn't bring back her parents, or any of the others. She threw another piece of ice, and it shattered against a frost-furred rock.

The penguins were undisturbed by her fury. They gazed at her with vague curiosity, as if she were a mild-mannered walrus. She pulled out the fish pasty she had stowed in her pocket and fed it to them in scraps. Soon she was surrounded by a honking horde that groomed her boots and rubbed their beaks on her coat. Most animals took a fancy to her, and it seemed ice-dwelling creatures were no different. Gradually their squawks calmed her, and she found herself smiling at their antics.

"Wouldn't do that if I was you," said a voice. Mac marched past, scattering penguins as he went. He came to a stop in the middle of the congregation, then took a notebook from his coat and scribbled something in it.

Ember made no reply, but Mac kept talking anyway. "You don't want to trust Adélies. They might look like cute wee things, but they have the hearts of lions. Nasty little tyrants, they are."

One of the penguins rubbed its beak against her knee. "Yes, they seem quite vicious."

"I've seen things I won't soon forget," Mac said in his ominous way. "Don't say I didn't warn you."

"All right." Ember wished Mac would go away. "I won't."

Another penguin waddled up to Ember and buried its head in her side. She didn't understand what it was doing until it withdrew its head, her flagstone clutched in its beak. It had taken it from her pocket!

Ember made a lunge, but the penguin raced off. It jumped onto an ice floe that Ember couldn't reach without using her wings. Other penguins clustered around it like spectators in a square, tilting their heads curiously. Ma—et *Scientia* was all Ember could read around its beak.

Mac turned toward her, and Ember snapped her gaze away from the penguins, her heart racing. Given the Scientists' aversion to anything related to magic, she doubted they would be pleased to find the penguins playing with an artifact from Chesterfield, even if it was just a bit of paving stone. She would wait until Mac left, then try to get it back.

Mac scanned the rocks. He made another note.

"What are you doing?" she said innocently.

"Your aunt is conducting a study on penguin migration," Mac said. "I'm tallying the birds wintering here and noting their general condition."

Ember thought this sounded interesting. "Can I help?"

"No." Mac swiped at his glasses, seeming to focus on her for the first time. "As a matter of fact, I don't think you're supposed to be out here at all, young lass. Are you?"

Ember wished she could swallow the truth rising in her throat. She was just opening her mouth to answer—and land herself in more trouble—when a voice rang out.

"Ember!"

Ember turned. To her dismay, Nisha was making her way toward them. She was bundled in a jacket in a shade of purple that coordinated with both her glossy boots and the swirl of ribbons in her hair. Ember felt a shiver of nervousness. She had always been intimidated by girls who knew how to coordinate.

"Moss and I were looking for you. We could use some help with the fort." Nisha held up a thermos proudly. "I have hot chocolate!"

"Er . . ." Ember glanced at Mac, who continued to gaze at her suspiciously. Nisha looked from one to the other, and then her eyes lit with a combination of understanding and mischief.

"You did say you would help us," she said in a cajoling tone. "And your aunt thinks you're with us. She didn't give you permission to go off by yourself."

Ember stared at Nisha, realizing that she was simultaneously rescuing her from Mac and obligating her to spend time with her and Moss. Ember didn't understand her at all. Other children were put off by Ember's unfriendliness, or because they were intimidated by her famous father. She thought of how strange it had felt to stand up to the Doll Twins, to take someone's side. She wasn't used to sides— she was used to standing alone.

Nisha turned to Mac. She was wearing eye shadow and pink powder on her cheeks, which only made her pretty face look more angelic. "Hello, Mac. My mother says that you were a great help with the drilling equipment yesterday. She very much appreciated it."

Mac gave a mollified grunt. "You shouldn't be spending your time with that boy, lass."

Nisha looked affronted. "Moss is my friend!"

"And you should choose your friends more carefully." Mac shuddered. "That bairn makes my skin crawl. When he wandered into the Firefly, I told Myra she'd regret taking him in. He's unnatural."

Ember blinked. "Wandered in? Are you saying Moss just *appeared*?"

"Aye," Mac said. "I remember the night too well—just over two years gone. A storm was raging—terrible fierce. You couldn't sleep through the racket, so we all sat together in the common room, drinking tea and whisky and trying to forget there was only an inch of metal and glass between us and certain death. None of us spoke much. All you could hear was the snow moaning about the station, like a horde of miserable ghosts." He paused. "Then there was a knock on the door."

In spite of herself, Ember was spellbound. "What did you do?"

"What do you think?" Mac gave a sharp laugh. "Jumped out of our skins, that's what. Your aunt was the first to her feet, and she opened the door. And what do you think we found? A boy framed against the dark with his hair full of snow, wearing naught but his skin."

"Where did he come from?"

"Ah, that's the question," Mac said. "Where indeed? None of us had ever laid eyes on him. The last ship set sail for England days before, eager to beat the ice. And you can't walk ten yards in a winter storm without getting lost and catching your death. Quite the mystery, isn't it?"

Ember looked at Nisha, expecting to hear the story contradicted. But the girl only shook her head, looking distressed.

"Well, Moss must know where he came from," Ember said.

"No," Nisha said sadly. "He can't remember a thing before that night. Not even his own name. Moss is just what he decided to call himself."

"There's all sorts of stories told about him." Mac lowered his voice conspiratorially. "Some say he's not from this century, even. That he's from an ancient Viking expedition that wrecked in the Amundsen Sea, and that he froze inside the ice and woke up again when it melted four hundred years later. They say that when the survivors of that wreck ran out of food, they ate each other one by one, but nobody bothered to eat him on account of his size."

"Blech," Nisha said.

"The Vikings never came to Antarctica," Ember said.

Mac tapped his nose. "Maybe they did, lass. Maybe they did."

Ember rolled her eyes. She thought it silly that she would know more about history than an old man, who after all had seen a lot of it himself, but then most adults were like that. They knew a lot about one or two things, and all that knowledge left no room in their heads for anything else. That was how it was with her father, who could talk for hours about Silverwood's *Treatise on the Third Era of Magic* (not that anyone ever wanted him to), but when she had asked once why people had decided to keep cats and dogs as pets—and not, say, owls or opossums, which were surely just as useful—he had stared at her blankly.

"He can't be a Viking," Nisha said. "He speaks English. I don't know what the Vikings spoke, but it wasn't English."

It was such a sensible thing to say that Ember looked at Nisha in surprise. Mac gave her a lofty look, as if he knew more about Vikings than she ever would, secret things, but both girls could tell that Nisha had him.

"There's a better explanation, anyway," Ember said. "Moss must be a Stormancer."

Mac smiled his lofty smile. "We discounted that. The boy's been tested by a renowned Magician, who found no trace of ability. Besides, those storm-chaser types don't start to show it until they're older."

Ember chewed her lip. That was true enough. Lionel St. George had come into his powers earlier than most, but even he had been fourteen before he could cast a single spell. Still, there must be some other explanation. Boys didn't just fall from the sky.

"That one's trouble," Mac said ominously. "Mark my words. Ah!"

To Ember's astonishment, one of the penguins had marched up to Mac and matter-of-factly slapped its wings against his boot.

"Why, you little devil," the Scientist said.

The penguin gave him another slap.

"Ah! See what I mean? You turn your back for an instant—"

"I think he can smell your pockets," Ember said, suppressing a snort. The penguin didn't reach Mac's knee.

But Mac wasn't listening. He lunged at the penguin, and it scampered off, chittering defiantly.

Nisha took Ember's hand and pulled her away. Once they were out of earshot, she muttered, "Ignore him."

"But I don't understand—it's like he's afraid of Moss."

"Mac's very superstitious. He's afraid of a lot of things. He hides in his room on the thirteenth day of every month and burns peppermint candles—did you know?"

Ember shook her head. "Why did Moss call himself Moss?"

"I don't know. I mean, he's obsessed with anything to do with plants. He spends most of his time in the greenhouse, helping Professor Maylie with her experiments."

"But who looks after him?"

"All the Scientists do. Your aunt gave him his own room at the station—it's right across from mine." Nisha smiled at her. "I'm so glad you're going to play with us. I've always wished there was another girl here! Kitty doesn't count, of course," she added, spitting out the name of the girl Doll Twin. Oh, your hand is so warm!"

Ember, befuddled, let Nisha lead her along the coast to a cave cut into the rock. Moss's head popped up from behind a bank of snow that he must have piled there himself. He greeted Ember shyly. Ember thought he looked even more colorless than yesterday, as if the wan sunlight had bleached him.

Moss and Nisha showed Ember what they were planning—to build a dome against the cave using rolls of snow piled atop each other. Nisha had worked out the precise number that would be required and wrote out the equation for Ember in the snow with a gloved finger. Overwhelmed by Nisha's confident friendliness, Ember silently set to work rolling snow. In truth, she didn't understand the point of what they were doing—why didn't Nisha and Moss just play inside, rather than going to the trouble of building an outdoor shelter? She suspected, though, that if she asked, they would just give her strange looks.

Nisha talked as she worked—a lot. Ember learned that Nisha's parents were Elizabeth and Gurjit Singh, the renowned glaciologists, and that they had been in

Antarctica for over a year. She also learned that Nisha wanted to be a mathematician when she grew up, or possibly a physicist, and that her twin sister had died from an illness several months ago.

Nisha fell uncharacteristically silent after that, and Moss, with a sharp glance in Nisha's direction, changed the subject before Ember could ask any questions. Moss himself spoke little, allowing Nisha to talk as much as she liked and dictate the construction of the fort, which Ember sensed was their usual way of doing things. Ember kept sneaking glances at Moss. He didn't look much like a Viking to her.

"Let's see," Nisha was saying, "if we wish to build a fort with a minimum height of twelve feet, assuming our snow bricks are approximately eight inches high—Ember, your bricks are a little small, I'm afraid—we'll need eighteen layers of bricks."

"How will we build a twelve-foot-high fort?" Moss said. "We're not half that tall ourselves."

"Easy. We'll build a staircase with the—"

"Hang on," Moss said. "Didn't your parents say you can't stay outside for more than an hour? Isn't that a new rule?"

Nisha's expression darkened. "There are so many new rules, I can't keep track. Never mind. I'll stay out as long as I want to."

"Have you ever seen an ice dragon?" Ember said. She

hadn't been paying attention to the conversation.

They both stared. Ember flushed. Her natural inclination to honesty also made it difficult for her to avoid voicing whatever was on her mind, even if it wasn't an appropriate time for it.

Nisha, however, recovered quickly. "No. My mother has, but only from far away. It's dangerous to get too close to their hunting grounds."

"Have they ever attacked anyone?"

"Oh yes." Nisha was nodding. "Not while I've been here. But there are stories. Every few years, a Scientist goes missing—usually near the South Pole. That's where most ice dragons live, your aunt thinks, though they fly to the coast to feed."

"Two Scientists were killed last year," Moss said. "They were researching magnetism."

"But how do they know it was dragons that killed them?" Ember said. "Did someone see it happen?"

"They didn't need to see it." Nisha lowered her voice, as if afraid that a dragon might overhear. "The bodies, they—they were torn apart. There's nothing else in Antarctica that could do that."

"Well," Moss said. "There is one other possibility."

"I don't want to talk about them," Nisha said with a dramatic shudder. "Not for anything! It's too horrible."

"But—" Ember began.

"Well, all right," Nisha said. "There are the—" She paused. "The grimlings."

"Grimlings?" Ember repeated. "What's that?"

"No one knows," Nisha said. "That's what they say the German expedition called them, back in the eighteenth century. A few Scientists have seen them, though most think they're hallucinations. Scientists, you know. But a few others—including your aunt—think there's more to the sightings than that."

"Well, what *are* they?" Ember said impatiently.

"It's like Nisha said," Moss replied. "Nobody knows. They live in the crevasses, maybe—deep inside the ice. They're small, and have no eyes . . . just ears to hear when something walks over them, and mouths full of sharp teeth they can eat you alive with. They travel in swarms, like insects, and some people say they can take the shape of other things—dragons, monsters. Even people."

Somehow, when Moss talked about grimlings in his quiet voice, it was more frightening than when Nisha did. The older girl gave another shudder.

"We shouldn't be talking about them," she said, though her cheeks were flushed with excitement. "It's bad luck."

Ember didn't remind her that she had made fun of Mac for his superstition. She just went back to work, filing away this new information. Antarctica, she was beginning to realize, was stranger than she could have imagined.

SIX

EMBER MAKES ANOTHER ENEMY

*There were two primary subspecies of fire dragon: Old World and
Australian. The Australian fire dragon was a bizarre violet creature that
preferred traveling on its belly like a snake, and dug burrows in the
desert soil. It is probable that in ancient times, many other subspecies
roamed our planet, which have since been lost to memory. . . .*

—*TAKAGI'S* COMPENDIUM OF EXOTIC CREATURES

In the days that followed, Ember helped Nisha and Moss
finish the snow fort. She went to school, and she even did
her homework with Nisha in the library, among the warm
yellow lamps and rustling pages that contrasted strangely
with the whirling snowflakes and long-shadowed mountains that loomed beyond the Firefly. She answered Nisha's
questions about Chesterfield and the famous Lionel St.
George. She ate dinner with Aunt Myra sometimes, when
her aunt wasn't busy, though she didn't try to ask about
dragons anymore—her aunt kept up such a steady stream
of talk that it wasn't really possible anyway. Ember found
herself preferring the nights when her aunt was busy with
her research, and she ate dinner alone.

She did all those things, but she wasn't really paying attention to any of it. She missed London, and her father, and Puff. Even worse than that, though, was the dark mood that had settled over her. It was like dragging around an extra shadow, one even crankier than the shadow in the corner. Her dreams were full of the fire dragons' cries, echoing behind her as she fled. Sometimes they were threatening. Other times, they were merely sad. Calling her back.

———————

A week after the fire dragons, Ember woke early and couldn't fall back to sleep. She didn't feel like going to school, and if she didn't have to do things she didn't like back in London, why should she here? Cheered by her rebelliousness, she pulled on her coat and boots. She crept past the Scientists huddled by the fire in the common room, darting so quickly through the dancing shadows that they didn't see her.

Once she was out of sight of the station, Ember spread her wings and let herself drift over the snow. The stars blazed and the Antarctic cold was like velvet against her skin. It had been several days since she'd felt it—Aunt Myra still wouldn't take her on any field trips, and had even forbidden her from playing outside, claiming it was too dangerous.

She landed on the shore where it jutted out into the sea,

forming the edge of the headland that guarded the harbor. The sea lapped against ice and snow with a sort of slurping sound. A honk floated out of the darkness.

One of the penguins tottered up to her. Ember recognized it as the one who had stolen the flagstone; its chest feathers had a distinct ruffle. The penguin seemed pleased to see her—it rubbed its beak on her boot.

"You!" Ember said. She had forgotten all about the penguin—she hoped it had dropped the flagstone into the sea where the Scientists would never find it. "You almost got me into trouble, you know." She scratched its head, which always worked with Puff, though she had no idea if penguins liked it. The bird eyed her sideways.

A larger penguin waddled up. It seemed about to muscle in to claim its share of attention. The first penguin chittered angrily. It drew back its wing, and—

Zap!

It was a sound that had no business coming from a penguin. Ember leaped back in alarm as the larger penguin went sailing through the air, struck by the unnatural force of the first penguin's slap. With a surprised squawk, the penguin lowered its wing, which sparked and hummed with a strange light.

No. With lightning.

"Oh no," Ember whispered.

The second penguin stood up, shaking snow off its back. It seemed unharmed, though little bolts of electricity skittered through its feathers. Another penguin standing nearby gave a squawk and fell over, as if shocked.

"Oh no," Ember said again. Her thoughts flashed back to the flagstone, which had looked perfectly ordinary, identical to all the others that lined Chesterfield's winding paths. She had taken it from her father's office—she had just assumed he had found a broken one somewhere, and decided to use it as a paperweight! But he must have charged it with magic, perhaps intending to use it for a spell he had never gotten around to casting. And now the penguins, either by breaking the flagstone or pecking at it, had absorbed that magic.

The first penguin rubbed its beak against her boot again. Ember couldn't imagine any scenario in which Mac or the other Scientists would find this amusing, nor one where she would escape blame. After all, who but Lionel St. George's daughter would do something like this?

The penguins waddled off calmly, as if lightning bolts were their traditional way of resolving disputes. *It will wear off,* Ember thought with an edge of hysteria. *Please let it wear off.*

In the meantime, there was nothing she could do except hope the Scientists didn't notice that their research subjects had been electrified.

Someone shouted in the distance. The sound echoed by raucous laughter, and then a gunshot. Lord Norfell. Lord Norfell, who would surely be one of the first hunters to bid on the captive fire dragons. Ember felt a dark sort of anticipation—she had thought she'd missed her chance to make herself his enemy. Moving silently through the dark, she followed the sounds to where the ground leveled off at the base of a mountain.

There at least twenty men were gathered, their breath rising through the frosty air like clouds of white smoke. Lord Norfell was mounted on a sled attached to a team of dogs. Two others had their own dogsleds aligned with his, while a small group affixed a target to a post driven into the snow. Several figures watched from a hill overlooking the field, including two Scientists Ember recognized. And there was another, smaller figure—Moss. The boy had a satchel slung over his back, as if he was just getting back from somewhere. He watched the men below with a frown.

Ember's first instinct was to flee—but then a small voice whispered about her vow, and she crept closer, heart thundering.

Another boy stood a short distance from the men, his arms crossed, scanning the landscape restlessly. He blinked when his gaze met hers. He was nobody Ember had seen before, and was oddly dressed in a long green coat that resembled a cape at the bottom, and had golden stars on the epaulets. His boots were tall and shiny, and in addition to the bow and quiver slung over his shoulder, he wore a sword at his belt.

The boy strode toward her, his cape billowing. His tawny eyes were large and deep set, reminding Ember of an owl peering out of a thicket. His tangle of hair was golden brown, curling around his ears, almost the same shade as his skin. For some reason, Ember felt herself blushing.

"Excuse me. Who gave you permission to be here?" the boy asked Ember, in a voice that managed to be both polite and rude at the same time.

Ember frowned. "Who gave *you* permission?" Her tone was rather less polite than his.

He looked surprised, then he smiled. "You're joking. I like that. Most people don't joke around me."

Ember gazed back at him blankly. In her pocket, the doorknob gave a rattle. Ember's hand flew to it. She had discovered it by her door that morning, despite having left it in her suitcase, and this had alarmed her so much that she had resolved to carry it with her wherever she went. She couldn't risk losing her door to Chesterfield.

"Is that Takagi's *Compendium*?" the boy said. He was staring at Ember's other pocket—the book was sticking out of it. She was currently memorizing the entry on lantern fish.

Ember hadn't thought there were any other children who had read Takagi's *Compendium*. "Yes."

"Takagi's all right," the boy said. "She's not as thorough as Littlewood, though."

"Littlewood?" Ember snorted. "His sketches are terrible. You can't tell a griffin from a rhinoceros."

The boy laughed. "That's true enough." He gave Ember an appraising look, which she returned. "I don't meet many people who know much about zoology," he said, echoing Ember's own thought. He motioned to the men. "They're about to start practicing for the hunt. You can watch with me." And he extended his arm to Ember.

Ember stared at it, confusion warring with alarm. At that moment, the doorknob gave an unmistakable lurch. The boy's gaze sharpened on Ember's other pocket.

"Is that magic?" A note of excitement entered his voice. "Let me see it."

Ember disliked being ordered about, even when she was in a good mood. "No."

The word came out more bluntly than she had intended. The boy's eyes darkened. The doorknob went still, as if it too was taken aback; then it began to rattle again. Ember's heart thudded as she realized that the boy must be Prince Gideon—it explained why she hadn't seen him at the station, as well as his thoughtless bossiness. Also, she suspected that the doorknob was the sort to get excited in the presence of royalty.

"I am the crown prince of these lands," the boy said, drawing himself up to his full height. Ember found herself wondering why she had initially perceived his face as kind. His mouth was pinched, as if habitually held in an irritated frown, and in his eyes was a gleam of cruelty. "Let me see it, I said."

"No," Ember repeated. Her lurking anger snapped its jaws. "Your Highness."

Prince Gideon's face was as pinched as a mole's. "Who are you? Who are your parents?"

Ember was feeling calmer with each passing minute. She was relieved by his unpleasantness—she had no idea how to respond to a kind prince, but a cruel one was straightforward. "I'm Ember. Myra St. George is my aunt."

"St. George?" The prince's voice was scornful. "That explains it. Did you come here to spy on us?"

Ember was baffled. What reason could she have to spy on Prince Gideon?

Realization dawned on the prince's face. "You don't know, do you? About the hunt."

Ember gazed at him blankly.

"I suppose that isn't surprising," the prince said. "It's not open to commoners, you see. We keep it quiet. My father's trying to convince the queen to expand it, but she keeps listening to the Scientists—they say that if we allow too many hunters to come here, ice dragons will go extinct."

Ember felt as if she'd plunged into the icy sea. "You're— you're hunting dragons."

"An annual hunt with a select group of men is all my grandmother will allow," the prince said. "For now. We set sail for the dragons' hunting grounds the day after tomorrow. The third annual Winterglass Hunt."

"Winterglass?"

The prince raised his hand. For a moment, Ember thought he was offering it to her again, but then he removed his thick glove, and a ring flashed. It was inlaid with a cluster of stones the color of starlight on water, a swirl of silver and shadow and winter sky. Ember gasped. She had never seen anything like it.

"Pretty, isn't it?" The prince replaced his glove. "You can tell your aunt that this will be a record year. And that there's nothing she can do about it. My grandmother has already said that the hunt can go on as scheduled. Clearly she wasn't that impressed by your aunt's letters. Nor was the Senate."

"Her letters?" Ember's thoughts whirled. Aunt Myra had written to Queen Victoria?

"I'm participating this year," the prince said in a lofty voice. "My father gave me permission."

"You?" Prince Gideon looked no older than her—and his father would allow him to take part in a dragon hunt?

The prince regarded her coolly. Then he fixed an arrow to his bow and turned toward the target the men had erected. It was quite a distance away, and there were several people still clustered about it. This did not seem to bother Prince Gideon one bit. He loosed the arrow, and a man jumped as it whistled past his ear. It struck the target dead center.

He turned to Ember, smiling. She gave him a glare so

venomous he took a step back. If she had burst into flames then and there, turning Prince Gideon into a royal pile of ash, she wouldn't have been sorry. She couldn't believe it. Even here, at the bottom of the world, dragons weren't safe.

"The Scientists are right," she said, her voice shaking. "Ice dragons will go extinct if you allow hunting here."

"You share your aunt's views, do you?" Prince Gideon said. "What is wrong with you people? A dragon would rip you apart at the first opportunity. They're vicious beasts. They've killed Scientists, you know, Scientists just like your aunt—or don't you care about that?" He slung the bow over his shoulder. "I hope they do go extinct—and I hope that I'm the reason for it. I want to be the person who kills the last dragon in the world."

He stormed away. Ember didn't move, didn't breathe. She just stood there, her hands balled into fists. But then her anger dropped away, and hot tears slid down her cheeks. How many ice dragons lived in Antarctica? How long would it be before they too were gone, and all that was left of dragons was a memory, a story in a book?

One of the hunters strode past. He did a double take when he saw her. "Girl, what do you think you're doing? This is no place for children."

"Sir Abraham?" one of the other men called, and the hunter waved him off. He had a deeply lined face and the most dignified mustache Ember had ever seen. It was immensely thick and droopy, as if it bore the weight of the world.

"Are you taking part in the Winterglass Hunt?" the man said, in the same way you would ask, "Are you currently purple?"

"The practice field is restricted to participants only," he went on. "Move along, now. It's not safe for children."

Ember felt as if something was surfacing from deep inside her. "What did you say?"

"I said, it's dangerous here." Sir Abraham frowned. "Are you from the research station? Can't those flighty Scientists keep an eye on their—"

"No." Ember's heart pounded. "What did you say before that?"

The man looked exasperated. "I asked if you were taking part in the Winterglass Hunt. Only hunters are permitted here, so I suggest you move along."

Ember looked at Lord Norfell, easily visible with his flame-colored hair, laughing with the other men. Prince Gideon, standing nearby, glowered at her—he was her sworn enemy now too. She thought of all the dragons that would die because of them, of all the dragons who had died—not just because of this hunt, but others like it.

Sir Abraham gave her a strange look. "Are you all right, child? Are you sick?"

"No," Ember said. "Sir Abraham, is there an age limit for the Winterglass Hunt?"

"There was." He was still eyeing her strangely. "Until His Royal Highness decided he wanted to compete." He tilted his head in Prince Gideon's direction, a look of disapproval on his face. "Now Prince Cronus has decreed that anyone as young as twelve can take part."

"Are there any other requirements?" Ember pressed. "Does it cost money to enter?"

"No. Prince Cronus takes a cut of all the winterglass we collect. As long as a man's of noble blood, he can take part. Of course, only the most dedicated hunters would come to a place like this. . . ."

"Noble blood," Ember murmured. "Thank you, Sir Abraham." She darted away, leaving the man staring after her.

Once out of sight, she broke into a run and leaped into the air. Her anger hadn't left, but it had changed into something else, like water shaping itself into ice, sharp and jagged. The remnants of the aurora hung in the violet sky, green bars that billowed like a lion's mane.

She couldn't help the fire dragons, or undo what had happened to the others. But perhaps here, unexpectedly, she could do something else. Perhaps she could save another dragon's life, or more than one. The stars shone brighter the higher she flew, as if they were mirrors reflecting her excitement back at her.

She was going to join the Winterglass Hunt. And she was going to sabotage it.

SEVEN

THIEVES AND GRIMLINGS

*Fire dragons lived alone or in pairs; however, in inhospitable
environments, such as the Kalahari Desert, they were
known to form small clans, banding together to defend
themselves against threats and rivals. . . .*

—*TAKAGI'S* COMPENDIUM OF EXOTIC CREATURES

E mber could tell something was wrong as soon as she
saw the Firefly.

Before sunrise, the research station looked like its
nickname. It crouched in the shadows like a many-legged
insect, lit from within, its golden glow spilling across the
ice. Usually it looked peaceful—now it thrummed with
activity. Scientists darted to and fro behind the glass,
while others clustered by the door wearing headlamps and
snowshoes, as if they were about to set off on a long trek.
One of them was Mac, who let out a low whistle as Ember
trudged up.

"Well, well!" he said. "There's the lass. What do you
have to say for yourself?"

Ember never knew what adults meant by this. "Noth-ing?" she tried.

"Nothing!" Mac shook his head. "Nothing, she says. After causing such a commotion, is that the best you can do?"

Ember, who had never in her life been the cause of a commotion that didn't involve things being set on fire, merely stared at him. Mac took her by the arm. "Och! Come on, you. Your aunt's in a black humor about all this."

"All what?" Ember asked, but Mac just said, "Och!" again and shook his head despairingly.

Ember was annoyed. Her giddy excitement was still with her, and she wanted to go somewhere to work out a proper plan. She didn't have a moment to lose—the hunt began in two days.

Ember followed Mac to the common room, which, to her surprise, was deserted—apart from her aunt, who stood pacing by the fire, her boots managing to thud even against the thick carpet. She was wearing her most hideous gray suit, the long skirt making a sort of huffing sound as she moved, like an old man clearing his throat.

She spun around when Mac entered. When she saw Ember, her lower lip trembled, and then she seemed to steel herself. She placed her hands on her hips, and for some reason the gesture caused Mac to scurry from the room. "Where," she began in an ominous voice, "have you been?"

"Down in the field with the hunters," Ember said. She knew Aunt Myra was going to lecture her again, and her answer came out sullen.

"The hunters?" Aunt Myra said. "You went to watch them? Why on earth would you do that? What were you thinking? Do you have any idea how dangerous they are?"

Ember's mouth fell open. She wasn't used to having questions hurled at her like sharp stones. Which one was she supposed to answer first?

Her aunt stamped her boot, causing the neat pyre of logs in the fire to collapse in a shower of sparks. "I specifically stated that you were not to leave the station unsupervised, not even for a moment, and this morning Mac tells me that you've been sneaking out every chance you get. Now I learn that you missed school to watch the hunters?"

"Nisha and Moss said—" Ember began.

"Nisha and Moss are allowed to play outside," her aunt snapped. "You are not."

This was so clearly unfair that Ember was momentarily struck dumb. Aunt Myra paced before the fire, appearing to wrestle with her temper. When she spoke again, her voice was carefully steady. "Apparently, from now on, we will need to monitor you. We have no nursemaids here, of course, but the scientists' assistants can perform the duty on rotation."

Ember drew in her breath. She was to be watched? Like an infant that might at any moment put something dangerous in her mouth? She was twelve years old!

"That's not fair," she said hotly. "I only want—"

"What you want is nowhere near as important as your safety," Aunt Myra interjected. "If you continue to disobey my instructions, I will have to write to your father."

Ember stared. Aunt Myra was going to write to her father and tell him—what? That Ember was behaving like a spoiled child? Didn't she understand that none of this was what Ember truly wanted? Her pulse beat in her ears. She had never felt so angry in her life.

"I don't care if you do," she declared. "While you're at it, tell him that you keep me locked inside all day, and that you won't even talk to me about your research—or anything else that matters!"

Aunt Myra looked as if she had walked into a wall. There was a small silence. "Ember, I . . . my research, I mean, isn't something that would interest you—"

"You're studying *dragons*," Ember almost shouted. "Why wouldn't that interest me? Now I find out that you're writing letters to Queen Victoria and trying to stop the Winterglass Hunt. Why didn't you tell me? Don't you know how much I want to help? It was hunters like those men who killed my parents!" Ember's anger flowed through her like a river, wild and unstoppable. Only it wasn't just anger at her aunt now—it was Prince Gideon, and Lord Norfell; it was Nisha and Moss, for their confusing kindness; and even her father, for not knowing how to unwrinkle the world with a wave of his hand or turn back time to correct a mistake he had made when he was a teenager.

"You didn't think of that, did you?" she said. "You didn't think of me at all. Why did you invite me here, if you were going to treat me like some experiment you got bored with?"

Aunt Myra actually took a step back. She stared at Ember for a long moment. Then her jaw quivered, and to Ember's astonishment, she began to cry.

She sank into the chair by the fire, burying her face in her hands. Ember, who had been so full of fury a second ago, now felt it fall from her like a weight, leaving only weariness and a dull, untraceable sorrow.

"I'm sorry, Ember," Aunt Myra said finally, brushing her tears away. "I've made a mess of everything, haven't I? I don't—I don't know how to look after children! I don't even know how to talk to them. You especially."

"Because I'm not a real child," Ember said, her voice flat.

"No!" Myra said it so sharply that Ember jumped. "No, Ember—because you're Lionel's child. Do you have any idea what my brother would do to me if I let any harm come to even one hair on your head?"

Ember was confused. Though she had heard stories about her father attacking bandits or treacherous fellow Stormancers, she had never witnessed him hurt anyone (apart from insects, toward which he was ruthless). Myra seemed to guess her thoughts and gave a wry, shaky smile.

"He would look terribly disappointed and give me

one of his bumbling, nervous lectures," she said, "then he would tell me he forgave me, and that I must take extreme care with all the *other* hairs on your head, and then he would give me a hug." She sighed. "And through it all, without even meaning to, he would make me feel three inches tall."

Ember hadn't been expecting this. She gazed at her aunt with new eyes.

"Lionel always did have that way about him," she said ruefully, dabbing at her eyes with her sleeve. "Even when we were children. I remember one time I pushed him into a mud puddle at a party—I thought it would be a good joke! And what did he do? He apologized to our mother's guests for not setting a better example. Then when I cried about it later, he found me and apologized to *me* for not being more delicate with my feelings. Now he's the most celebrated Stormancer in the empire, and I'm—what? Still the embarrassing little sister he has to apologize for, while *he* can't do anything wrong."

"He gets things wrong," Ember said awkwardly. She chose the most recent example that came to mind. "Didn't you hear about the spell he cast to restore Lady Trembleworth's youth? She'll have to go through life with an upside-down nose now."

Myra sighed. She blew her nose into a handkerchief.

"Is that why you've been avoiding him?" Ember said. "My father said that since you got out of prison, you won't see him."

Myra made an exasperated sound. "I'm avoiding him? That's rich. He's the one who always has some excuse not to visit. And would it kill him to answer a letter in less than three months? Or let me pay him back for bailing me out of prison?"

These questions seemed directed not at Ember but at some invisible version of her father, and she wisely avoided answering.

Aunt Myra rested her forehead on her palm. After a moment, her shoulders began to shake, and Ember thought she was crying again. But she wasn't—she was *laughing*.

"Upside-down nose," she said.

A smile crept across Ember's face. "Yes. But better than sprouting two extra ears, which is what happened when Lord Flightley wanted to cure his bald spot."

Aunt Myra doubled over, and Ember laughed too, though extra ears were far less funny when you were actually confronted with them. Aunt Myra's laughter was warm, and so loud it shook the floor.

Into the surprisingly companionable silence that followed, Aunt Myra said, "Ember, I haven't done this properly. I'm sorry. It's not that I didn't want to talk to you—the thing is, I didn't want to risk treating you like some research subject. I've spent years studying dragons, and I thought I might . . . well, make you feel uncomfortable. I wanted you to feel like an ordinary girl."

"But I'm not an ordinary girl," Ember said. "And in any case, why didn't you think to ask what I wanted?"

"I don't know. I suppose I was so caught up in keeping you safe, and getting your father to trust me again, that I forgot to find out if you were happy here." She paused. "*Are you happy here?*"

Ember considered. She thought of the icy mountains, begging to be explored, the curious penguins, the twilight sky. And all that Science! "I don't know. I suppose I could be, if—if things were different." If she was a normal girl enjoying a holiday. If she could return home whenever she wanted, without being a danger to anyone. She didn't say any of that, though.

"If you didn't feel cooped up, I wager," her aunt said, shaking her head again. "Is that why you went down to watch the hunters practice? I can't imagine you getting any enjoyment out of it."

Ember swallowed. In her anger, she had almost forgotten about her plan. If Aunt Myra got angry at her for going near the hunters, she certainly wasn't going to react well if Ember told her she was planning to join the hunt. "I—I didn't know they would be there."

Aunt Myra expression softened. "I should have told you about the Winterglass Hunt. I'm well aware of how your parents died, and I shouldn't have left you to find out about it that way. But, well—I hoped I wouldn't need to. I've been trying to stop it, you see."

Ember remembered the letters Aunt Myra had written. "To stop it?"

"Oh yes," her aunt said darkly. "Come with me. I

should have shown you this days ago."

Ember followed Aunt Myra to her room, which she had never seen before. Aunt Myra's room was—well, calling it a mess would be kind. It reminded Ember of her father's study, except that instead of books on Stormancy, used teacups, and piles of papers, it was crowded with scientific equipment—magnifying glasses and carbon paper; protractors and compasses. In the corner was a set of scales on which, unnervingly, two small bones were balanced. A single painting hung on the wall: Ember recognized her father, then a teenager, and her grandmother. There was also a girl who looked only a little older than Ember, who she recognized as Myra from her piles of hair and flushed cheeks, as if she had sprinted there. The painting was clearly old, but someone had cleaned and reframed it.

Ember's eyes went to a shelf in the corner. On it was a necklace of sapphires and gilded pearls, a silver hairbrush studded with sapphires, and another roughly hewn sapphire the size of a goose egg. Aunt Myra seemed to have a penchant for them. "What's that?"

"Nothing." Aunt Myra hastily stepped in front of the shelf. "Just a few, ah, mementos."

"Mementos," Ember repeated.

Aunt Myra glanced over her shoulder. Her eyes went a little misty. "From some of my more successful heists."

"Won't you get in trouble for keeping them?" Ember said.

"Well, as they've already sent me to jail for it, there's

not much else they can do. Bit of a loophole, that."

Ember didn't think this was what "loophole" meant, but said nothing. Aunt Myra unceremoniously swept her arm across the desk, sending books and telescope lenses tumbling down to join the chaos on the floor. "Sit," she said, motioning to a chair.

Ember sat. Aunt Myra perched beside her and flipped through a sketchbook. Once she found the page she was looking for, she handed it to Ember.

Ember drew a sharp breath. She was staring at a blurry photograph of a dragon, spectral and magnificent, thinner than fire dragons and more sinuous, like water given form. Somehow Ember could sense the gleaming silver-blue of the dragon's scales. She felt cold just looking at it.

"This was done by Professor Walcott," Aunt Myra said. "There are others, though."

"How did they get so close?" The image looked as if it had been taken mere yards away from its subject.

"It was perfectly safe," Aunt Myra said. "The dragons don't attack. They ignore us, for the most part, once they're sure we aren't hunters."

Ember stared. "What?"

"It's true," her aunt said. "The stories are wrong. They aren't bloodthirsty beasts. And what's more, I think they can speak to each other. We heard them using words— none that we could understand, but words nonetheless. They're thinking creatures, not animals."

Ember's breath caught. Did this also explain her own

strange existence? Were fire dragons, too, cleverer than anyone thought? Ember's father had often speculated that this was the case, though Ember's own intelligence could very well have resulted from a quirk in the spell, much like Montgomery's sense of self. (Unless, of course, all doorknobs had a sense of self that they never had the opportunity to express, which Ember supposed was impossible to know with certainty.)

"I've told all this to Queen Victoria," Aunt Myra said. "Unlike the rest of her family, she actually has an interest in this place—and I think I'm beginning to get through to her. Several senators are on my side. If I could just get more evidence . . ."

"Do you really think she'd stop the hunt?" Ember said.

"I do. She's already placed limits on the number of ice dragons they can kill each year. Of course, even if dragons were little more than unthinking beasts, it would be wrong to hunt them to extinction. Dragonglass, though, is so profitable that most are prepared to ignore that. But if we can prove to the queen that dragons can speak and reason and feel just like people, I think we can convince her to protect them."

"But why would she?" Ember said. "Even if you can prove that ice dragons are smart, they've killed Scientists in the past. Torn them apart, Nisha said. Would the queen forgive them for that?"

"Those Scientists were killed by *something*," Aunt Myra

said. "The dead tell no tales, and there are things in this world more dangerous than dragons."

"Like the grimlings?" A shiver went down Ember's spine.

Aunt Myra nodded and passed Ember a sketch.

Ember squinted at it. The sketch showed a mountain peak under a starry sky. Before the artist stretched a field of ice, perhaps the edge of a glacier, and rising up out of a crevasse was—

"What *is* that?" Ember said.

It looked like smoke, but the smoke had mouths in it. Hundreds of mouths. They yawned open, round and hungry and sharp, as if trying to devour the stars.

"That is the only documented sighting of what some have been calling the grimlings," Aunt Myra said. "It's possible this was the only time they've been observed by someone who lived to tell of it."

They fell silent, both gazing at the sketch. Ember looked away first. The sketch aroused a revulsion so deep it rattled her bones.

"Who drew this?" she said.

Aunt Myra gave a dark smile. "I did."

"You?"

"Of course. I wouldn't ask one of my Scientists to take that sort of risk. That's the first rule of leadership. When something threatens the lives of my people, I'm going to solve it, not ask someone else to." She frowned. "As it was, I couldn't get close enough to understand what I was seeing."

"Where was this?"

"On the Tacroy Glacier. The same place several dragons were killed in the last Winterglass Hunt."

Ember frowned. "What does that mean?"

"I don't know," Aunt Myra said. "I'm a Scientist, so I don't assume two things are connected just because they match up. But it is interesting, isn't it? Could the grimlings be drawn to places where dragons have died? If so, why?"

"Nisha said they can take other forms," Ember said. "Is that true?"

Her aunt sighed. "Yes, Nisha has been listening to some of the more outlandish rumors. It's true there have been sightings of strange . . . figures. They only appear after dark. Professor Binder has seen one. 'Pale and thin,' he called it. But I'm not convinced. The darkness here does things to the imagination."

Ember examined the sketch. "I don't think Queen Victoria is listening to your letters. Prince Gideon said that—"

Aunt Myra snorted. "Don't tell me you spoke to the princeling."

Ember nodded. "He's taking part in the hunt."

Aunt Myra shook her head darkly. "I suppose that shouldn't surprise me. His father has always cared more about showing up his relatives than he does about his son."

Ember blinked. "Prince Gideon's father doesn't care about him?"

"I shouldn't think so, as he's not plated in gold, or otherwise of value to him. Gideon's mother was a Turkish princess—she was Cronus's second wife, and every bit as rich as his first. She died in an odd sort of accident, just like the other one. Nothing to connect it to her husband, of course, though there were rumors I won't go into. Cronus didn't waste any time mourning her loss—remarried another rich princess right away, and had a batch of new sons. They all live in England, where Cronus spends most of his time, leaving Gideon alone here. I would say it's a shame for a boy to be separated from his parents, but when that parent is Prince Cronus, I think it would be healthier for Gideon to spend even less time with him. That's not the sort of man a boy should look up to."

Ember considered this silently. Prince Gideon was horrid, to be sure, but she couldn't help feeling a twinge of compassion for him. She couldn't imagine having a father like Prince Cronus.

They stayed there for another hour or so, until the purple light brightened to deep aquamarine. Ember liked how Aunt Myra talked to her. It was as if she viewed her as an equal—she didn't use simple words or a special voice the way many of the professors at Chesterfield did. Finally Aunt Myra glanced at the clock and declared that it was time for Ember to go to school.

"Aunt Myra," Ember said as they stood to go. "Do you really believe that your research can stop the hunt?

Dragonglass is so valuable. And everyone is convinced that dragons are monsters."

Her aunt gave a slow nod. "It's true that saving these dragons will be no easy task. But it's also true that even the mightiest train can be derailed by a single penny. In my experience, most people confuse impossible with difficult. All we can do is try."

Ember mulled this over. She paused by the door, her gaze falling on an old tintype photo on the dresser. It showed a young woman in a rather short dress holding two wine bottles to her mouth, while around her crowded several men and women making faces or holding up their own bottles. One man appeared to be mooning the camera.

"Where did that come from?" Aunt Myra slammed the photo facedown, her cheeks a brilliant red. "I say! I don't know who any of those people are."

"Well, the one in the middle looks like you," Ember pointed out.

"I don't think—I mean, Scientific gatherings can be a bit . . . you know."

Ember did not know, but she thought she was beginning to understand a few things about her aunt. "You don't have to dress like that," she said. "I won't tell my father."

Aunt Myra nervously adjusted her hideously respectable jacket. "Like what, dear? Amos!" she called to the man leaving a room across the hall, who started. "How are the soil samples looking?" And with that, she thundered away.

Ember trailed after. She felt a whisper of guilt about not telling Aunt Myra her plan. But there was no way her aunt would allow her anywhere near the Winterglass Hunt. She thought of the captive fire dragons, and her resolve hardened. If she could do something—anything—to save the ice dragons from a similar fate, she would. No matter what her aunt thought.

EIGHT

EMBER GAINS
TWO SECONDS

*Considering the former abundance of fire dragons,
and their wide extent over the globe, it is surprising how little
is known of their habits and behavior.*

—*TAKAGI'S* COMPENDIUM OF EXOTIC CREATURES

E mber stayed up half the night, scheming. She discarded several ideas, such as setting fire to the hunters' ship (risky, given that she'd have to be on board to do it) and setting off flares to warn the dragons that the hunters were coming (she didn't know how they'd react to flares—what if they were curious and came to investigate?).

Just as she finally drifted off to sleep, she had been awoken by a murmur of sound from the wardrobe, and the soft *scritch-scritch* of claws.

She was out of bed in an instant, staring at the wardrobe door. Montgomery was asleep under her bed. Her thoughts turned to the Red Labyrinth between the worlds—had one of its creatures somehow escaped into her wardrobe?

Heart pounding, she inched open the door. Puff

uncoiled herself into the room, stretching first her front legs, then her back. "Eat!"

"Oh, you naughty cat!" Ember said. "You found a way through the portal!"

It was the only explanation. Cats had no respect for doors, and were good at slipping through the smallest of gaps. Puff must have used that talent to winnow her way through the portal, even though it was dormant.

The cat purred, winding herself around Ember's legs. She couldn't take Puff back to London—at least not immediately, given the wrinkled state of the fabric of the world. So she tiptoed out to the quiet kitchen, which was empty, and gathered a saucer of milk, a piece of raw fish, and some of the liver and gravy left over from dinner. She took the smelly feast back to Puff, who devoured everything.

"Eat," the cat said approvingly. She bounded onto Ember's pillow and began washing her face, as if they were back in Ember's room at Chesterfield.

"Father will be worried about you," Ember scolded. Lionel St. George doted on the white cat. He allowed her to sleep on his favorite chair and jump on his desk, even though she overturned the inkwell and got black paw prints everywhere. If Puff sat on his lap in the evening, Lionel generally refrained from moving until she was finished. Ember had often marveled at how the most renowned Stormancer in the Empire had, in truth, less power than a small, spoiled cat.

"Now now now," Puff muttered through her purrs.

Ember buried her face in the cat's fur. Eventually, soothed by Puff's familiar snores, she drifted into an uneasy sleep, haunted by the glowing eyes of dragons that circled in the darkness.

———————

Ember could barely concentrate during school the next day. Madame Rousseau had to call on her three times before Ember could provide the correct answer to her question (the date of Captain Robert Scott's expedition to the South Pole). At one point, Madame Rousseau asked in a digni-fied voice if Ember had decided to write her next essay about the carpet, as she kept staring at it. The Doll Twins snickered. They had been keeping to themselves lately, and Moss had reported, with a shy glance at Ember, that Baxter, the boy, had not once tried to stick his head in a textbook. Ember ignored them—they were the least of her worries right now.

The Winterglass Hunt was tomorrow.

Ember felt lightheaded. Her stomach was so twisted up that she hadn't been able to eat breakfast. A small, elab-orately folded piece of paper landed in her lap, and she jumped. Confused, she looked up at the ceiling.

Someone sighed. Ember turned to find Nisha watching her. She held her usual thermos of hot chocolate in her hand—the paper, Ember realized, had a small smudge of brown on it. Nisha carried hot chocolate with her almost everywhere. She had declared it the world's most Scientifically perfect food.

Nisha mimed unfolding the paper.

Puzzled, Ember did. On it was written: *The library. Five o'clock.*

She suppressed a groan and glanced back at the other girl, whose expression was uncharacteristically serious. She raised her eyebrows as if to say, "Well?"

Fortunately, Ember was spared the need to reply. Madame Rousseau hit Nisha with a tricky algebra question, which she answered with ease, though she couldn't have been paying attention. Ember turned back to the blackboard and pretended to be fascinated by the equations.

She slipped out the door during the second it took Nisha to pull on her coat. The Winterglass Hunt was tomorrow, and she still hadn't figured out a proper plan. She sneaked past her aunt, too, who was in the storage hexagon gesticulating wildly at her assistants. Once she reached her room, Ember breathed a sigh of relief. Being around people all day was exhausting.

She froze in horror. Puff lay on her side on the rug, her tufted paws wrapped around a small object she was cheerfully muttering threats at.

"Oh, Puff, no!" Ember cried.

"Mine!" the cat wailed as Ember pried Montgomery from her claws. "Mine mine mine mine mine—"

Ember hurried the poor doorknob over to the light to

examine its injuries. They weren't severe, but the keyhole was scratched, and the stem had gnaw marks all over it.

"I'm sorry, Montgomery," Ember said, and meant it. "I promise that I'll fix you up. Please calm down."

The doorknob would do no such thing. Ember had never seen it so furious—not only did Montgomery attempt to roll out of her hands, but it refused to be packed into her bag, shaking itself vigorously when Ember tried.

"Please," Ember said, half in tears after a dozen failed attempts. She couldn't leave the doorknob behind—it was her way back to her father, and Chesterfield, and she would need it in case of an emergency. "You have to come with me tomorrow—"

The doorknob, at its wits' end, gave a mighty shake, flying into the air and whomping her in the face. Puff caterwauled with delight as her forbidden quarry tumbled to the ground, and then Ember was wrestling with both of them—the muttering, murderous cat and the slippery doorknob, which seemed to have decided that it would sooner die inflicting injury on its enemies than allow such an insult to its dignity to stand. Occupied as she was, Ember did not at first hear the knocking on her door, which grew more insistent as the fight progressed.

"Ember?" came a muffled voice. "Are you all right?"

"Die!" Puff yowled with horrible glee, sinking her teeth into the doorknob.

There was a startled silence from the other side of the door. "What?"

The cat let out an evil wail of triumph. "Quiet!" Ember snapped. She managed to seize Puff by the scruff of her neck, lifting her hissing and spitting into the air. The doorknob rolled exhaustedly under the bed to nurse its wounds. Ember marched to the door and threw it open, then flung the cat into the corridor—past Moss, who stood outside, gaping. With a hiss, Puff scampered off into the shadows.

"By the Sciences! What on earth was all that?"

Ember shoved her scratched hands into her pockets. "Ah—just the cat."

Moss was staring at her face. Ember realized that she likely had a black eye from where the doorknob had struck her.

"She's a very naughty cat," she added.

"I didn't know that you had a cat," Moss said slowly. "Pets aren't allowed at the Firefly."

"Well, you know cats." Ember was increasingly desperate to change the subject. "If there's a rule, they'll break it. Did you want something?"

Moss seemed about to argue further, but Ember gave him her best blank stare, and he shook his head, his face solemn. His hair was tangled with leaves as usual, and there was dirt under his fingernails, as if he'd been scrabbling around in garden soil. He looked at Ember's half-packed bag. She hastily stepped in front of it.

"Would you come with me?" he said.

Ember, silently cursing her inability to lie her way out of things, followed him to a room at the opposite end of the hall. It was the same size as hers, only it held a bunk bed. Hanging on the wall was a chalkboard covered in mathematical equations. In one corner was a sketch of a lion. It was beautifully done, but faded with age. Whoever had written out the equations had carefully gone around it.

"Is this your room?" Ember said.

"Nisha's," Moss said. "She used to share it with her sister."

That explained the bunk beds. Though Ember found it strange that both were made up and piled with stuffed animals, as if the room was still occupied by two girls. She recognized several of Nisha's ribbons tied to the headboard of the lower bunk. On the wall beside the upper bunk was a row of sketches, done in the same hand as the lion on the chalkboard. They were slightly yellowed, their corners crinkled with age.

"Would you like to sit down?" Moss said in a formal voice, gesturing awkwardly to a chair.

"Thank you, no," Ember said, equally awkward and formal. They gazed at the floor like two dinner guests who had run out of small talk. Ember thought of asking about the made-up bunk beds, but decided against it. Both Nisha and Moss changed the subject whenever Nisha's sister came up, though Moss had told her, quietly, how she had died: from a cold contracted after a field trip with her parents, which had turned out to be pneumonia. Ember wondered what it would be like to know someone who had died—while her birth parents were dead, she couldn't remember them. She wondered if it was better or worse that way.

"Nisha said you ignored her note," Moss said suddenly, in a rush. "She didn't think you would talk to her, so I decided to come myself. I came to say that you can't do this."

Ember blinked. "What?"

"Join the hunt," Moss said. "You just can't. Those dragons aren't hurting anyone, and I don't want to see them killed just so some toff can have his pocket watch jeweled."

"I—" Ember was stunned. "How did you—"

"I heard you talking to Sir Abraham," Moss said. "Professor Maylie sent me out to collect seaweed—she uses it as fertilizer. Didn't you see me?"

"I—yes, but . . ." Moss had been at least fifty feet away. How could he have heard what she had said to Sir Abraham? But before she could puzzle over it, Moss rushed on.

"Tell me you're not actually planning to join the hunt." He was speaking faster and faster. "All the Scientists are against it. Even Professor Maylie says it's inhumane, and she doesn't have many opinions that don't relate to flowers or photosynthesis—"

"You don't understand," Ember said, alarmed. She had never heard Moss utter this many words all at once—it was as if they were bursting out of him, like water from a dam.

"No, *you* don't understand," he said. "I thought we

were friends. That means you should listen to me. Are you doing this to impress Prince Gideon? Or is it—"

Ember grabbed his arm. She didn't know what else to do to make him stop talking. Moss's skin was disconcertingly cool, and he flinched under Ember's warm hand. She quickly released him, feeling as if she'd touched a stone.

"Prince Gideon is a clod. I couldn't care less about impressing him. As for the rest of it," Ember added quickly, in case he decided to get going again, "I didn't know we were friends. I didn't agree to that."

Moss looked perplexed. "You don't agree to be friends with someone," he said. "You've been my friend since you saved me from Baxter."

Ember didn't know what to say to this. "Moss, did you tell anyone that I was thinking about joining the Winterglass Hunt?"

"Just Nisha. And she—"

"You can't tell anyone else." Ember's voice was low and fierce. "My aunt will never let me go."

Moss's mouth twisted. "But—"

"I'm not joining the hunt to kill dragons," she interrupted. "I'm going to sabotage it."

"To *sabotage* it?"

"Yes." Determination stirred within her. "I want to make sure it goes so badly that no hunter in his right mind will want to come back."

Moss stared. "Are you—will they let you join?"

"As long as you're of noble blood, and at least twelve, you can join," Ember said. She folded her arms and gave him a stubborn look. "My father's a baron, and I'm twelve. So I'm joining. My aunt won't stop me, and neither will you."

Moss was silent for so long that Ember wondered if he'd been struck dumb. Then, slowly, a smile spread across his face.

"That's brilliant," he said. "What do you want me to do?"

This was the last thing Ember had expected him to say. "To do?"

"I'm good with plants," Moss said. "Really good. Maybe that can be useful. I know all the ones you can eat—and the ones you can't." A sly note entered his voice.

Ember's mouth fell open. "I don't want to poison anyone!"

"Not poison. But I could give someone a nasty stomach-ache. Can you imagine all those tough hunters setting out on the ice, bows drawn, and then suddenly all they can think about is finding a bathroom?" He laughed. "And you know Nisha's good at math, right? I mean, really good. She can do trigonometry in her head! I'm sure that can be useful somehow."

Ember was flummoxed. She hadn't even considered the possibility that Nisha and Moss would want to help her. In truth, she hadn't really thought about them at all.

"Thank you," she said finally. "But I don't think that's a good idea. Surely your parents wouldn't be very happy about it."

She realized her mistake a second too late. Moss's face flushed, and he looked at the ground.

"I mean . . ." She felt as if the words were twisting up inside her. Finally she said, "I'm sorry. I forgot that you don't have parents."

Moss forced a smile, but it was too bitter to count. "Maybe I do," he said. "But wherever they are, they don't know about any of this, do they?"

"It's kind of you to offer to help," Ember said. "The thing is, I don't—"

"Hang on!" Moss said, his expression lightening again. "If we're going to talk strategy, we need Nisha here. She's like a general!"

Ember, who had watched Nisha command the construction of an architecturally sound, twelve-foot-high snow fort, was aware of this. "I—"

But a second later, Nisha was there, having been lurking in the corridor the whole time. "I heard everything!" she declared. "Oh, this is so exciting, Ember! I have so many ideas!"

"Already?" Ember said faintly. She was beginning to feel that things were spiraling out of control.

"Of course! Have you considered speed and distance equations, for example?" she said, brushing a purple ribbon aside. "And the weight of the sleds divided by the number of dogs and their maximum payload? If we can alter those ratios even a little—not enough for the hunters to notice, of course—the dogs will be too tired to pull the sleds after a day or two!"

Moss hooted with laughter. "Leaving them stranded in the middle of nowhere with a bad case of the trots!"

They were both laughing. Ember burst out, somewhat desperately, "But you can't come with me! It just won't work!"

Moss and Nisha stopped laughing, and an awkward silence fell.

"But you need us," Moss said, exchanging looks with Nisha. "You need a second."

"A second?"

"Yes—every hunter has one. Someone to prepare your food and set up your tent and organize your supplies. Were you going to do all that by yourself? While single-handedly sabotaging the hunt?"

"I—I never thought about that," Ember said. Now that she had, the prospect alarmed her. She had no idea how to set up a tent, and she had never cooked anything in her life. All her meals at Chesterfield were prepared by servants. Her father often joked that he was so terrible at cooking he could burn water, and Ember had formed the impression that it was a rare and difficult art, like playing the violin or locating a horn-toed tree frog in the Amazon.

She suddenly realized the magnitude of what she had been planning to do, and how unprepared she was. She flushed, thinking of her pack back in her room, into which she had thrown a few sweaters, and not much else.

Nisha was nodding. "And it makes sense for you to bring both of us, because after all, Moss and I are only half the size of the other seconds."

"Are you sure seconds aren't supposed to be . . . well, adults?"

"I'm almost an adult!" Nisha stuck her fingers in her hair and draped it floppily atop her head. "There. Don't I look eighteen at least?"

Ember shook her head despairingly. "You don't know what you're getting yourselves into."

"I've gone camping with Professor Maylie," Moss said. "She buries seeds out on the glacier and then studies which ones survive the winter."

"And I can cook!" Nisha said. "Well, sort of. I've never done it, but I've watched my mother. She and Aditi used to cook together." She fell silent.

"I know how to travel in Antarctica," Moss promised. "I'll help Professor Maylie pack her gear."

And with that, Ember was out of arguments. She felt faintly stunned. Apart from her father, and now Aunt Myra, she had never heard anyone speak of dragons favorably. For a moment, her vision swam. She felt an unfamiliar sort of pleasure listening to Nisha and Moss invent increasingly outlandish ways to sabotage the Winterglass Hunt, particularly as they were clearly deferring to her, seeming eager to see which ideas she approved of. It was all extremely strange, though not exactly bad.

"Nisha?" There was a quiet knock on the door, and then a thin, bespectacled man pushed it open. He looked quite a lot like Nisha. "Your mother's looking for you."

"Why?" Nisha's voice was more impatient than seemed necessary—the man was so soft-spoken that Ember couldn't imagine him offending anybody. "What have I done now?"

The man gave her a mild look that Nisha returned with a glare. He sighed. "Nothing, honey. But you said you were interested in seeing the canyon. Your mother's given her team the day off, so she has time to—"

"I wanted to go to the canyon last week," Nisha interrupted. "With Moss and Professor Maylie. I don't want to go now. Ember and I have plans."

"Ember?" The man adjusted his glasses, as if he'd only just noticed she was there.

Nisha sighed. "Ember, this is my father, Professor Singh."

"Hello, Ember," the man said gravely. He shook her hand, as if she were an adult. "Your aunt talks about you often. It's a pleasure to meet another child with an interest in Science."

"We're going to do our homework in the library," Nisha said. She added pointedly, "Unless that's not allowed?"

Her father gave Ember a wan smile. "That's fine, honey. I'll let your mother know."

He went out as quietly as he had come. The door barely clicked.

Ember expected Nisha to offer an explanation, but she carried right on as if her father had never been there. "So how are we going to do this? How about we brainstorm?" Her face lit up. "I'll be the notetaker!"

"All right, look," Ember said. "It's all well and good to come up with ideas, but we can't properly plan anything until we know what we're dealing with. I don't even know where the hunters are going."

"I'll talk to Madame Rousseau," Nisha volunteered. "She's friendly with the prince's steward—I bet he knows everything."

"Good," Ember said, nodding. "Now, Moss, you said you've gone camping with Professor Maylie. Do you think you could borrow her supplies without her noticing?"

The boy nodded. "She keeps everything in one of the storage sheds."

Nisha was bouncing up and down, ribbons dancing. "This is so exciting!"

Ember wasn't sure about that. But as the three of them went to the library, chattering together in hushed voices, she was surprised to realize that the panicky fear she had felt only an hour ago had shrunk to the quietest of murmurs.

"What are you grinning about, girl?" Mac said as she passed him in the firelit common room.

"Nothing," Ember said, smothering her smile—which in truth was a fearsome thing, half a grimace.

She was going to make good on her vow. She would become Lord Norfell's enemy—Prince Gideon's too. She would ensure this was the most disastrous dragon hunt that ever was.

NINE

THE HUNTERS
AND THE HUNTED

The popularity of fireglass peaked in the 1840s, during which the global fire dragon population was reduced by half. Scientists convinced the queen to pass a ban on dragonglass imports in 1851, but illegal hunting continued apace. The last documented sighting of a fire dragon in the wild was by the naturalist William Hawkley in 1869.

—*TAKAGI'S* COMPENDIUM OF EXOTIC CREATURES

The next morning, long before sunrise, they tiptoed out into the dark.

Ember felt like a spy. She and Nisha met Moss in the shadow of one of the outbuildings, where he had loaded Professor Maylie's gear onto a small sled. They didn't speak, though Nisha snorted occasionally with suppressed giggles.

Ember's guilt twinged as they followed the path to the harbor. She had left a note in her room, which Aunt Myra would find when she returned from her mapping expedition to the Consternation Hills. Ember hoped she would be back before her aunt returned, though she doubted this would spare her from the full force of Myra's fury when she discovered what Ember had done.

She, Nisha, and Moss had been up late the previous night, brainstorming ways to sabotage the hunt. Nisha had written down every single one, no matter how difficult or improbable. Ember had quickly felt overwhelmed. Part of her wondered what she had been thinking—how could she hope to have any effect on the Winterglass Hunt without the hunters immediately discovering what she was up to?

Nisha, however, had merely put down her pen and said calmly, "All right. There's only three of us, and we don't have much time. Ember, I don't see how we could set fire to the hunters' supplies without them noticing. Moss, I doubt that Professor Maylie has enough exploding mugwort to be useful, and if she did, I don't think it would be a good idea for us to carry it around." Moss's face fell. "It's best if we don't think big," Nisha went on. "We should think small. If we can create enough delays and disruptions, it will throw them off—maybe even enough to make them cancel the hunt."

Speaking quietly, she crossed out half their ideas, then wrote new ones underneath. Ember added suggestions of her own, while Moss drew sketches when they were helpful. Finally they sat back, looking at the list. Nisha gave Ember a dark smile, which she returned. They spent the rest of the evening creeping around the station, gathering supplies.

The hunters' ship loomed over Great Bother Bay. Ember had never seen such an enormous kiteship—most of the ones in London could carry no more than ten passengers, having been built to navigate narrow canals, not cut through treacherous ice. This one bore at least two dozen sails, ominously gray and billowing like storm clouds, in contrast to the gaudy colors in fashion in the city. The kiteship flew the British flag, as well as the coats of arms of Prince Cronus and Prince Gideon. Men stomped up and down the gangway, carrying trunks and packs and weaponry, while sailors shouted orders from the deck. Nobody paid them any attention as they crept through the lantern-lit harbor. A few snowflakes drifted down, fat as rose petals.

Moss grimaced. "Looks like Prince Cronus came to see his son off."

Ember followed his gaze. A tall, richly dressed man strode down the snowy path, shadowed by a shivering entourage of royal guards and noblemen, Lord Norfell among them. The man had large blue eyes and golden hair, and was handsome in an uncomfortable sort of way, his skin taut over sharp features, his mouth a harsh line. Apart from his paler coloring, the man's resemblance to Prince Gideon was striking.

Prince Gideon trotted along at his father's side, dressed in the same green cape and sword. His cheeks were flushed with excitement. He said something to Prince Cronus, and his father bent his head to listen, though his expression was impatient. He gave a short reply that made his followers nod their heads in unison and Prince Gideon stand up straighter. He walked with his hand on the hilt of his sword, just as Prince Cronus did.

They paused at the foot of the gangway, and Prince Cronus said something to his son, giving him a clap on the shoulder. The noblemen bowed to the younger prince, then turned to follow the elder. Lord Norfell fell into step beside Prince Cronus, speaking quietly and rapidly.

Moss and Nisha bowed as Prince Cronus passed. Nisha elbowed Ember, and she dropped into a hasty curtsy. Prince Cronus's eyes slid over them and the gawking sailors, registering so little interest they could have been an assortment of rocks. His attention made Ember feel small and oddly unhappy.

She looked at Nisha and Moss, and saw her own feelings reflected in their eyes. "At least he's not coming on the hunt," Nisha muttered.

Ember's unhappy feeling lingered, as if Prince Cronus had left a cloud of darkness trailing after him, like a squid. "Let's go," she said, shaking it off.

But once they had dragged their sled up onto the deck, they were stopped by one of the hunters. He was a large, bearded man, and while dressed in fine clothes, gave off a terrible smell.

"Children!" he bellowed. "What in the name of the gods are you doing here?"

Ember fell back. Several men standing at the railings

turned to look, as did the two women Ember had seen on her first day, both clad in polar-bear furs. Her knees trembled. She still wasn't used to being stared at.

"Miss St. George?" said a voice. Ember's left wing twitched. She turned, and met the amused gaze of Lord Norfell where he stood at the top of the gangway.

Her knees continued to shake, but Ember ignored them. With as much dignity as she could muster, she said. "Hello, Lord Norfell. I'm here to join the hunt." She gestured to Nisha and Moss, who stood pale and wary behind her. "These are my seconds."

A murmur swept over the deck, mixed with laughter. Ember tucked her hands into her pockets before they could get any ideas from her knees.

Lord Norfell, after a moment of blank surprise, was smiling again. But his smile was no longer condescending—it was almost impressed.

Ember raised her chin and fixed him with a cold look. *Just you wait*, she thought.

"What's all this?" Prince Gideon strode forward, then froze at the sight of Ember. "What are you doing here?"

"She says she's joining the hunt," Lord Norfell said in an unreadable voice.

Ember braced herself against Gideon's stare, which registered first shock, then scorn. "Did your dreadful aunt put you up to this? Is this some joke of hers?"

The hunters chuckled. As recently as last week, Ember would have quailed under their mocking gazes. But she thought of the fire dragons, and her anger rose again. It gave her the courage to lift her chin and reply evenly, "No."

Prince Gideon gave her a disdainful look. "The Winterglass Hunt isn't for little girls."

"Why?" she said. "Little boys are allowed."

The prince flushed. Lord Norfell let out an odd cough that sounded like it was covering something else.

"Your Highness," he said, "there's nothing barring Miss St. George from entering the hunt. Her father belongs to the nobility and she is of age. Unless you wish to petition your father to change the rules?"

Something told Ember that Prince Cronus wouldn't appreciate being bothered about her, and perhaps the prince came to the same conclusion, for his expression darkened. He gave her a look that was half irritated and half curious, as he had on the day they met.

"Why are you here?" he asked.

Oh no. Ember froze. The truth rose inside her, and she pushed it down. But it rose again, and Ember was on the edge of speaking when Nisha exclaimed, "Why is she here? Why are any of you here? For the dragonglass, of course!"

The prince's tawny eyes narrowed. "Your aunt won't approve."

Ember's thoughts raced. "My aunt won't approve," she agreed. "But my father sees things differently than she does. He gave me this."

She drew off her glove, revealing her fireglass ring. It

flashed in the lantern light, throwing a red gleam across the prince's face.

"I want to join the hunt," she said. "No matter what my aunt thinks."

The prince frowned. He looked Ember up and down, as if searching for something. "All right," he said unwillingly. "Though I doubt you'll even be able to get within shooting range of a dragon. If you can't keep up, we'll leave you behind."

"I can keep up." Ember returned his gaze coolly until he turned away. Several of the hunters looked uncomfortable. They clearly didn't like the idea of children taking part in a dragon hunt, but they couldn't very well protest without looking as if they were questioning the prince's presence too.

Lord Norfell lifted Ember's bag, the picture of gallantry. "I'll show you to a cabin."

Ember glared. "Why did you help me?"

Lord Norfell gave her an inscrutable look, hidden behind a sly smile. "Because it seems you're at a disadvantage, Miss St. George. Don't you think you could use all the help you can get?"

The kiteship flew across the water, making good time with the clear weather. The sun rose and then settled low in the deep blue sky, stretching the kiteship's shadow over the icy sea. The soft-spoken captain told Ember that they would reach the dragons' hunting grounds that evening. They would anchor offshore, and then next morning load their supplies onto smaller boats and set out for the rocky cove a mile or two from where the dragons had last been sighted.

Ember spent most of the day pacing the deck, light-headed with nervousness. Meanwhile, Nisha and Moss dashed back and forth along the railing, exclaiming at everything. They seemed to see the hunt as a grand adventure, which gave Ember a twinge of jealousy. For she knew it for what it was: life and death. She folded her arms and tried to imagine that she really was a spy, a hardened spy with ice water in her veins. She wondered what it felt like to have ice water in your veins—it didn't sound particularly pleasant.

The hunters walked the deck too, some solitary, others clustered in small groups and hooded against the breeze. They paid Ember little attention aside from the occasional frowning glance, as if she were a harmless but ill-favored dog. Ember eavesdropped on their conversations whenever she could. Aside from the prince and Lord Norfell, there were seven hunters, plus their seconds and a number of personal servants. The women in the grotesque polar-bear-skin cloaks were Lady Valle and Lady Tennenbaum. There was Sir Abraham, who was often in the company of the Marquis de Montvert, a French nobleman with a permanent scowl. Then there were three professional hunters: Mr. Black, Mr. Crawford, and Mr. Heep. Based on what Ember had overheard from the sailors, most of the bets were on these three, with some saying they would kill a dragon apiece, others that they would come back with several. Many of the hunters carried their bows with them—this was the only weapon that worked against dragons. Bullets bounced off their scales, but arrows tipped with dragon bone did not.

Ember watched the Antarctic coast glide past. Blue shadows nestled into the snowbanks, and icicles hung down over the water. Mountains, tufted with cloud, reached up to the darkening sky. Ember didn't think she'd ever seen such a beautiful place. They sailed past an iceberg with turrets like a castle, on which a dozen seals rested. They eyed the ship from their fragile battlements. One of the hunters shot at them, and they scattered, barking.

"Waste of arrows," said a cultured voice. To Ember's dismay, Lord Norfell appeared at the railing beside her. "Some people aren't taking this hunt seriously."

Ember suppressed an urge to step back. Lord Norfell was richly dressed in what looked like country riding clothes topped with a fur coat and burgundy cape. He wore his customary expression of sly amusement, as if every situation he encountered was a joke only he was in on, but behind it was something Ember couldn't read. He had brought twice as many bows as anyone else, in various sizes, all decorated with precious stones and engraved with his initials.

"But you are?" she said in a cool voice, the way a hardened spy would.

Lord Norfell smiled, tucking one ringed hand into his pocket. "There are few things in life I take seriously. But the Winterglass Hunt has become an important source of income for my family. Our estate has had its share of difficulties. Debts, you know. It's hard to maintain a lifestyle. It's frustrating, to say the least, that the queen has placed limits on this hunt. We should be able to kill as many dragons as we can catch."

Ember swallowed her anger. She wondered if there was anything Lord Norfell didn't think he was entitled to.

"My father," he went on, "used to fill our coffers with the profits he made hunting fire dragons, but after they went extinct—well, we had to start selling off our lands."

"I'm sure that was very difficult for you."

If Lord Norfell noticed her tone, he didn't let on. "Oh, we got by. My siblings married well. I found part-time work in Stormancy."

"Stormancy," Ember repeated. Despite herself, this piqued her curiosity. Stormancers were rare.

"I have a bit of a gift for magic, though I confess it didn't entertain me for long." He nodded at her. "No doubt my abilities are nothing next to your father's. All those experiments . . . quite impressive. Quite impressive."

Ember shivered under Lord Norfell's opaque gaze. She

wanted to move away, but before she could make an excuse, the man went on.

"Stormancy involves too much tedious theory, too many restrictions. I wasn't sad to give it up. Technically, I'm barred from practicing magic—I had a little disagreement with the International Stormancy Alliance. There is one area in which I always excelled, however, and that was in detecting magic. I was always able to sniff out other Stormancers' spells . . . you could say I have a nose for it. I'm sure you understand my meaning."

Ember's heart slowed.

"Why, your father, of course." Lord Norfell's smile had lost its slyness, and was nothing more than a crease in his face. "No doubt he has the same ability."

Now Ember very much wanted to get away. Her left wing was twitching like a fish out of water. She felt a bit like that herself—as if the very air was suffocating her.

"Quite the man." Lord Norfell finally turned to regard the coast, his gaze sliding away like some slimy thing. "And a very private person. You know, I don't recall ever hearing that he had a daughter. I understood him to be a bachelor."

Ember's throat was dry, and she had to clear it before she could speak. "My mother's dead. She died after giving birth to me." It was what her father had always told her to say to anyone who questioned her. While her identity was known at Chesterfield by those who needed to know it, her father didn't publicly discuss his family situation. This wasn't an uncommon practice among Stormancers, who attracted powerful enemies, so no one had ever guessed there might be other reasons for Lionel St. George to keep his daughter's existence quiet.

"Ah! How sad," Lord Norfell said. "That must be difficult for you. How lucky you have been to have your father, at least, to protect you all these years."

Ember was frozen. Somehow, in shifting position, Lord Norfell had moved closer to her. He loomed above her like a shadow. Was he close enough to feel the warmth radiating off her skin? He reached out a hand as if involuntarily, an eerie curiosity in his eyes.

"What is this about, Norfell?" said a voice.

Ember stumbled back, released from her paralysis. Lord Norfell's hand dropped, and he turned to face Prince Gideon with his usual impish smile.

"Your Highness," he said, bowing slightly. "Miss St. George and I were simply swapping stories. You see, her father shares my old profession."

"She didn't look terribly interested in your stories." Distaste flitted over Prince Gideon's face as he looked at Lord Norfell. "I expect you'll want to prepare yourself for tomorrow." The dismissal in his voice was clear. He could have been addressing an idle servant.

Lord Norfell bowed again. "Much to do, indeed." He winked at Ember, as if they'd shared a good joke, and then strode away.

"Are you all right?" Prince Gideon regarded Ember uncertainly. "What was he saying to you? You looked like a cornered rabbit."

"I–" The lie stuck in Ember's throat. Her heart pounded. Every instinct told her to run, to hide—but where could she hide on a ship full of dragon hunters? "He was talking about magic. I—I didn't exactly understand."

"Well, if he was threatening you, you must let me know," the prince said.

Ember stared at him. "Why do you care?"

The prince's face closed. For a moment, Ember thought she saw a flicker of hurt, but then it was gone. He gave her a cold look, any trace of concern gone from his face, and strode away.

———

"Ember! We're all ready to go—we were waiting for you," Moss said as she entered their cabin.

"I think it's dark enough now," Nisha said. "We've kept an eye on the stairwell—hardly anyone goes down to the lower deck, so we should be safe."

Taking a close look at her, Moss said, "Is something wrong?"

Ember sat heavily on her bed. There were two bunk beds to a cabin, so the three of them were sharing a room. She was trembling all over.

"Are you sick?" Nisha slapped her hand to Ember's

forehead, then just as quickly drew it back. "You *are* sick! You're burning up!"

"I'm not sick," Ember said. "I just—Lord Norfell . . ."

He knows, a panicked voice said. *He knows. He knows. He knows.*

And yet it was impossible—wasn't it? Lionel St. George could sense the presence of spells, it was true, but he didn't always know how they had been cast, or what had been altered. Still, even if Lord Norfell didn't know she was a dragon, it seemed clear he suspected there was something unusual about her. She felt as if the room was closing in on her. She had thought she understood the dangers she faced in joining the hunt, but she hadn't, not at all.

"Him!" Nisha spat. "I don't trust him one bit. He came up to us and started asking all these strange questions about you. Course, we just made everything up—by the way, you and your father live in an enchanted zeppelin that circles London every thirty-six seconds. Moss and I visited last Christmas, and we both got terribly airsick."

Ember was barely listening. She couldn't stop shaking—she put her hands under her thighs to still them and forced her thoughts away from Lord Norfell. Right now, there was the plan to focus on. "All right. We've got to do this quickly."

Nisha rubbed her hands together. Moss grinned. After a moment, Ember smiled back, her own excitement kindling.

They filed down the stairs to the lower deck. Ember

had to keep a close eye on Nisha, who often tried to grab on to Ember's shoulder or stand too close. It was awkward: Nisha had already brushed her arm against Ember's wings once, though the other girl had merely furrowed her brow and asked Moss if he had pulled on her coat.

They reached the room where the cannons were stored, which was low ceilinged and smelled of gunpowder. There were six of them, three on each side of the ship. "You know what to do?" Ember said quietly.

They nodded. Moss had already retrieved the pack he had stowed down there earlier and was untying the straps.

Ember darted back out into the hall and made her way to the forward section of the ship. Her part of the plan was trickier: she had to get inside the locked room where the hunters' extra gear was stored and break as many arrows as possible. It wouldn't be enough to call off the hunt—the hunters had their own stores in their cabins—but it would limit their firepower.

She had a pocketknife with her, small enough to pick a lock, but she wouldn't be using it.

Ember reached the door of the storage room. Her heart was pounding again, and she tried not to think about all the things that could go wrong with their plan. She held out her hand, allowing a flame to flicker to life in her palm.

Ordinarily, she avoided summoning fire—fire meant danger, destruction. She forced herself to remain calm as it danced against her skin. She was not going to burst into flames. She was not.

The lock was iron, but it began to glow and warp as Ember heated it. After a moment, she tugged on it, and it snapped. She pulled the door open—

There was a shout from above. Ember jerked back. She launched herself into the air, pressing herself into the shadowy corner where the ceiling met two walls. And just in time—Mr. Crawford and Mr. Black stampeded by below, into the storage room. They charged out again, jabbering at each other. Ember caught only one word:

Dragons.

Ember swooped back to the ground, landing awkwardly. She cast a longing look at the storage room, but fearful that more men would be on their way, she darted back up the stairs. She ducked into her own cabin and leaned against the door, waiting for her heart to slow. When she left the room, she almost walked into Sir Abraham.

"Steady on!" The man squinted down at her. "Eager to get your first look at the dragons? Well, come along."

Ember glanced down at the stairwell—she needed to check on Nisha and Moss. But she couldn't very well do so with Sir Abraham watching her, so she allowed him to lead her upstairs to the deck.

There everyone was abuzz with excitement. Sailors and hunters alike were crowded about the ship's prow, some clutching binoculars in thickly gloved hands. Ember, straining to see around them, finally—and reluctantly—went to stand near Prince Gideon, from whom everyone kept a respectful distance. The prince gave her a cool look, then turned back to his spyglass.

Ember followed his gaze and gasped.

In the distance, upon the snowy headland, a glittering shape crouched. It was like a fragment of starry sky, sharp and spectral. Then it opened its wings and took flight.

An ice dragon.

The creature glided down to a rocky shore where two others lurked. The size of the dragons was difficult to guess from that distance, and Ember could make out few of their features beyond the gleam of silvery scales. She guessed they were smaller than the fire dragons she had seen, and certainly they were more willowy—while the fire dragons had reminded her of slinking cats, these creatures moved like wisps of cloud. She couldn't stop staring.

"Have your men ready the cannons, Captain," Prince Gideon said.

Ember started. Her first reaction was horror for the dragons' sake, and then she remembered Nisha and Moss. Were they still below? What if the plan was discovered?

"Surely we're too far away," she said, trying to keep her voice steady.

The prince smiled. "Let's find out, shall we?" He turned to the hunters gathered at the prow, and said in a carrying voice, "Any dragon killed by cannon fire is property of the Crown."

There was some grumbling at this. The hunters' bows would not work at this range, which meant the prince had an unfair advantage. But the hunters couldn't very well do more than grumble.

Ember opened her mouth to argue further, but the prince raised his hand at one of the sailors, who gave an answering nod. Prince Gideon stepped up to the railing, a cold smile on his face.

"Fire!" he shouted.

TEN

SABOTAGE

*Fire dragons were worshipped as gods by certain tribes
in the South Pacific, who believed that to kill a
dragon was to invite ruin into one's household and curse one's
descendants with illness of both body and spirit. . . .*

—*TAKAGI'S* COMPENDIUM OF EXOTIC CREATURES

What followed was a dull whump, whump, whump, and then a cloud of ice, blown by the wind, sprayed across the deck.

The hunters yelled and shielded their faces. "What happened?" Prince Gideon cried as the cloud cleared.

"I don't know," Lady Valle said. "But I think the dragons escaped your cannons."

Indeed, the dragons hadn't even moved—Ember doubted they were aware they'd been fired on. She had to face the railing, choking on her laughter, as Prince Gideon stalked about, yelling at everybody.

A sailor dashed onto the deck. "Your Highness, the cannonballs, they're—well . . ."

"Well, what?" Prince Gideon snapped. The sailor was holding one of the cannonballs—a black, round thing about the size of his palm. The prince seized it, and let out a strangled sound. Narrowing his eyes, he flung the cannonball against the mast with all his might. Mr. Crawford, leaning against it, jerked aside with a shout.

The thing shattered like ice—because it *was* ice, shaped and dyed to mimic the appearance of a cannonball.

"They're all like that, Your Highness," the sailor said. "I can't find the real ones."

And you won't, Ember thought. *Unless you search the bottom of the sea.* Nisha and Moss had succeeded. Of course, it had been largely Nisha's idea—she was the one who had insisted on measuring the circumference and diameter of real cannonballs, and replicating these measurements to produce snowballs of exactly the same size. That way, if the prince didn't end up using them, their appearance would ensure no suspicion was raised during the voyage.

Ember could barely breathe. Her plan was working! She watched the dragons lounging by the shore—they were alive, at least for now, because of her. Before that moment, her plan to sabotage the hunt had been a formless thing, made of air and hope. She realized that part of her had always expected to fail—after all, the Winterglass Hunt was so much bigger than she was, powered by the machinery of the empire.

"Even the mightiest train can be derailed by a single

penny," her aunt had said. Could she be that penny? The feeble sound of the snowballs erupting seemed to echo through her mind like a trumpet.

"You." The prince rounded on Ember, his eyes flashing. "You did this."

Ember gazed at him blankly, relieved beyond words that he hadn't phrased it as a question. "Me?"

"I doubt that the child is to blame, Your Highness," Sir Abraham said in his gravelly voice.

"Surely not." Lady Valle's pale eyes flashed to Lord Norfell and Lady Tennenbaum. "Besides, we've already seen evidence that not everyone is focused on our mission."

Lord Norfell alone among the hunters hadn't seemed disturbed by the false cannonballs—he had watched with barely suppressed amusement, which faded fast as the other hunters rounded on him. "Are you implying I would attempt sabotage on His Majesty's ship?"

"Someone has clearly done so," said the Marquis de Montvert. "I for one suspect the Scientists. Any one of them could be responsible for this. We all know of their sanctimony and softheartedness where these beasts are concerned. Every person in the research station should be questioned upon our return."

Several of the others nodded. The prince was silent for a long moment. He fixed his cold, tawny eyes on each of them, one by one, and though he was only twelve, and barely as tall as the fairylike Lady Tennenbaum, more than one of the hunters looked away. He held Ember's gaze the longest, and she stared back stubbornly, chin jutting.

"We set out first thing tomorrow morning," he snapped. "An hour earlier than scheduled. Those who aren't ready will be left behind." With that, he strode away.

The prince was true to his word. The next morning—if a black sky with only the faintest stain of blue could be called morning—they clambered into cold rowboats weighted with supplies and set sail for shore. From there, they would make for the dragons' hunting grounds by dogsled.

Ember's hands trembled as she stepped onto one of the sleds. She had never ridden any sort of sled before, let alone one pulled by four massive dogs. Sensing her fear, the closest dog looked over its shoulder at her. Several of the hunters, bundled in layers of coats and scarves and furred boots, were squinting in the darkness. Ember's eyesight, though, was excellent—she could see at night as well as Puff.

The prince gave the command to start. The other hunters fell in behind him, allowing him to lead the way. The seconds and servants followed. The prince handled his dogs well, calling crisp commands, which was irritating.

Ember's dogs broke into a run when the others did, but they soon fell behind. The lead dog was acting strange, growling and snarling at the others and veering sharply back and forth. The other dogs followed her lead, as they were trained to do.

"Steady," Ember called as the frosty air whipped her face. "Steady!" Her voice was thin with fear—she felt as if she were riding an unbroken horse.

The lead dog growled. With a yip, she broke away from the other hunters' sleds entirely and plunged into the darkness.

"Haw!" Ember yelled, which meant left. The dog ignored her. She was heading for a heap of rubble and boulders at the base of a mountain. To Ember's horror, beyond the boulders the ground disappeared, a glacial rift that could be hundreds of feet deep.

"Whoa!" Ember shouted. Terror made the word stick in her throat. "Whoa!"

The dogs paid her no heed. They were all going to plummet off the glacier, or be dashed against the rocks. Realizing that she had no way of saving the dogs, Ember flung herself off the sled. She rolled across the slippery ice, losing all sense of direction, while behind her the sled struck stone with a tremendous crash. She barely managed to grab the edge of a boulder before she tumbled into the rift.

Ember screamed. Her legs dangled in thin air. The rift wasn't horribly high, after all, but certainly enough to break a leg or ankle. One of her wings, tangled up by the roll, was caught painfully under her arm. Frantically she tried to free herself. Her hand kept slipping on the rock as the ice melted under her too-warm grip.

"Hang on!" A hand gripped the collar of her jacket and hauled her onto the glacier.

Ember lay there a moment, panting, relishing the feeling of being on solid ground. She was shaking all over. The dogs were whining, but they seemed unharmed. The sled was destroyed, pieces of it scattered everywhere.

Ember glanced up at her rescuer, and was astonished to find Prince Gideon looking back at her.

"Are you all right?" he demanded. His face was pale.

"I—I think so." Her right wing ached, but she didn't think it was broken. The rest of her felt fine, though she didn't think she would be able to stand for a while.

"I saw your dogs break away from the group," Prince Gideon said. "I turned my sled around right away. What happened?"

"It was the lead dog," Ember said. "It was like she was possessed. . . ."

The prince's tawny eyes narrowed. He seemed a different person than he had been yesterday: thoughtful and decisive and completely without malice. He whistled for the dog, who was rubbing her back against the rock. She came to him grudgingly, twitching and uneasy. Ember had never seen a dog behave that way. Prince Gideon shone his lantern on the dog's paws, then her back.

He froze, and then yanked at something tangled in the dog's fur. He examined the thing for a moment, then held it out to Ember. It was the size of a pebble and cruelly spiked, covered in fur and specks of blood.

"Burrs," Prince Gideon said. "They're all over her."

"Oh!" Ember hurried to the dog's side and began pulling at the burrs herself. The prince did the same, his fingers surprisingly gentle. He stroked the dog's muzzle as she whined.

"No wonder she was acting that way," Ember said. "She was in pain, poor thing."

"Where did they come from?" the prince murmured. "These look like burdock. It doesn't grow in Antarctica."

The dog buried her head in the crook of his arm. "There, there, Nell," the prince said in a voice that was so kind Ember could barely believe it was his. "I'll sort you out." He seemed to remember that Ember was there, and turned back to the burrs, flushing.

"Is she your dog?" Ember said curiously.

"They're all my dogs." The prince's voice was formal again, edged with disdain. "Only true-bred Antarctic sled dogs have what it takes to survive out here. Once I find out who did this, I'll make sure they're sorry."

He leveled Ember with a hard stare, and she bristled. "Are you mad?" she said. "Why would I have injured my own dog? I almost went over a cliff, if you didn't notice."

"I've noticed that you aren't very bright," the prince said. "Joining a hunt like this when you have no idea what you're doing. Perhaps you thought this a funny joke."

Ember glared at him. "Anyone with half a brain can see that someone doesn't want me taking part in the hunt—I'd take a hard look at the other hunters, if I were you. Unless you're the one who did it."

"I would nev—" the prince began hotly. Then he seemed to make an effort to control himself, hiding his anger under a mask of scornful dignity. He tossed another burr onto the snow, then rose, murmuring for the dogs to follow him. They did so, tails wagging, seeming delighted to trot along at their master's heel.

"Ember!" Moss drew up his sled and dashed to her side. "What happened?"

"I wish I knew." Ember cast a grim look at the broken sled, and then at the prince's retreating back. "But we might not be the only saboteurs on this hunt."

ELEVEN

THIEVES IN THE NIGHT

Several ancient cultures speak of "shadow dragons"
(China: "coal dragons"), which are said to be kin to the fire dragon,
beasts of ash and darkness that breathe fear itself, enough to reduce
the most stalwart of men to quivering children. Most Scientists, however,
believe the tales to be little more than myth.

—*TAKAGI'S* COMPENDIUM OF EXOTIC CREATURES

They approached the hunting grounds as quietly as possible—which was not very, given their numbers. Ember's heart was in her ears the entire time, so loud she felt certain the hunters would hear, but of course they didn't. They didn't seem to notice her at all. Which suited her just fine.

Fortunately, the rocky beach where they had spotted the dragons was empty in the moonlight. Despite the danger of the dragons returning at any moment, Prince Gideon ordered them to set up camp behind a sheltering cluster of rocks, and stationed guards upon the nearby hills. They lit a fire too, which stained the snow red. The hunters clustered around it as the seconds prepared their tea. Some were jovial, boasting about previous hunts and telling bawdy jokes, while others were drawn and serious, gripping their bows and repeatedly glancing over their shoulders into the darkness. Though it was nearing midday, the sun had not yet risen, and the sky was the cool navy of early twilight. Winter, and the total darkness that came with it, was rapidly overtaking the continent.

Ember tried not to pay attention to the dozen or so silent, burly men who had their own separate cluster of tents. These were not hunters—they were butchers. They had been hired to strip the winterglass from any dragons that were killed and carry it back to camp. The hunters were not expected to get their hands dirty.

Moss did most of the work constructing their tent, while Nisha stood back and delivered mostly unhelpful instructions. Ember, for her part, was too nervous to focus on anything. She wandered away from the firelight. The earth wheeled below the stars, which formed a glittering carousel of snakes and centaurs and dead heroes and other constellations she couldn't name.

She reached the small bluff that overlooked the rocky beach. To her dismay, Prince Gideon was there, crouching by several of his dogs. He was examining their paws, muttering to them in that same weird, kind voice. She was about to turn around, but then she remembered something that had been nagging at her. Sighing, she came forward, allowing her normally silent feet to crunch against the snow.

He glanced up, and his eyes narrowed. "Good day,

Your Highness," Ember said, bowing her head. She tried to keep the mockery out of her voice, but was only partly successful.

Prince Gideon looked suspicious, but at least he didn't snap at her. He gave a grudging nod and turned back to the dog.

"I never thanked you for rescuing me," Ember said. "That was rude. So: thank you."

It wasn't easy to say it, but her father had always impressed upon her the importance of showing gratitude. The prince might be horrible, but he also may have saved her life.

"You don't have to thank me."

"I know," Ember said, more saltily than she had intended. The prince actually smiled. She remembered that he had smiled once before when she had spoken bluntly to him. She guessed that a prince wouldn't get much honesty from people—maybe it was a novelty for him.

"I've thought about it, and I don't actually believe you had anything to do with the cannons," Prince Gideon said. "It was silly of me to accuse you before."

"That's . . . all right," Ember said, surprised.

"You're not capable of organizing something like that," the prince said.

Her eyes narrowed. "Thanks."

He laughed—a little dismissively, but it wasn't an unfriendly sound. Ember settled on the snow, not too close to him. One of the dogs approached her, and she patted it.

The prince pushed his hood back, watching her. "I raised these dogs myself."

"Oh," Ember said. Was Prince Gideon actually making conversation? "They're very handsome."

"Dogs are important out here," he said. "A good dog can save your life in a place like this. A disobedient one can doom it. I spend most of my time with them. When I'm not in my library."

Ember remembered that the prince had read Takagi's *Compendium* and that the sailor had said he was a bookworm. She frowned. Somehow it seemed like an insult to books.

"I often survey my lands by dogsled," the prince continued. "I went all the way down to the pole with this one."

Ember stared. "You've been to the pole?"

"Yes. It was colder then than it is now, too. Every few years we get a warm winter like this. Something about ocean currents."

Ember didn't see how the weather could be described as warm. As a fire dragon, she could put up with the cold, but she still felt it. The hunters shivered almost constantly. How could the prince have endured that sort of journey? "You went by yourself?"

Prince Gideon shrugged. "I have to know this place, don't I? I'm going to rule it one day. Perhaps very soon— my father hates it here. He's spoken of passing the territory directly to me and retiring to England for good."

Ember thought this over. "And you don't? Hate it, I mean?"

"It's my home. I was born here." He looked at the mountains, over which the green aurora rose and fell like musical notes. An unexpectedly peaceful look passed over his face. "It's mine."

Ember thought of what Aunt Myra had said about the prince's father, and of the lonely castle she had seen from the ship. She had felt an odd sense of kinship with the prince then—he was someone who was just as alone as her. Now she wondered if, in fact, he was more alone than she had ever been.

"Of course, it won't be home for long if my grand-mother decides to abandon it," the prince went on.

"Abandon it?" It took Ember a moment to realize what he meant. "You mean the queen wants to leave Antarctica?"

"It costs a lot to defend a place like this," the prince said. "My grandmother's advisers all think it was a mis-take to take Antarctica from the Germans. It isn't exactly a profitable part of the empire. But if we can get this hunt up and running, it can be. That's why it's so important. I'll do anything to keep this place."

"Because it's your home," Ember murmured.

Prince Gideon blinked, as if he'd almost forgotten she was there. He began to tell her the story of his trip to the pole. Ember listened quietly, though much of it seemed far-fetched. She doubted, for example, that he had repaired a broken ski on his sled by weaving dog hair together. Despite his arrogant tone, he kept sneaking glances at her as he spoke, as if to judge her reaction. Ember wondered how long it had been since he had spoken to someone his own age. Or to anyone who wasn't a servant.

The prince's fingers were gentle as he examined the dogs' paws for injuries. Ember didn't think she had ever met someone like Prince Gideon. She knew there were people who had a hidden meanness inside them, lurking under layers of kindness—Professor Riggles at Chesterfield was like that. He was chipper and sunny with everyone, but she had once seen him react with a sudden, startling fury when one of the servants spilled his wine. Prince Gideon was the opposite. He seemed to have a kind streak buried under a lot of nastiness.

Finally one of the men came to ask the prince about something, and he rose, brushing the snow from his knees.

Ember went back to her tent. Moss had pitched it near the bluff, a little apart from the other hunters'. Nisha stood back, watching Moss work. She smiled at Ember.

"He's cute," Nisha said.

It took Ember a moment to realize who Nisha meant. "Gideon?"

"Haven't you noticed?" Nisha sighed. "Too bad he's so awful."

Ember hadn't particularly considered whether Prince Gideon was good-looking or not. Now that she did, though, it seemed obvious that he was, and for some reason, this annoyed her. She wanted to change the subject.

"Is he cuter than Moss?" she said in an innocent voice. She had noticed how Nisha blushed whenever Moss stood close to her—it was difficult not to notice.

Nisha made a sharp sound, gesturing dramatically at the tent where Moss was arranging their belongings. Her flaming cheeks were answer enough.

"I think the prince likes you," she said. "I was listening."

Ember's jaw dropped. "I don't—of course he doesn't! How did you come up with that? All he did was brag."

"That's what boys do when they like you," Nisha said.

"Well, that's the stupidest thing I've ever heard."

Nisha nodded. "Do you like him? I mean, you can still think he's awful either way."

Ember, her cheeks now flaming to match Nisha's, had had enough of this. She said quietly, "We need to change the plan. I didn't have a chance to damage the hunters' weapons on the ship, which means that if those dragons appear, they're doomed."

Nisha thought about it. "If we could sneak into their tents while they're sleeping—"

"It's too risky. If anyone sees us, the prince will know we were behind the cannons, and then there goes any hope of sabotaging the hunt."

She and Nisha batted ideas around, each more unlikely than the last. Moss joined them after securing the tent. He was for putting something into the hunters' food— he had brought along herbs with a variety of unpleasant side effects—but Ember couldn't see how they could do it without being detected.

Nisha fiddled with the ring on her finger. It was studded

with a small sapphire, which sparkled in the firelight. The sapphire made Ember think of Aunt Myra. She froze.

"What?" Nisha said, as a slow smile spread over Ember's face. Ember motioned Moss closer, and told them her plan in a hushed voice. It was a straightforward one:

Theft.

As it happened, the hunters weren't overly careful with their belongings. Whenever one of them left something unattended—a book, a pair of spectacles, even a spoon—Ember, Moss, or Nisha would take it, and either drop it from the bluff into the sea or bury it under a rock.

They waited until darkness had fallen again—which it did after only three or four hours of daylight, the sun barely scraping the horizon—and then set to work. Unfortunately, most of the things they were able to steal were small, but Ember hoped they might at least succeed in causing confusion.

After pocketing Lady Valle's bracelet (she had left it on a rock), Ember paused outside Lord Norfell's tent. The man had wandered off somewhere with Lady Tennenbaum, and most of the others were still clustered around the fire. She remembered the vow she had made on her first day in Antarctica, and a grin spread over her face. Feeling every inch a hardened spy, she tucked the bracelet into a corner of his tent, then kept walking, pretending to admire the view.

Ember doubted that she would be able to sleep as she settled into her blankets that night. The sky stayed clear, though the wind had picked up, brushing over the treated leather of the tent like hands that might at any moment decide to strike. The scouts had reported that a storm was massing to the south, though it might well change direction.

"I can't stop thinking about the sled," Nisha whispered. The girl was curled on her side between Ember and Moss, facing her. "Those burrs . . . who would have done that?"

"I know." Ember didn't like being reminded of the accident. It made her afraid, but in a strange way. Afraid that they were missing something important, something that lurked close but just out of her range of sight, like a poisonous jellyfish. "Maybe it wasn't meant for me. Maybe someone was trying to hurt Lord Norfell, or one of the other hunters, to cut the competition."

"Do you really believe that?" Nisha said.

Ember didn't answer. She didn't know what she believed.

"I think we should talk to the servants," Nisha said. "I bet one of them saw something."

Ember nodded slowly. "It's worth a try."

Nisha was quiet for a while. "Are you afraid?"

"Yes," Ember said, wishing she didn't have to admit to it. To her surprise, Nisha smiled.

"That's what I like about you," she said. "You always tell the truth."

She squeezed Ember's hand. Ember tried to draw her hand back, but Nisha had already fallen asleep, still holding on to her. After a moment, she closed her eyes too, their fingers woven together.

The next morning Ember awoke disoriented. Where was she? Was that Puff at her feet, digging her claws into her skin?

Ember opened her eyes and remembered. She was not at Chesterfield, with Puff asleep against her legs and the sounds of the university drifting in through the window. She was in Antarctica, surrounded by miles of snow and glacier and icebound sea. It was still dark, of course, and she wondered what time it was. The hunters were awake— she could hear them talking in raised voices.

"*Psst*," she said, nudging Nisha. The other girl muttered irritably and pulled her blankets over her head.

Ember gasped. Her feet, poking out of her blankets, had turned an unhealthy white. It took a few minutes to rub the feeling back into them.

She shivered. She was more protected from the cold than most, but it was clear that even she would have to be careful. The Antarctic winter was vicious; so vicious, it seemed, that it could best even a fire dragon.

Ember shook Moss awake. He alone did not seem to be shivering, and smiled when he woke, as if he had spent the night in a luxurious mansion. They pulled on their outer layers and stepped outside.

The hunters were clustered around the fire, which threw dancing shadows over the ground. Lord Norfell stood on one side, Lady Valle on the other. The larger group of hunters, Ember noticed, stood on Lady Valle's side. Prince Gideon was nowhere in sight.

Lady Valle seemed to be gesturing with something that sparkled in the light. Ember smothered a smile. She knew what this was about.

"—then where were you last night, Norfell?" Lady Valle was demanding as Ember and Moss approached. "If you're so innocent in all this, surely you can answer that simple question."

Lord Norfell cast a sidelong glance at Lady Tennenbaum, who was flushing. "I, ah . . ."

"If the man refuses to provide evidence of his whereabouts, I say we search him." The Marquis de Montvert examined Lord Norfell with distaste. "He may be concealing more stolen items about his person."

"What need have I to steal from you, good sirs?" Lord Norfell burst out. He gave a short bow to Lady Valle, managing to convey slyness even in his distress. "And ladies, of course. I have enough jewels."

"A rogue may have other motivations than money," growled Mr. Black, a tall Irishman who wore several curved daggers at his belt. He scratched irritably at his neck. "My notebook, after all, was also found in your tent, along with Lady Valle's bracelet."

Ember glanced at Moss in surprise. He grinned and whispered, "That was Nisha."

"Clearly, there is treachery afoot," Lord Norfell said. "Someone wishes to rouse suspicion—"

"Speaking of treachery," Mr. Black said, "did anyone happen to see Lord Norfell lurking belowdecks before the cannons were tampered with? As he seemed to find that incident so amusing."

Sir Abraham huffed. "This is getting out of hand. I don't think it's fair to leap to that, Black."

"Why not?" Lady Valle demanded viciously. "If he's capable of theft and bald-faced lies, why not sabotage?"

The hunters continued to argue, their voices increasingly loud. They were all distracted; no one was paying attention to the tents. Even the prince's attendants were standing about, watching the commotion. Ember, seeing her opportunity, motioned for Moss to stay where he was. What she was going to do demanded absolute stealth.

Ember ghosted through the shadows, grateful that the moon had set. She reached the largest tent, which stood apart from the others, a flag waving from the pole. Prince Gideon's coat of arms.

Ember listened for breathing, but there was none. She slipped inside.

She waited for her eyes to adjust to the darkness, which they did quickly. Prince Gideon's tent was painfully neat, the corners of his blankets so expertly tucked they could have been measured with a ruler. Ember would have expected a prince to bring a lot of fine furs and other luxuries, even to a place like this, but he hadn't—she could have been standing in a servant's tent. The only extraneous items were the books scattered across a low table. Most were dog-eared, with frayed covers. She saw several books on science, but there were also novels and a penny dreadful or two.

Ember wasn't here to examine the prince's library. She shoved her curiosity aside and quickly found what she was looking for.

The bow was heavy, surely far too large to suit Prince Gideon comfortably, and newly polished. She summoned fire in her palm, trapping it beneath her skin, where it glowed like coals. She didn't want to break the bow outright—she wanted the damage to go undetected. After giving it a moment's thought, she ran her hand over the wood of the bow, listening to it creak and groan as it dried.

She looked about the tent for the prince's sword, but he must have taken it with him. She found two smaller bows, and repeated the process. Then she crept out of the tent.

"What are you doing?"

Ember whirled. There behind her, looking larger under the bulk of his wolf-skin cloak, was Prince Gideon, standing with one of the scouts.

"I asked you a question," he said, stepping closer. His face was pale with anger. "You were inside my tent. Why?"

A direct question. Ember quaked under the fury in his gaze. The truth rose up in her throat, and she shoved it down.

"Why do you not speak?" Gideon snatched at her hand, clearly intending to see if she was holding something. His eyes narrowed in surprise as he felt how warm it was.

Ember yanked her hand back. "I—"

But at that moment, one of the scouts let out a shrill, echoing cry:

"Dragons!"

Ember looked up. She could see nothing, hear nothing. Then there was a great *whoosh*, and for a moment, the stars disappeared.

A dragon soared past, a mere ripple of glimmering scales. It looked down at them, and Ember gasped—the dragon's eyes glowed like the fire dragons', but the light was colder. Closer to moonlight than fire.

More dragons joined the first. They wheeled in the sky above, calling to each other—their voices sounded like enormous birds of prey. They had clearly been on their way to their hunting grounds, and now, finding them occupied, they were uncertain what to do.

Flee, Ember urged silently. *Flee, now.*

Bows twanged as the hunters took aim. One of the dragons gave a piercing cry and fluttered unevenly toward the ground. Several of the dragons fled, while others lingered, crying out. Prince Gideon strode past her, gripping his bow.

"Hold your fire!" he shouted to the hunters. "I'm to have the first shot, you idiots!"

The hunters listened to him—surprisingly few of them had fired in the first place. Ember didn't understand it, but as she and Gideon approached the fire, she realized something was wrong.

Many of the hunters were not even holding their bows. Lady Valle and Mr. Black were scratching at their hands and necks, swearing. Mr. Heep was hopping up and down on one foot, trying to tear off his boot. The marquis clawed at himself, his jacket half off. Several of the seconds seemed to be affected too. Sir Abraham and Lady Tennenbaum stared at the rest as if certain someone would announce it was all a prank.

Ember rounded on Moss, standing at the edge of the firelight. He seemed to be suppressing laughter. "Moss?"

"I wasn't sure it would work," he said. "It's freckled ivy—I know we talked about putting it in their boots, but I thought I'd try sprinkling some on their tent flaps after they went to bed. They would have touched it this morning when they got up. It takes a few minutes to have an effect." He gestured with his chin. "I made sure to put extra on his tent."

Ember looked. Lord Norfell was on the ground, rolling back and forth over the rocks like a dog over a dead fish. "Ooh, ah!" he gasped as he furiously scratched at himself. "Ooh, ah!"

"What is going on?" Prince Gideon shouted.

"Your Highness!" one of the scouts called, dashing into the firelight. "There's a dragon down—it can't fly!"

Prince Gideon rounded on the others. "Everyone who hasn't completely lost their minds, follow me!" He took off at a gallop, giving a shrill whistle. Two of his dogs fell into step behind him, as did Sir Abraham, Lady Tennenbaum, and three of the seconds.

Her heart in her throat, Ember raced after them, as did Moss. The other dragons had fled, the sky now empty of everything but stars and a distant line of clouds.

When she came into view of the beach, she gasped. An enormous glittering shape lay there, scrabbling at the rocks. When it saw them, it let out a cry.

The dragon was beautiful—willowy and elegant, with a long, curving neck topped with a head more pointed than the fire dragons'. Its silver-blue scales shone as if dusted with starlight. Even the hunters seemed momentarily awestruck.

The dragon gave another cry, and tried again to hoist itself out of the shallow water. One of its wings bent at a strange angle. Tears stung Ember's eyes as she watched the magnificent creature struggle against the tide.

Before any of them could say a word, Prince Gideon stepped forward and raised his bow.

The bow snapped.

A scream rent the air. But it didn't come from the dragon—it was Lady Tennenbaum, standing next to the prince. The enormous bow had burst spectacularly into shards, and a piece had flown free and struck Lady Tennenbaum in the head. She sagged against Sir Abraham, who let out a curse.

"Your Highness!" one of the seconds exclaimed. Prince Gideon had fallen when the bow exploded. He stared at his hand—two of the fingers were bent strangely.

"What happened?" Sir Abraham cried, cradling the unconscious Lady Tennenbaum in his arms. "Who is responsible for this?"

No one answered. Ember looked at Moss, who was pale and grim. She knew her own face likely mirrored his. She hadn't meant for the bow to hurt anyone. But now that it had, she couldn't bring herself to feel sorry.

Fly, she begged the wounded dragon silently. *Please fly.* If it could only escape before the other hunters recovered—

Gideon drew himself shakily to his feet, cradling his injured hand. With his left, he unsheathed his sword.

"Stand back," he ordered his seconds.

"Your Highness!" Sir Abraham's eyes bulged. "You can't possibly be—"

"It's injured," Prince Gideon said. "It won't put up a fight."

"Please, Your Highness, you can borrow my bow—"

"I can't draw a bow," the prince snapped. His eyes were narrowed against the pain, his jaw clenched as he gripped his sword. "This . . . this is what my father would do."

He strode toward the beach.

"No!" Ember cried. She started forward, but the prince's second grabbed her arm, holding her back.

"The prince knows what he's doing," the man said, though he sounded far from certain. "He'll be all right, girl, don't worry."

Ember wept as the prince drew closer to the dragon.

After trying and failing to pull itself out of the waves, it lay half on its side, watching the prince with large, glowing eyes. The rocks were stained red.

"Why isn't it doing anything?" Ember said through her tears.

"It's hurt," the man holding her said, though this was hardly an answer. Ice dragons could breathe clouds of frozen vapor, cold enough to kill any living thing in their path. Yet the dragon didn't attempt to do so. It just lay there, its massive bulk dwarfing the prince. Was it too badly hurt? In the last seconds before it happened, the dragon closed its eyes.

Ember couldn't watch. She had fallen to the ground. She felt Moss's arms go around her, and then for a time she was aware of nothing. But she surfaced again, and felt the cold ground, which mirrored the cold inside her. All she could think about were her birth parents. Was this how they had died, all alone, at the hands of some horrible prince? She hated Gideon, then, with all her heart—the hatred was like a furnace inside her, a dark flame that she didn't think would ever go out.

TWELVE

THROUGH THE
FALCON'S CAGE

*Fire dragons continue to grow for at least thirty years,
and live to well over one hundred. A captive dragon in India lived
to 151. The beasts' longevity has no doubt given rise to the phrase,
"As long as a dragon's memory."*

—*TAKAGI'S* COMPENDIUM OF EXOTIC CREATURES

It was Sir Abraham who helped her to her feet and led her, clumsy and stumbling, back to camp. Lady Tennenbaum had recovered—Ember was dimly aware of her cooing and tsking over her. They seemed in agreement that Ember had fainted from fear for Prince Gideon's life. How relieved she would be, the lady said, when the shock wore off and she realized that he had successfully slain the dragon! Ember ducked inside her tent without speaking a word, and was aware no more.

She awoke properly some hours later, wrapped in blankets. Nisha and Moss were there, whispering, but Ember didn't stir. She didn't want to talk to anyone. She had failed. True, they had saved the other dragons, for it was likely that more would have been killed if the hunters hadn't been distracted. But that didn't change the fact that a dragon had died. Oddly, though, her thoughts kept drifting from the dragon to Chesterfield. She wished she had never heard of the Winterglass Hunt, or Prince Gideon, or any of it. She missed home so much she felt it would choke her.

It was her stomach that eventually forced her to move—it gave a mighty rumble, reminding her that she had missed breakfast and lunch. Grudgingly, Ember sat up.

"You're awake!" Nisha was at her side in an instant. "I'm so glad—we were worried! Are you all right?"

Ember was silent, and for the first time, her honesty didn't rise up inside her. Her honesty didn't know the answer any more than she did.

"That horrid Prince Gideon," Nisha said. "I wish I had been there with you—but then, I'm glad I didn't have to watch. Moss threw up. Do you want some hot chocolate?"

Ember wanted to lie back down and close her eyes and have nothing more to do with any of them. But she couldn't. She had failed the dragons once. She couldn't fail again.

She shook her head. "Where's the prince?"

"Off with his scouts and a few of the hunters. They don't think the dragons will return here, so they're going to try to track them south. The other hunters are preparing the dogsleds for an expedition."

Ember swallowed. "Then I have to go with them."

"*We* have to go with them." Nisha grinned her warm grin. She took Ember's hand. "Are you sure you're all right?"

For a moment, Ember thought about telling Nisha everything, but fear stopped her. If Nisha knew what she was, would she still want to help her? Nisha wanted to protect the dragons, but that didn't mean she wasn't afraid of them. Would she still see Ember as her friend? To her surprise, Ember found herself frightened at the thought of losing Nisha's friendship. It would be too painful on top of everything else.

"I'm all right," she said. "I just . . . want to be alone right now."

She went outside. It was late afternoon, and daylight had come and gone. Some yards away, hunters were clustered around the fire, while others seemed occupied with the dogsleds. The sky was mottled with clouds, which obscured most of the stars. A few snowflakes fell. They were gentle and soft, but a knife edge in the wind promised worse to come.

Ember had forgotten to don her coat, but she didn't feel like turning back now. She squeezed the pocket of her sweater and felt Montgomery's reassuring outline. The fabric of the world must have ironed itself out by now. Even if it hadn't, she didn't care. She had never felt so alone in her life, and she needed her father, and home, even if just for a few moments.

She made her way to the sleds, keeping to the shadows. The hunters paid her little notice anyway, and when one did glance her way, Ember made her expression dully curious, as if she had merely come to watch their preparations. Finally, she found what she was looking for.

The Marquis de Montvert had brought one of his prize falcons with him—it sat in its large cage on his sled, shivering. Though the creature was native to the Arctic tundra, it seemed to be bested by the Antarctic chill, and Ember was sorry for it. When no one was watching, she lifted its cage from the sled and darted away, murmuring to it to keep silent. It did, its black eyes wide with uncertainty.

Ember crept down to the shore and knelt behind a boulder. Here, with the stars hidden by the clouds, there was almost total dark, a towering, empty dark that Ember had never seen before, that was at once comforting and terrifying. Antarctica pressed against her back like a crouching monster.

Ember lifted the falcon out of the cage. It whistled softly, its talons gripping her wrist. Then, suddenly realizing its freedom, the bird took off over the water—back toward the prince's ship, which lurked somewhere in the mist, where the soft-hearted captain would scold it and spoil it with treats. Ember watched it go.

There came a familiar squawk.

Ember turned. A half-dozen Adélies clustered at the edge of the beach, waves lapping at their feet. Bold as anything, they strode up to Ember, eyeing the cage as if certain it was a tuna in disguise.

"You again!" she exclaimed. One of the birds had very ruffled feathers—it was the one who had stolen her flag-stone. "Did you follow me?"

The bird gave her a cunning sideways stare. It honked as she scratched its head. She hoped the magic had worn off.

"You stay here," she warned the penguins, in case they got any ideas. But it is impossible to tell if a penguin is getting ideas, and in the end, she just had to hope they wouldn't follow.

She was certain that it was night in London—early evening, she estimated, so she wouldn't pose a danger to anyone. That wasn't what gave her pause. The knob on the birdcage door was small—much smaller than Montgomery, and Ember felt a tremor of doubt as she unscrewed it.

"What do you think?" she murmured to the doorknob. They had patched things up since the incident with Puff, after Ember had spent three hours laboriously sanding and painting Montgomery's injuries. The doorknob, though, would never return to its former mint condition, and it knew it. It had a glum, self-conscious air as Ember affixed it to the birdcage. To her surprise, Montgomery fit the cage door perfectly, though it did look rather silly there.

"Sorry about this," Ember murmured. The doorknob maintained a long-suffering silence.

Holding her breath, Ember turned the knob to the right.

The door swung open. Beyond it, Ember beheld not the wire bars of the back of the cage, nor the falcon's perch, but the firelit wood and hangings of her father's office. She drew in a sharp breath. Wonderingly, she turned the cage around. From the back, she saw only bars and the open cage door.

Now for the tricky part. Ember knelt before the cage and squeezed her head in. The door should not have been wide enough for her shoulders, but then somehow it was, and she was pushing through. Once she had her arms in, Ember grabbed on to the edge of her father's rug (a gift from a Moroccan sultan) and dragged herself forward like an ungainly seal onto dry land.

As she did, she became aware of an odd sort of silence—not the silence of an empty room, but that of several people who had just drawn in a collective breath.

Ember looked up. Her father sat at his desk, blinking, and in the chairs opposite were two of his students, a young man and woman whom Ember recognized vaguely. Their jaws hung open.

"Er," Lionel St. George said. "Well! I think that's enough for today, Miss Montague, Mr. Basra. I trust you now have the information you need to complete your assignments?" He rose without waiting for a response. "Good! I'll see you both in class tomorrow."

He held open his office door. His students bumped into their chairs as they made their way from the room, their eyes fixed on Ember. Lionel shut the door behind them.

"Ember!" he exclaimed, rushing over to the door to the secondary hallway. He took her hands and pulled her into the office. As he did, Ember risked a glance behind her—instead of the secondary hallway, she saw the dark, snowy beach of Antarctica, the gawping penguins, a cage door attached to nothing, and her own legs, which seemed to hover in midair in a ghostly way. It was a disturbing sight, as it made no logical sense whatsoever, and she tried to forget it.

She fell into her father's arms, her tears starting almost immediately.

"What's happened, my dear?" he said. "Tell me everything."

Ember choked out the story of the hunt, and Prince Gideon and the dragon. When she spoke of Lord Norfell, her father went very still. But he said nothing until she was finished.

"That's quite a tale." His voice was carefully even, but Ember could tell that underneath it, he was very angry—though not at her. Lionel St. George rarely became angry, though Ember had sometimes heard the other Magicians remark that, when he did, it was best to stay out of his way. "I'm very sorry you had to witness that. Still, you no doubt saved the lives of a great many dragons. I'm proud of you. You did the best you possibly could."

"But I—" Ember stopped. *"Did'?"*

"There's no question of you going back to Antarctica," he said. "I feel—well, I feel absolutely dreadful for allowing you to go there in the first place. To think that I threw you into the path of that man Norfell . . ."

Ember didn't know what she had been expecting her father to say, but it hadn't been this. She felt as if she were falling. "But I have to go back! I have to—"

"I cannot allow that," he said, and though he didn't raise his voice, the words stopped her like a wall of stone. "I'm sorry, my dear."

He didn't say a word about her sneaking away to join the hunt, but it hung in the air nevertheless. Ember lowered her head. A weight settled over her, terrible and cold. She looked back at the door, the dark beach where an empty cage sat. One of the penguins seemed to be pecking at it.

"I'm sorry," she whispered. She said it to the dragons as much as to her father.

He let out a long sigh. For a moment, he looked older than his years. "I can't be angry at you for doing what you thought was right," he said. He went to the portal and knelt at the height of the birdcage. He reached an arm through, and when he withdrew it, he was holding Montgomery. He murmured in stormspeech, and then he closed the door to the secondary hallway. When he opened it again, Antarctica was gone.

Ember couldn't believe that she had left everything behind—not only the dragons, but Nisha and Moss. They would be so worried about her! "What will happen now?"

"I'll send your aunt a telegraph," her father said. "It will reach her in a few days."

"Have you figured out how to fix the spell?" Ember said.

His face fell. "No. But I believe I'm close. That dragon's blood will be the breakthrough, I can feel it."

Ember thought of how many times she had heard him speak of breakthroughs, only to have them come to nothing. "But it's summer. What if I catch fire again?"

Her father's brow furrowed. "Yes, I'm afraid we are substituting certain danger for probable danger. But we'll work something out. The important thing is that you're safe."

But you aren't safe from me, Ember felt like saying. Nobody is. But she couldn't, not with her father looking so grave.

"Father," Ember said, "if I don't go back, and those dragons die, it will be my fault."

Her father stared at her. "How could you think such a thing? Of course it isn't—"

"Yes, it is." The words burst out of her in a torrent. "It was my fault my parents died. And if I can save those ice dragons, and I don't, their deaths will be my fault too."

Her father grew very still. When he spoke, it was slowly and deliberately. "Ember. Your parents' deaths were not your fault."

"They died protecting me." Her voice broke. "That

makes it at least partly my fault."

"Ah, Ember." Her father ran his hand through his hair. "It is the duty of every parent to die protecting their children, if it comes to that. I would do the same. There is much evil in this world, and you are not to blame if it crosses your path." He let out a long breath. "Perhaps it's time I gave you something. . . ."

He paced over to his invisible desk. It was a little smaller than the visible one, shoved into a corner of the room beneath the best window. There Lionel did his secret magical research that he didn't want the nosy professors at Chesterfield to know about. He also kept a variety of mysterious trinkets and talismans from his travels in the drawers, which, in addition to being invisible, were locked.

Lionel spoke a few words in stormspeech, and the desk flickered into view. It was piled with notebooks and papers covered in his elaborate, loopy writing, as well as several empty teacups that had no doubt been there for some time, given that the servants couldn't see them. He unlocked the lowest drawer and removed something that flashed briefly in the light.

"What is that?" Ember said. There was something familiar about that flash of light—

Her father placed the object in her hand, covering it between their two palms. It was a pendant of some sort, affixed to a leather chain.

"It was your mother's," he said quietly. He drew his

hand back, and Ember gasped.

She was holding a fire dragon's heartscale—a complete one. It was roughly the shape of a teardrop, and fit perfectly in Ember's palm. Veins of gold ran through it like rivers of molten light.

"I found it when I found you, along with that bit of scale from your birth father," Lionel said.

Ember touched the ring she still wore. The ring was one thing—dragonglass was usually divided and sold in small pieces. An entire heartscale was almost unheard-of. She thought of Prince Gideon, who would no doubt be showing off the heartscale he had taken from the ice dragon. Her grip tightened.

Her father kissed her forehead. "I was going to keep it safe for you until you were older. I intended to study it further—you see, there's some sort of magic tangled in it, magic that doesn't seem to be present in worked dragonglass. I suppose the hunters and jewelry makers don't sense it—or if they do, they simply don't care. But I think, in light of all that's happened, it's time I let you look after it."

Ember placed the heartscale around her neck—the chain was only a little long on her. She marveled at how it shone even in shadow. What she held was worth a fortune. Thinking that drew her mind back to the hunters.

"Do you know Lord Norfell, Father?"

"I don't recognize the name," he said. "If that man was ever a Stormancer, he must have used an alias, which is not something that bodes well. There have been Stormancers barred from practicing magic. There was a man by the name of Nordock who, some years ago, was charged with sentient experimentation . . . that is, transforming human subjects against their will into a variety of gruesome forms. He fled the country before he could be arrested."

There was a knock at the door. Her father went to answer it and spoke to someone briefly.

"I'll be right back, my dear," he said, returning to her side. "Some business with Professor Donnelly." His expression was harried—Professor Donnelly, a wheezing, perpetually red-faced man who regarded himself the foremost Magician in the empire, was the ringleader of a clique that was constantly campaigning to have Lionel St. George permanently removed from Chesterfield, claiming he was a menace to the scholarly community. It was partly true, but fortunately Professor Donnelly was so unpleasant that few were inclined to listen to him.

Ember nodded, and her father disappeared, pulling the door shut behind him. Her gaze traveled around the familiar office, taking in the backward clock, the rich tapestries, the shelves of books. She had missed Chesterfield so much! And yet she couldn't be happy to be back, not like this, which was worse than not being back at all. It was as if she had returned home as a ghost, unable to enjoy any of the things she loved. She had left part of herself back in Antarctica.

Her gaze fell on Montgomery.

Her father had left the doorknob on his visible desk, next to a pile of books. Her heart thudding slowly in her chest, Ember lifted it.

As if in a dream, she strode to the door to the secondary hallway. It wouldn't work. It couldn't. Could it? While she had no interest in magic herself, Ember had absorbed enough during her life at Chesterfield to recognize a number of spells—including the one her father had used on the portal to Antarctica. Removing portals took time—possibly hours. Her father hadn't done that—he had merely closed it.

Ember removed the doorknob on the door to the secondary hallway. She turned the screws around Montgomery, her fingers trembling.

It won't work, she thought. She wasn't sure if she hoped for this to be true or not. Montgomery had been connected to Chesterfield—if attached to any door, it would open onto Lionel's office. So what would happen if it was attached to the other side of the office door? Montgomery couldn't open onto the office again—that would create a paradox. Magic, Ember knew, hated paradoxes and tried to avoid them whenever possible. The most logical thing for Montgomery to do, then, was to reverse the portal Ember had just used.

Ember turned the knob to the right, and the door swung open.

Beyond it was a dark beach, the snow a smudge upon

the night. An icy breeze stirred Ember's hair, and she shivered.

She glanced back at the cozy office—the flicker of firelight, the squashy furniture, the curtains drawn against the early summer night. Snowflakes spilled into the room and popped in the fireplace like corn. Ember's hand went to the scale around her neck. If she returned to Chesterfield, it wouldn't be as a ghost.

She went through the portal.

THIRTEEN

PENGUINS

Fire dragons subsisted entirely on vegetation. Grass, leaves,
and birch bark were among their favorite foods. Interestingly, this
has only added to their fearsome reputation, for it was often
said that when a dragon kills a man, it does not do so out of hunger.

—*TAKAGI'S* COMPENDIUM OF EXOTIC CREATURES

Reemerging onto the beach was an awkward thing to do. While it looked as if you could simply step into Antarctica from her father's office, this was deceptive: though the portal was stretchy, it was only the size of the birdcage door. Ember had to crouch on her hands and knees and slither and slide through. She finally tumbled onto the snow, scraping her elbows on the cage in the process.

She had retrieved Montgomery on her way back, and tucked it into her pocket. Then she closed the birdcage, and Chesterfield disappeared.

Ember sat there for a moment, half unable to believe what she had done. She had never defied her father before—not in any way that mattered. She felt ill, worse still when she thought about her father returning to his office and discovering what she'd done.

She tucked her mother's scale beneath her sweater, and it rested against her heart, warm and oddly familiar.

Now she had to hide the empty birdcage. The penguins had gone, and the snowy beach was deserted. Ember wandered up the beach, finally finding a spot between two large stones that created a shadowed hollow. She piled more stones on top of the cage, then stood back to admire her handiwork.

She turned and nearly walked into Prince Gideon.

She stifled a yelp of surprise. The prince stood with his arms crossed, his eyes cold. His right hand was bruised and bandaged, two of the fingers set with splints. It must have hurt to set the bones—they had brought no doctors along. Behind the prince stood his second, a hulking, grim-faced man with a scar running across his face. And next to him was Lord Norfell.

"Where were you?" he demanded. "Norfell saw you come this way, but when he followed, you vanished. He thought you'd run away."

"I . . . I just . . ." Ember fell back. She still felt sick over disobeying her father, and it took her a moment to gather her wits. Her eyes went to the glittering thing around Prince Gideon's neck. She realized with horror that it must be the ice dragon's heartscale. It was a blue so rich it seemed to transcend color, threaded with glittering silver. Heartbreakingly beautiful, and somehow alive in the darkness.

Gideon smiled. "Magnificent, isn't it? The first of many, I hope. My father will be pleased."

Ember's hatred thrummed in her veins. "Is that all you care about?"

The prince regarded her thoughtfully. "No," he said. "I also care about loyalty. It's important that my subjects are loyal to me, and through me, to my grandmother, Queen Victoria. My father is always very strict in punishing disloyalty. I intend to be no different."

Ember's heart sped up. Had he guessed about the cannons, and everything else? Did he know she was a spy? She didn't feel anything like a spy just then, certainly not a hardened one. The prince was gazing at her strangely, his eyes traveling from her boots to her hair and back again.

"Lord Norfell tells me that you have a spell placed on you," he said. "A very strange spell, something he's never seen before. Would you care to tell me what it is?"

He said it calmly enough, though his gaze was wary, as if Ember were a feral dog that might lash out at any moment.

Ember's heart was pounding wildly now. She knew she was in greater danger than she'd ever faced in her life. She took another step back. Calmly, slowly, Prince Gideon's second moved to stand behind her. Lord Norfell stood with his foot propped easily against a rock, surveying the landscape as if he owned it, as he always did, though his expression was an odd mixture of relief and anger. What did he know? How much had he told the prince? She guessed that he hadn't confided in Gideon out of loyalty, but to ensure that the prince would be motivated to find her if she had indeed run off.

"No," she said.

"No?" the prince's face went blotchy. "You dare to say no to me?"

"My . . . my father swore me to secrecy," Ember stammered. "I'm . . ." She swallowed. "I'm under a spell. But it isn't a danger to anyone. My father cast it when I was a baby, to save my life."

Prince Gideon's eyes narrowed. "You're going to have to do better than that. Especially given that I know what you've done."

"What?" Ember made a feeble attempt at an innocent tone. She wished that someone, anyone, would come— though would it matter if they did? She faced Prince Cronus's heir, the grandson of Queen Victoria herself. There was no one who could rescue her.

Gideon removed something from his wolf-skin cloak and tossed it at Ember's feet. It was a piece of his bow, warped and charred.

"You were in my tent this morning," he said. "I saw you. You did something to my bow. Didn't you? Admit it."

Panicked as she was, Ember felt powerless to stop the truth rising in her throat. "Yes."

Prince Gideon seemed to make a visible effort to control himself, wincing as he unclenched his injured hand. "And you were behind everything else, weren't you? The cannons . . . those strange rashes. The thefts. You've been attempting to sabotage this hunt from the beginning—no doubt on the orders of your miserable aunt."

"I wouldn't leap to that conclusion, Your Highness," Lord Norfell said. "Whoever—whatever—she is, she may have her own motives. I think it best to examine her thoroughly, rather than waiting to speak to her aunt."

Gideon turned back to her with an awful smile. "Lord Norfell thinks you're not even human," he said conversationally. "That you're some sort of . . . creature. I suppose that's why you have so much sympathy for dragons."

Before she could stop him, he grabbed her hand.

"Hmm," he said. "I noticed this before—your skin is hot. Some side effect of your father's spell? Or something more? What else are you hiding?" He grabbed at her hair, as if to test if it was real, and Ember jerked out of his grip. But his fingers brushed against the heartscale at the back of her neck.

Ember was paralyzed with terror. The prince's brows knitted together in confusion. He took her by the shoulders and wrenched her around, pulling her scarf down. She jerked out of his grip, crying out. But not before he had seen.

The prince fell back a step, a strangled sound rising from

his lips. His eyes were wide with horrified understanding.

"Your Highness?" said his second.

"Hold her." The prince's voice was hoarse.

Ember didn't even feel the man grip her arm. She couldn't think. She could only stare at the prince. If he told Lord Norfell what he had seen—if he told *anyone* what he had seen—they would kill her on the spot. She saw the same realization pass over the prince's face as his gaze darted to Lord Norfell. His eyes clouded. For a moment, Ember thought she saw a flash of the boy who had talked to her as he tended to his dogs. The boy who had saved her on the glacier. But then it was gone, so fast that Ember thought she had imagined it.

"What is it, Your Highness?" Lord Norfell said. His dark eyes ran eagerly over Ember. She knew in that moment, with a bone-chilling certainty, that he suspected that she was a dragon. He couldn't know for sure, though, or he would have told the prince.

Prince Gideon shook his head, as if to clear it. "Nothing." His voice was strained. "I dislike having to touch the creature, that's all."

Hope blossomed in her chest. But when he turned back to her, the prince's expression was black.

"Get yourself dressed properly," he commanded. "Then my second will ensure that neither you nor your irritating friends are able to cause any more trouble." With that, he was gone.

Prince Gideon ordered his men to roll a boulder over to the fire. Then he had Ember tied to it, along with Nisha and Moss.

Ember had protested. She had tried to argue that Nisha and Moss had nothing to do with sabotaging the hunt, that it had all been her idea, but the prince had acted as if she hadn't spoken—as had the other hunters. Only Sir Abraham had objected, his dignified mustache frowning at them all, and demanded to know why the prince felt it necessary to tie up children.

"Of course it's necessary," Prince Gideon had snapped. He hadn't looked at Ember once since the beach. "These criminals have confessed to sabotage. We must prevent them from doing further mischief that may endanger not just the hunt, but our lives. Don't be so squeamish, Sir Abraham. The saboteurs are perfectly unharmed and will be safely escorted back to the ship tomorrow at first light."

And then no doubt safely held at the castle for questioning, Ember thought darkly. Like Nisha and Moss, she was bound at the waist and hands. The chill of the ice-caked boulder seeped into her back, and if she was cold, she could only imagine how the other two felt.

Her father had been right. She never should have come back. She felt a terrible weight settle over her—the weight of her father's disappointment. She could have borne it if it had meant the dragons were safe, but they weren't. She had failed them *and* her father. Ember slumped against the rock, too miserable even to cry.

"Unfortunate business, this," Sir Abraham said. He lifted a steaming mug of tea to Ember's mouth. She gave him a stony look, and he sighed. "Miss St. George, given the circumstances, I think it would be advisable to show some—"

"You can just stuff it," Nisha snapped loudly and unexpectedly, drawing stares from the hunters at the fire. She had been almost silent throughout the ordeal, her face pale with shock as the prince's servants had bound her.

"Nisha!" Moss hissed.

"You heard me," she went on, her voice growing louder and louder. "She doesn't want to talk to you. You're a beastly person—you all are. How dare you do this to us? I hope the dragons eat you alive. I hope they start with your toes and then work their way up. Good riddance, I'll say! You might be a nobleman, but Ember has as much class in one finger as you probably do in your entire family tree!"

Sir Abraham had gone pale. Even his dignified mustache seemed whiter. With a sharp gesture, he dashed the tea against the ground and stalked off. Several of the hunters at the fire sniggered.

Ember looked at Nisha. The other girl was breathing hard, her face red. "Are you all right?" Ember whispered.

Nisha shook her head once, sharply. A tear slipped down her cheek. Finally she said, "I just c-can't stop thinking about my parents. I n-never even told them where I was going, and now—now I've been arrested by the prince!"

Ember bit her lip. "I'm sorry. I hope they won't be too angry."

"You don't understand," Nisha said. "Ever since Aditi d-died, they don't let me out of their sight! But they also don't—they don't talk to me, not the way they used to, and sometimes I think they wish that I had been the one who died instead of her. And I just get so angry. I wish everything could go back to how it was before."

Ember was astonished. She hadn't known that Nisha felt any of these things—but then, she realized with a stab of guilt, she hadn't really been paying attention. She had been so concerned with her own worries and plans that she had barely asked Nisha anything about herself, or Moss, for that matter. Now here they were, held captive alongside her, having risked their own safety to help her.

"That's not true," Moss said. He had to talk past Ember, who was tied up in the middle of them. "Your parents are worried about you—just as worried as they would be for Aditi."

Nisha sniffled. "I wish she was here. She was always braver than me. I thought I could be as brave as her by coming with you, but . . . now I just feel more alone."

Moss said quietly, "I miss her too."

Nisha buried her face against her knees, and would not respond to either of them again.

"I knew she shouldn't have come along," Moss

whispered to Ember. "I should have tried to stop her."

"It doesn't seem fair to stop her, and then go yourself," Ember said.

"Nobody cares where I go." He said it in an offhand way, and then he flushed, as if hearing his own words.

Ember didn't know what to say. Moss gazed into the darkness, the flush lingering on his cheeks.

"Do you really not remember anything before you showed up at the Firefly?" Ember said. She had been longing to ask since they'd met but hadn't had the courage.

"No," Moss said wearily.

"It's just . . . my father met a man once whose memory had been altered by magic," Ember said. "Someone had switched his memories with a vole's, which are just about the worst memories to have—all voles think about are tunnels and being eaten alive by birds. But when he was asleep, sometimes he'd dream about his old life. Do you ever dream?"

Moss was quiet for so long Ember didn't think he would answer. "Sometimes," he said.

"About what?" Ember prompted.

"It's nothing specific, it's just . . ." He swallowed. "Darkness. Somewhere dark—underground, maybe. I'm lost, and I'm . . . I'm hungry."

Ember felt an odd sort of shiver trace its way down her back.

"That's all I remember," Moss said.

"Maybe if you tried harder," Ember pressed, but he shook his head. "Don't you *want* to get your memories back?"

"Not if they're memories of this place."

Ember was surprised. "I thought you liked it at the Firefly."

Moss sighed. "I want to live where things grow. I want to see trees and flowers, and feel the rain. I've never even seen rain before. I'm tired of snow and ice and darkness. I don't think I ever liked it here, even when I was . . . whoever I was before."

"Why don't you?" Ember said. "I'm sure the Scientists would be happy to pay for a boarding school—"

"It's not that. I don't know what it is. It's like . . . it's like there's something holding me here." His hand clenched at the snow. "I don't know why, but I thought that if I joined the hunt with you, I might find some answers. I feel like they're out here, I just don't know where."

"Hmm." Ember wondered if her father would be able to sort out Moss's memories. But thinking about her father only made her miserable again, and she said no more. The three of them sat there in silence, thinking their separate thoughts as they gazed into the darkness. Ember found herself puzzling over their conversation. Both Moss and Nisha felt alone, even though they weren't—they weren't the last of their kind, after all, and Nisha had both her parents. She decided eventually that there must be different kinds of alone, just as there were different species of lantern fish.

She dozed fitfully, dreaming of the captive fire dragons, only she wasn't observing them from a distance—she was one of them, chained to the floor in that awful ship. She pulled and pulled, and cried out, but no one heard, and no one came—

Something started her awake. It wasn't a noise—it was a feeling. A faint throbbing in her thumb, and a twitch in her left wing. Nisha was shivering in her sleep beside her, and the wind moaned over the ice like a lonely ghost.

She turned her head and found Lord Norfell crouched in the shadows not three feet away.

"Hello, Miss St. George," he said in his elegant voice. "I'm glad to see you're awake. It would be unsportsmanlike to do this any other way."

Ember felt as if the night's chill had settled in her stomach. They were nearly alone—the hunters had retired to their tents. The fire, burning low, was being tended by two of the prince's servants, whose backs were turned.

She opened her mouth to shout, but Lord Norfell said, "They won't come. I've given them reason not to." He laughed, a short, sharp sound like a branch breaking. "Quite a few reasons, actually. Shiny golden reasons. As for the others . . . they can't hear you."

He was right. Snow fell steadily, muffling the camp, and the wind was rising. If she shouted, she wouldn't be heard from the tents.

"Wassat?" Nisha stirred beside Ember, lifting her head and blinking away the snow in her lashes. She cried out when she saw Lord Norfell. "What do *you* want?"

"This doesn't concern you," Lord Norfell said. "Close your eyes and sleep like a good girl."

"Don't tell her what to do," Moss snapped. He must have awakened when Nisha did. There was sleep in his voice, but the glare he leveled at Lord Norfell was steady.

"What do you want?" Ember said.

"I want the truth." Lord Norfell's gaze slid over her. "That is, of course, why I encouraged the prince to let you join the hunt. So that I would have more time to study you, to see if my hunch was correct. I won't deny I found the mystery entertaining."

Ember watched him as a hen watches a fox, her muscles braced for flight. But she was bound, and couldn't flee.

"As it turns out," he went on, "it was." He lifted a dagger from the snow beside him. To Ember's horror, there was a small bloodstain on the tip.

"Yours, I'm afraid," Lord Norfell said. Ember followed his gaze to her right hand—a drop of blood beaded from a nick on the thumb. That was what had woken her! The night's chill had only partly numbed the pain.

Lord Norfell murmured something to the dagger in stormspeech, which sounded twisted and wrong in his voice. The remaining blood evanesced into a curl of smoke, and then it vanished.

"I doubt I need to explain that human blood wouldn't do that," he said with a smile.

"Leave me alone." Her voice was barely above a whisper. "If you try anything, my father—"

"Ah, your famous father." Lord Norfell looked as pleased as a child placing the last piece in a puzzle. "Brilliant man. And like most brilliant men, he likely thinks himself high above the rest of us . . . so high that the spell he placed on you couldn't possibly be detected by anyone else."

"What are you talking about?" Nisha's voice was louder. "Are you mad?"

Lord Norfell tutted. "Keeping secrets from your friends? I can't say I'm surprised . . . if they knew, they'd be doing everything they could to get away from you."

He calmly examined the cutting edge of the dagger. All of Ember's focus swung to the blade—everything else disappeared.

"I happen to know a lot about this sort of magic." Lord Norfell continued in the same tone. "More than most Stormancers, perhaps. My experiments got me into a bit of trouble with the Stormancy Alliance, but they did teach me a few valuable lessons. Now, I doubt I'd be able to shatter your father's spell. But interestingly, there is another way. If you take the life of someone who is under a spell, that spell no longer has anything to hold on to, and it dissolves. I won't go into details on how I know this—those aren't stories for innocent ears, I'm afraid." He clucked his tongue. "I tried once, of course."

Ember blinked. Her brain wasn't working properly; her

thoughts were a tangle. But then she realized.

"You," she breathed. "You sabotaged my sled! You're the one who hurt those dogs." Her thoughts flashed back to her near escape, the sensation of falling, the prince hauling her to safety.

He shrugged slightly. "Yes, that was my doing. It was partly to test you . . . your ability to slither out of danger. I don't see much room for slithering now."

"Put that away!" Nisha cried. "How dare you threaten us, you vile, dreadful—"

"It's only fair for you to come clean with your friends." Lord Norfell went on as if Nisha wasn't shouting insults at him. "I'm doing them a kindness. They deserve to know what sort of creature they've befriended, don't you think? And I—well, I deserve to reap the reward for discovering your secret. You're mine by right."

And then, without warning, he drove the dagger toward her.

Nisha and Moss screamed. Nisha clawed at the ropes like a wildcat. Ember shut her eyes. An image of the fallen ice dragon rose before her.

I'm sorry.

But instead of pain, there was an odd sort of *zap*, followed by a gust of wind.

Ember's eyes flew open. Lord Norfell groaned—he lay in the snow a few yards away. Some force had knocked him backward and through the air. Several small shapes clustered about him, cocking their heads curiously at his prone form.

Penguins.

The penguin that had stolen the flagstone stood between her and Lord Norfell. It let out a honk, flapping its wings indignantly. Another penguin stomped up to Lord Norfell and began slapping his knee. Little daggers of lightning shot up his leg, and he shrieked.

Lord Norfell raised himself on his hands. Rage—a horrible, blank sort of rage—spread across his face as his eyes fixed on Ember. "You wretched little—"

The penguin gave him another slap, unleashing a bolt of lightning that sent Lord Norfell skittering over the snow. He staggered to his feet, and as one, the penguins trooped toward him. He fled, stumbling, over the snow, the penguins waddling behind.

"What in the Sciences—" Nisha began.

She was interrupted by a strange echoing cry. Another followed it—a sound like an enormous hawk, but of a higher pitch, sharp as ice shards. Ember wished she could cover her ears. Then there came the beat of enormous wings, which lifted the snow and dashed it across their faces in a painful mist. Ember looked up, squinting, and saw a dozen glittering shapes wheeling over the camp.

The dragons had returned.

FOURTEEN

THE STOLEN
HEARTSCALE

*Part of the attraction of fireglass is its hardiness. Neither bullet
nor dagger can penetrate it, but only the horn or bone of another dragon.
A dragon's scales are like armor made of diamonds.*

—*TAKAGI'S* COMPENDIUM OF EXOTIC CREATURES

Shouts filled the air. The hunters had heard the dragons'
cries and were spilling out of their tents. The Marquis
de Montvert was among the first to appear with his bow
in hand. He fired an arrow, which missed.

Nisha screamed. "The dragons! They've come back!
They're going to tear us to pieces!"

Ember thought this a likely conclusion, though part of
her wished Nisha wouldn't put it so bluntly. She scrabbled
at the snow with her feet—Lord Norfell's dagger lay barely
a foot away. One of the dragons unleashed a blast of ice
fog that engulfed one of the seconds. The man fell to the
ground, twitching.

Ember hooked her heel around the dagger. Gripping it

between her feet, she sawed apart the bonds at her wrists, then cut the rest of the ropes.

"Let's get as far from camp as possible," she said. Nisha and Moss nodded, but before they could move, Lady Valle stampeded past them, clutching her bow. She took aim at one of the dragons.

Not knowing what else to do, Ember flapped her wings furiously—they were stiff from cold and being tied up, but she managed to stir a gust of wind. Lady Valle's shot went wide, and she let out a curse.

"What was that?" Nisha yelped, brushing the hair from her eyes.

"Come on." Ember grabbed her hand and Moss's. Together they raced past the fire, past the tents—where Prince Gideon had just emerged, his expression a mixture of excitement and fear.

"To me, Brooks! O'Malley, get my sled ready! Good grief, what are all these penguins doing here?"

To Ember's horror, the prince was still wearing the dead dragon's heartscale around his neck—it flashed in the firelight. Was he mad? The dragons would see it!

"Gideon—" Ember began.

The prince whirled on her. "You! I thought I ordered—"

"Get down!" Moss shouted.

Ember didn't think. While the prince continued to yell at her, Ember leaped at him, using her wings for extra propulsion, and knocked him to the ground.

"What in the—" Prince Gideon began, but at that moment, a dragon swooped over them, passing so low its belly scraped the peak of the nearest tent and its icy breath rolled over them like fog.

Ember didn't pause. "Give me that scale!" she yelled, scrabbling at the prince.

"I will not! Get off me!"

They wrestled in the snow, tumbling over and over. The prince let out a sharp breath when he felt Ember's wings. His expression hardening, he grabbed one and twisted it, so hard that Ember cried out, her grip on him loosening.

The prince sprang to his feet. "How dare you lay hands on me! I will not—"

"They're going to kill you if they see that scale!" Ember snapped. "You stupid, arrogant . . ."

The words died on her lips. With a terrible silent grace, an ice dragon settled onto the snow behind Gideon.

The dragon was bigger than the one that had died on the beach. In the darkness, its scales shone like will-o'-the-wisps, while its eyes were fallen stars, cold and entirely white. There was nothing in its face that Ember could read—she could have been staring at the side of a frozen mountain. The dragon let out a long breath—not a killing blast of ice, but a frigid sigh that stirred the prince's hair and covered Ember's skin in gooseflesh.

Everything seemed to slow. Gideon, sensing the dragon at his back, reached for his sword—it wasn't there.

He hadn't had time to don it. Ember opened her mouth to scream a warning. The dragon's front foot darted out, its talons like icicles digging into the shoulder of Prince Gideon's coat.

The dragon sprang into the air, its powerful wings pumping so hard that Ember was momentarily blinded by snow. The last thing she saw was Gideon's face, his eyes wide with helpless terror. Then he and the dragon were gone.

FIFTEEN

SOUTH

Without its heartscale, the fire dragon would die. As if conscious of the vital importance of this organ, the dragon was exceedingly cautious in protecting it, preferring when in combat to fight with flame and talons only, keeping both head and neck out of reach of its opponent.

—*TAKAGI'S* COMPENDIUM OF EXOTIC CREATURES

"Follow them!"

"Did we hit any? I could have sworn—"

"Dammit, Black, get out of my way so I can take a shot!"

"Which way did they go?"

The camp was in complete disarray. Hunters ran this way and that—some wanted to follow the dragons, while others were for searching the vicinity to see if any of the beasts had been taken down by their arrows. The night was black—fat snowflakes swirled from heavy clouds; the fire had been reduced to embers by the dragons' wings. Penguins honked and slapped at anything that came within slapping range. They did little harm, but contributed to the general confusion. Mr. Heep, yelling something about the supplies, slammed into the Marquis de Montvert, who was running in the opposite direction. They were almost blind.

But Ember was not.

She was on her feet and racing back to her tent before the dragons' wingbeats faded. She emerged moments later, having shoved all her belongings into her pack. She darted toward the sleds.

She found Prince Gideon's easily enough. His dogs were clustered around it, whining and shaking. Someone had already half harnessed them—one of the prince's servants, no doubt. That servant was nowhere to be seen, having been swept up in the chaos of the camp. Ember wondered if any of them had even realized yet that the prince had been taken. Her hands trembling, she secured the dogs to the sled.

"What are you doing?"

Ember whirled. Moss stood behind her, holding a piece of firewood like a torch, which threw his sharp features into stark relief. His eyes widened when he saw the pack she carried.

"I'm going after him," Ember said.

She expected Moss to argue—to call her mad, to say that she couldn't think of risking her life like that. Instead he said, "Why?"

His voice held only curiosity. Ember met Moss's gaze and saw a coldness there that she had glimpsed before. He truly would leave Prince Gideon to die and not feel a shred of guilt about it.

"He held us captive," Moss said. "He threatened you. He refused to listen when you warned him about the scale. He deserves whatever happens to him."

Ember tried not to shiver at the cold logic of it. Moss was right. The prince was arrogant and cruel. He had killed one dragon, and given the chance, he would kill more. But she also remembered the tiny glimmers of kindness she had seen in him. Was that enough to make his life worth saving? Or did kindness factor into it at all?

"You're right," she said. "He deserves to be carried off by dragons—or worse. But I'm still going. I think . . . I think I'm the only one who can save him."

Moss said nothing. His blue eyes were the exact shade of ice in the afternoon, when shadows stretched long over the snow.

"Why do you always do that?" an angry voice demanded. Nisha stepped into the torchlight. "You have to do everything by yourself, don't you? Don't you trust us at all? After all we've been through! And you're just going to leave us behind?"

"I—" Ember fumbled for words. "Well—yes. Do you know how dangerous this is?"

"Do you?" Nisha retorted. "We helped you get this far. Admit it—you're glad we came along."

"Of course I am," Ember said, and then she stopped, surprised by how true it was. Without Nisha's strategizing and Moss's quiet encouragement, she could never have saved as many dragons as she had.

"I don't care about Prince Gideon," Moss said. "But I care about the dragons. If he dies, so does any hope of saving them."

The sickening truth of Moss's words hit Ember like a stone. Queen Victoria had been willing to listen to Aunt Myra, and to place limits on the Winterglass Hunt. But if the ice dragons killed her grandson . . .

Ember swallowed. Hunters would pour into Antarctica to wipe out Gideon's killers—with the queen's blessing.

Still, that didn't change the fact that it was far too dangerous for Nisha and Moss to come with her. It had felt like a game before. It wasn't a game now.

"I have to do this myself," she said.

Nisha folded her arms. "No."

Ember stared at her. "What are you—"

"Moss, the sled," Nisha said. Before Ember knew what was happening, Nisha had leaped onto the sled, while Moss hopped up on the back, yelling at the dogs to move. They did, grudgingly, still unnerved by the dragons' attack.

Ember was so astonished that, for a moment, she could only stare at the retreating sled.

"Hey!" she yelled, and dashed after them.

"We're going after the prince," Nisha yelled back at her, her ribbons flapping around her face. "Goodbye! We'll be back in a few days!"

Ember narrowed her eyes, beating her wings to

quicken her pace. She caught up with the sled in seconds. Moss started as she grabbed the handle.

"Whoa!" Ember called to the dogs. They slowed, then stopped. Moss watched her uncertainly. Nisha had her arms folded again.

"All right!" Ember snapped.

Nisha seemed to smother a smile. "All right, what?"

"All right, you can come with me," Ember said.

Nisha accepted this with a dignified nod. She shuffled over, leaving space for Ember to sit beside her on the sled. Ember plunked down, anger warring with the laughter rising in her throat. She looked at Nisha, whose glower melted into a giggle. Ember couldn't suppress her smile.

"What about your parents?" she said.

Nisha's face darkened. "They want to keep me locked up. I don't want to be locked up anymore." Her gaze grew distant, and she set her jaw. "This is what Aditi would do."

"Er," Moss said. "Where are we going, anyway?"

"South," Ember said. That was the direction the dragons had flown. "Hopefully we can catch up to them. I don't—I don't know what we'll do when we find them. I don't have a plan."

"We know," Moss said.

Nisha nodded. "That's why we're coming with you, of course," she said in an exasperated voice. "Because you need help."

Ember swallowed against the lump in her throat. Nisha

and Moss had already risked their lives to help her. And now this? She felt she should say something—thank them, perhaps, or warn them again. She couldn't find the words. But neither Nisha nor Moss seemed to mind.

"All right, let's go save those dragons." Nisha narrowed her eyes at the southern horizon. "And that useless prince too, I guess!"

SIXTEEN

LAND OF NIGHT

*In the prehistoric era, dragons were often hunted by humans for meat.
They were smaller than their modern descendants, and Charles
Darwin has speculated that human contact led to the evolution of the
dragons' impenetrable scales, as well as their size and ferocity. . . .*

—*TAKAGI'S* COMPENDIUM OF EXOTIC CREATURES

They traveled for hours, the sled dogs' paws light against the snow. After the dogs' initial hesitation, they seemed happy to run, to work off their nervous energy. The clouds lifted before morning, and the Milky Way illuminated their path, spilling across the sky like a river of pearls. Nisha slept, burrowed in blankets with her head against Ember's shoulder, but Ember kept glancing back, certain the hunters would pursue them. But she saw nothing but the empty expanse of snow. If the hunters were following, they weren't keeping up.

Eventually they had to pause to rest the dogs. Ember examined them thoroughly, checking their paws for any signs of injury as she had watched Gideon do. The lead dog was a beautiful half wolf that the prince had called

Finnorah, her fur silver and ivory. She didn't seem to want to stop, turning up her nose at the meat Ember offered. Whining, she pulled at her harness.

"You have to maintain your strength," Ember lectured. The dog stared at the empty horizon, as if expecting someone to appear.

"We'll find him," Ember murmured. She said it with more confidence than she felt. Finnorah nosed reluctantly at the meat. Ember felt like telling her that Prince Gideon wasn't worthy of so much concern, but she knew the dog wouldn't believe her. After all, Takagi's *Compendium* stated that a dog's defining characteristic was loyalty, not being a good judge of character.

Ember, Moss, and Nisha rummaged through the prince's supplies until they found food for themselves— hard bread, cheese, porridge, dried milk, and fruit. It was fortunate that the prince had been preparing for his own journey south. Though, Ember thought, if the prince was dead, using his supplies was a little creepy.

Ember shook her head. She couldn't allow herself to think like that. Prince Gideon wasn't dead. They were going to find him and bring him home, and the dragons would be safe—or at least, as safe as they'd ever been.

Nisha crouched in the snow over a map, a compass in her hand. Though she was wearing three coats, including an oversized man's fur she had found on the sled, she was shivering. Ember gathered a few scraps of wood into a pile and, when she was certain Nisha and Moss weren't watching, lit the fire with a wave of her hand. She whispered to the flames, asking them to consume the wood slowly.

"Oh, lovely!" Nisha crowded around the fire, warming her hands. "That was fast!"

"Nice to have some color," Moss said, and Ember nodded. She was growing tired of featureless snow.

"Actually," Nisha said, "white contains all the colors in the rainbow." She absently retied one of her ribbons. "So, if you think about it, that makes Antarctica the most colorful place on earth."

Moss went to the sled to examine the supplies. He wore only one coat, seeming unbothered by the chill even when the wind whipped around them. His pale hair, bleached by the moon, was the color of bone.

"Do you know how to read that?" Ember asked Nisha, gesturing to her map.

"Yes. Madame Rousseau always said that navigation was as important a skill as geometry or writing, at least out here." Nisha pointed at a spot. "We're here." She pointed to another spot. "The hunters' camp is here. I can tell by the mountains. That's the Shackleton Range, see." She gestured into the night. "And that's Whichaway. We could continue south all the way to the pole—there's a colony somewhere near it, the Scientists say. Do you think that's where our dragons are going?"

Ember fingered the heartscale through her coat. It seemed warmer against her skin, though perhaps that was only because of the cold hours she had spent on the sled. "I—maybe." She felt uncertain. She had seen the dragons fly south, but what if that was wrong? What if they turned around, or veered in another direction?

"That's a long way," Moss said, coming over to the fire. "Days. I don't know if the dogs will make it."

"They'll make it," Ember said with more confidence than she felt. "They've been to the pole before, with Gideon."

"Why do you think the dragons kidnapped him?" Nisha said. "I mean, they knew he killed their friend—he was wearing the heartscale, the idiot. Why not just, I don't know, turn him into a prince-shaped ice pop?"

Ember shook her head. "I'm not sure."

"Maybe they're going to put him on trial," Moss suggested. "Do dragons have trials?"

"Maybe they know who he is, and they want to scare his father," Nisha said. She and Moss kept up a steady stream of speculation, while Ember was quiet. She couldn't guess at why the ice dragons had taken Gideon—she didn't know how they thought. Were they anything like her? It certainly hadn't felt that way as she had faced the dragon that had taken the prince. Ember shuddered at the memory of its cold white eyes.

They set off again, Ember steering the dogs while Moss napped with Nisha in the sled. Ember wondered what time it was. She felt strange gliding over that featureless expanse of snow. The runners whispered, and the mountains loomed larger. It wasn't until they stopped for the night, hours later, that Ember realized why she felt so strange.

Though they had traveled all day, the sun hadn't risen.

The sky had purpled and then darkened again. They had passed beyond the invisible line that the sun, at this time of year, didn't cross. Now they were in the land of night. Ember had a sudden image of herself stuck to the bottom of the planet like a bug on an apple, and suppressed the urge to grab hold of the snow.

Ember helped Nisha and Moss put up the tent. The dogs rolled in the snow, trying to cool themselves after hours of hard exercise. Finnorah came to sit at Ember's side, and she scratched her ears.

Ember built the fire quickly, checking that Nisha and Moss weren't watching as she summoned an orange flame and let it catch on the kindling. She smiled at the dancing fire, which seemed to wave back at her. She had always avoided doing using her powers in London—she had been too afraid of losing control. After extinguishing her palm, she gazed at the dark sky, the snow that stretched in all directions, and let out a long, misty breath. She didn't have to be afraid here—at least, not of herself. The thought filled her with a sense of peace, which was strange, given all that had happened.

They sat around the fire, drinking tea boiled in melted snow. Moss had burned the leaves, but they were all too tired to care.

Nisha rubbed her wrists. "The prince's men tied those ropes too tight."

Ember felt a now-familiar stab of guilt. "I'm sorry. It's my fault you were tied up at all."

"It's the prince's fault," Nisha assured her. "Rotten snob. If we do rescue him, I get to punch him in his perfect teeth."

They were quiet for a moment. Then Moss said, "What did Lord Norfell mean, anyway?"

Ember said nothing, though her heart sped up.

"Ugh!" Nisha said. "Just thinking about that man gives me the creeps."

"He seemed to think Ember was under a spell," Moss said. "Did your father place a spell on you?"

He and Nisha both looked at her. Ember felt frozen by their gazes. But the truth rose up inside her as it always did.

"Yes," she said. Her voice was barely above a whisper.

"What sort of spell?" Moss pressed.

"I—" Panic overwhelmed her. She had seen Prince Gideon's horrified expression when he saw her heartscale. Would she see that same look in Nisha and Moss's eyes?

"Maybe she doesn't want to talk about it," Nisha said. She gave Moss a sharp look before turning back to Ember. "Do you?"

Ember shook her head mutely.

"Really, Moss," Nisha scolded. "That man tried to kill

her. He was going to stab her through the heart, or maybe slash her neck open! She doesn't need you reminding her about it."

Ember felt a rush of gratitude—though if it had truly been Lord Norfell she was upset about, she doubted that the graphic picture Nisha painted would have improved her mood. Moss mumbled an apology.

"What's that?" Nisha said in a brisk, changing-the-subject voice. "A necklace?"

Ember started. She hadn't realized that she'd been holding the heartscale, which was hot against her palm. "Oh, it's—" *Nothing*, she wanted to say, but the word stuck in her throat. And in any case, did it matter if Moss and Nisha knew about the heartscale? She didn't need to keep that from them too. She removed the chain from her neck and held it up.

They both gasped. Ember couldn't blame them—the scale was even more vibrant in the firelight. It looked like flame itself, frozen midflicker.

"Where did you get that?" Nisha murmured.

"My father gave it to me." Ember handed it to her.

Nisha held it up to the light, looking awestruck. "It's— it's a heartscale. And it's intact! This must be worth a fortune."

"Where did he get it?" Moss said. He too looked awe-struck, though as he took it from Nisha, he winced. "It's so hot," he said.

"He found it when he was out stormchasing," Ember

said, keeping her voice as neutral as possible.

Moss pulled his sleeve over his hand, using it to insulate his fingers from the heat of the scale. He held up the heartscale and gazed through it. "What's that?"

"What?" Nisha leaned against him, looking through the scale.

"Don't you see? It's like . . . light."

"I don't see anything," Nisha said.

Moss handed the scale to Ember. "Try it!"

Ember, frowning, held up the scale to the stars as Moss had done. At first, she saw nothing. The stars shone through the scale, their light tinged with red. She lowered the scale slightly, and then—

Ember drew a sharp breath.

A faint glow hovered in the sky beyond their camp— it looked like a trail of smoke, but it was luminescent, a silvery moonlight color. It seemed to lead south past the mountains, but how far it went after that, Ember couldn't tell.

She moved the scale around, examining the landscape. The same trail of light continued north, back toward the hunters' camp. Beside it, she realized, was a fainter trail, which ran almost parallel. But she could only see the light through the heartscale; when she lowered it, the sky was empty.

She looked down at her hand and started so badly she nearly dropped the scale.

Her hand *shone*. Shone like fire in the night; like sunlight spilling over the horizon. Ember looked at her other hand, and it glowed too. So did her arm, when she drew the sleeve back—the light was hidden by her clothes. It was her—she was glowing.

Ember looked at Nisha. She didn't glow at all—not her bare hands or face, or any other part of her. But Moss . . .

"What is it?" Moss said, his brow furrowed. "You look like you've seen a ghost."

Ember swallowed. His skin shone too, though the light was different than Ember's. It was a paler, cooler glow, and very faint.

"You see it, don't you?" Moss said. "What do you think it is?"

"I don't know," Ember murmured.

"Can I look again?" Moss said.

Ember tucked the scale back inside her coat with shaking fingers. "I—I think we should get some sleep."

Moss started to argue, but Ember was already walking away.

She gave the dogs their supper, then did another inventory of their supplies. All the while, her thoughts were whirling.

She drew the scale out again, and looked at the sled, the snow, the dogs. Nothing. She looked up at the sky, and there it was, that strange trail of light, still hovering in the same place.

Had it been left by the ice dragons? Were dragons able to sense the paths other dragons had taken, the way hunting dogs tracked their prey? Was that why it was visible through the scale? Instead of a trail of scent, did dragons leave a trail of light?

An idea struck, and Ember turned the scale toward her own footprints in the snow. Sure enough, a faint but unmistakable glow led back to the fire she had just abandoned.

Well. That explained Ember's glow. It explained the light in the sky.

It didn't explain Moss.

Moss was not a dragon. He didn't move like her, or possess any other dragonish qualities that she recognized. But beyond what her instincts told her, Ember knew that such a thing was impossible: she was the first and only dragon to be transformed into a human. Her father had invented the spell himself. It was unlikely that any other Stormancer had the ability to work that sort of magic.

But if Moss wasn't a dragon, what was he?

Sensing Ember's anxiety, Finnorah let out a whine. The dog crouched at her side, and Ember absently stroked her head. Her thoughts were a whirl. Before she could sort any of them out, Nisha called, "Ember? Are you all right?" and she had to rise and retire to the tent.

They spent the night shivering. Ember slept little. What if they didn't find Prince Gideon? What if all they found was a pile of prince-sized bones? How would she protect the ice dragons then? What about Moss—what *was* he?

Ember rolled over and gazed at him. Asleep, he looked like an ordinary boy, if unusually pale and slight as a shadow. She lifted the heartscale to her eye again, and watched him glow like moonlight.

Storm clouds gathered over the mountains as they set off the next morning (at least, Nisha's pocket watch said it was morning—the sky was purple ink). The dogs growled, nervous. They were heading toward the storm.

It loomed above them, towering clouds that hid the mountains behind sheets of white. Gusts of ice-flecked wind rolled over the sled in waves, and Ember's short hair flapped in her eyes. That wasn't what worried her—what worried her was the possibility that it wasn't an ordinary storm. Ember had seen magical storms, and they often looked like this: towering columns lit by lightning that danced and twisted like glowing snakes.

The dogs yipped, but they kept running, Finnorah leading the way. She barked fiercely at any dog that shied or struggled.

Ember pulled the scale from her coat. There—there was the trail of light. Leading directly into the storm.

She swallowed and urged the dogs on.

But after another quarter hour, even Finnorah was struggling. The wind was so fierce that the dogs were crouched almost on their bellies as they battled against it. Nisha and Moss had their scarves pulled up over their faces. Ember, steering the sled, had to crouch as low as she could, and even then, she was at constant risk of being blown backward.

Finally, she called for a halt beside a range of nunataks. The first blasts of snow had reached them, and it was icy, threaded with hail.

"We should set up the tent," Ember said, raising her voice to be heard over the wind. "We can't—"

That was all she had time for before the storm was on them, a cruel, ice-clawed pounce.

Ember could see nothing—not even her hand when she held it in front of her face. The world was reduced to snow and shadow. She was lucky to have been holding on to the sled—if she hadn't, she might not have been able to find it again.

Between gusts, her vision cleared slightly. Moss and Nisha were still crouched on the sled. Nisha seemed to be yelling something. The dogs circled, howling.

Ember fumbled for the tent. "Come on!" she shouted.

Moss hurried to help her. Nisha tried to stand, and then fell over as another gust crashed into them. Ember's heart was pounding. How were they going to get the tent up in this weather? How were they going to survive if they didn't?

As if in response, the wind gave a mighty roar, pelting the sled with hail.

Nisha stood and took an unsteady step forward. Lightning flashed, silhouetting her against the black clouds.

"Nisha?" Moss called. "What are you doing?"

"I thought I heard something," she yelled back.

Ember thought she had too. Among the pounding hail and thunder, there were voices. Whispers. She blinked. Figures loomed in the darkness. She caught a flash of reddish hair and a sly smile. A man stood before her, holding a knife. She screamed. Lightning flashed, revealing—

Nothing. There was no one there.

Realization struck. "Oh no," Ember murmured.

"What is that?" Moss said. He was looking in another direction, melting snow streaming down his face. "P-Professor Maylie? Are you hurt?"

Ember wrenched him around. "Ignore it."

"But I saw—"

"You didn't see anything. Look at me!" Ember grabbed his chin. "This is a magical storm. I've never been in one, but my father has. The magic makes you see things, things that aren't really there. You have to ignore it."

Moss's gaze darted around. But he gave a slight nod and helped Ember unearth the tent from the sled. Ember began driving the poles into the snow.

"Let me," Moss shouted into her ear, and Ember handed him the heavy folds of treated leather. But at that moment, the storm roared, and the wind snatched the tent from Moss's hands, sending it billowing away.

"No!" Ember screamed. Thunder boomed, and laughter echoed around them. She pressed her hands against her ears. The laughter sounded like Prince Gideon's. Then it twisted into screams.

It's not real. It's not real.

Nisha had her hands pressed against her ears too. She rocked back and forth, oblivious to the raging wind. Suddenly she looked up. Ember saw her mouth form a word that she couldn't hear.

Aditi.

"Nisha, no!" Ember grabbed her arm. "It's just a hallucination. She's not—"

But Nisha wrenched away and ran.

Into the storm, which descended over them again like a black veil.

"Nisha!" Ember screamed. It was no use—she couldn't even hear her own voice through the raging, churning wind. She and Moss clung to each other, blind and deaf. Though the sled was mere feet away, Ember could no longer tell where to look for it—all sense of direction had been swept away by the storm. She felt a moment of pure panic, imagining Nisha trapped out there—she would be completely lost. But she and Moss could only sit, grip each other's hands, and wait. Dragons surged around her, dragons that shrieked and fell from the sky, dead. Lord Norfell stalked among the shadows, appearing sometimes in the distance, and other times at her back, his dagger raised. Ember wanted to scream, to run, but she knew that if she did, the illusions would follow. Moss seemed to be crying.

After an interminable time, the wind died slightly, and Ember could see again. The cold was so ferocious that even she was shaking. She squinted into the whirling dark, trying to find Nisha. But she saw no movement, and all evidence of her trail had been swept away.

"Nisha!" Moss shouted. He stood, his pale hair a smudge against the darkness. "Nisha!"

"We have to go after her," Ember said. She fumbled around in the sled, finally locating a length of rope. "Here."

They knotted the rope around themselves, then tied the other end to the sled. "Stay here," Ember murmured to Finnorah, who was huddled with the other dogs in a miserable pile. The husky licked her hand.

Ember and Moss set out. They walked to the end of the rope—about thirty feet or so—then traced a wide circle around the sled, shouting Nisha's name. Disoriented by the storm and the tricks it played, she could have gone in any direction.

"What now?" Moss said, once they had shouted themselves hoarse. Ember opened her mouth to reply, but a thundering laugh, only vaguely human, drowned her out.

Moss gave a cry. The wind knocked him off his feet, and his weight on the rope took Ember down with him. She felt the rope catch on something sticking out of the ground—a rock, or a sliver of ice—and then it suddenly went slack.

"No," Ember gasped. She pulled the rope toward her until she reached the frayed, jagged end.

They were no longer tied to the sled.

There came a shout in the distance—it was impossible to tell which direction. "Nisha!" Moss yelled. Then he was charging into the storm.

Ember was on her feet in a heartbeat, racing after him. She grabbed his arm and spun him around. "What are you doing?" she yelled. "We have to stick together!"

"But Nisha's out there." Specks of ice clung to Moss's face—tears.

"We don't know if that's her," Ember said. "And even if it is, we won't be any help to her if we get ourselves lost."

She looked around. She thought she knew where the sled was, but she wasn't certain. In this weather, they could walk right past it. How long would the storm last? How long could Nisha and Moss survive in this bitter cold, without blankets or shelter? As if in response, the storm howled louder, and the visibility dropped again.

Moss's eyes darted this way and that. The visions had him again. Acting on some instinct, Ember lifted her hand to the scale around her neck—

The scale.

Ember raised it to her eye with trembling fingers. There, on the snow—a faint glimmer of light. Or rather, two faint glimmers, one silver and one golden—a path that led to where they stood. The wind had swept away their footprints, but it seemed that it could not destroy this.

Ember let out a relieved breath. At least she could find the way back to the sled! But that didn't help Nisha.

"What do we do?" Moss said through his tears.

Ember swallowed. There was only one thing she could think of, and it frightened her more than anything. But Nisha . . . She thought of her warm laugh, their hands twined together. How she had fought to save Ember from Lord Norfell. Ember couldn't abandon her. She wouldn't, not without trying everything.

She stepped away from Moss. "Stand back," she warned.

She looked down at her hands and concentrated. Flames flickered on her palms. Moss drew a sharp breath, but she ignored him. Ember let the fire travel from her hands up her arms. To her amazement, she found that she was able to tell it not to burn her clothes, and it obeyed, shimmering over her coat and hair like harmless heat haze. She let the fire spread until she was entirely alight, clothed in flame from head to toe.

"Brighter," Ember whispered. Would the fire obey? Or would it extinguish itself in a blinding burst, melting everything in the vicinity?

But the fire listened. It brightened, burning white-hot in the darkness. Moss threw an arm over his face with a shout.

"Brighter," Ember said, her heart thundering at her success.

She was a living torch, the flame reaching up a dozen feet into the sky. The storm raged, but it couldn't touch the fire, which gobbled up any snow tossed its way with a vicious hiss. Finally Ember heard a girl's voice shouting, and then a moment later, Nisha charged out of the storm. Nisha, flesh and blood and not an illusion, her face streaked with tears. She was clutching their lost tent.

"I saw the fire!" she exclaimed. "Oh, I thought I would never find my way back! How did you—"

She froze, her gaze shifting from Moss to Ember, standing at the heart of an inferno.

Ember extinguished herself with a single sharp gesture. A plume of steam engulfed her, and when it cleared, both Nisha and Moss were staring at her with identical expressions of shock—and fear.

"It's all right," Ember said. She wanted to run from the look in their eyes, but she forced herself to stand her ground. "I'm . . . I'm not dangerous. It was the only thing I could—"

She couldn't finish, for Nisha had leaped on her, wrapping her in a fierce hug. And Moss, to Ember's astonishment, was laughing.

SEVENTEEN

MISFITS

*The fire dragon's flame was a mystery until 1799, when entomologist
Priscilla Hencefort argued that it is, in fact, a superheated form of
bioluminescence similar to that found in fireflies. Her studies proved once
and for all that dragons are Scientific, not Magical, beasts.*

—*TAKAGI'S* COMPENDIUM OF EXOTIC CREATURES

E mber led them back to the sled, following the glowing trail she and Moss had left in the snow. There
they erected the tent in the shelter of a boulder, and dived
inside to wait out the storm.

It was a long wait. Ember didn't like to think about
what would have happened if they hadn't found Nisha—as
it was, even wrapped in blankets in the relative warmth
of the tent, the other girl was shivering. Moss, as usual,
seemed unaffected. The three of them huddled together in
the darkness, as beyond the tent, voices called their names
and wicked laughter rang out. Finally the wind's howl died
to a moan, and the voices faded to whispers.

They crept outside. Small patches of sky floated between

the clouds, and the snow had dwindled to a few fat, lazy flakes. Nisha immediately dove back into the tent, yelping in the icy wind. She didn't reappear until Moss and Ember had built a blazing fire and boiled water for tea.

"What other spells can you do?" Moss asked.

Ember blinked. "What?"

"Well, you're a Stormancer," he said. "I don't know why you didn't tell us. No wonder you weren't afraid to go after the prince!"

"Er," Ember said. This was the moment, then. Nisha and Moss would either hate her after this, or they would not. But even if they didn't, it was hard to imagine them trusting her as they had before. She sat frozen, her heart thudding. How did real spies reveal their aliases? She imagined they did so in a dramatic yet nonchalant fashion. She doubted it involved being sick all over their own boots, which was a real danger in that moment.

"She's not a Stormancer!" Nisha rolled her eyes. "She's a dragon. Obviously."

Moss stared. So did Ember.

"I . . . ," Ember said. "What? How?" Sentences seemed to have abandoned her.

"Oh, please," Nisha said. "Do you think I'm dense? Your father is renowned for his ability to transform animals— my parents used to scare me and Aditi into being good by telling us that the monster frog of Merseyside would come and get us. And then there's the fact that you feel like you're on fire all the time." She snatched at Ember's hand, holding it between her two cold ones like a mug of cider. "Ah! That's better. Oh, and did you know you smell of smoke? Just a little. It isn't that noticeable."

Ember flushed, for she hadn't known that. "Still," she said. "That could hardly be enough to—"

"Well, there's also the invisible wings," Nisha said. "That's a bit of a giveaway. I suppose your father thought they would come in handy, did he?"

"Well, no." Ember was completely befuddled. "He made a mistake with the spell."

"I wondered if that was it," Nisha said. "But I didn't want to say anything. That would be rude, wouldn't it? Imagine pointing at someone's arm or ears or something and asking if their parents had made a mistake. Still, your father does have that reputation. Did you hear about Lady Trembleworth's nose?"

"I don't understand." Moss's brow was furrowed. "If you're a dragon, why did your father send you here? Surely it's dangerous with all these hunters around."

"It's more dangerous in London," Ember said. "On account of my bursting into flames."

"Interesting!" Nisha cocked her head at Ember as if she were a geometry problem on Madame Rousseau's blackboard. For a moment, the intelligence in her eyes was intimidating, and Ember remembered every time that Nisha had recited an obscure fact from memory, or made a complex calculation in her head in seconds. She began to wonder why she hadn't guessed that Nisha might have figured out her secret. "Is it because of the climate? I read that fire dragons are more dangerous in the summer."

"What happened to your parents?" Moss said. "Why did Lord St. George adopt you? Is he a dragon too?"

"Of course he's not a dragon!" Nisha said exasperatedly. "They can't do magic."

"How do you know?" Moss said. "They're extinct— well, almost. And ice dragons have barely been studied."

"Dragons are *Scientific*," Nisha said. "Everything about them can be measured and explained."

Ember felt numb. She watched Nisha and Moss argue without hearing them. Finally she said, "Aren't you angry that I lied to you?"

Nisha seemed to think. "A little," she admitted. "But I just figured you had a good reason not to tell us."

"You probably thought we'd be afraid," Moss said.

Ember nodded silently.

"I can understand that." He looked away, and Ember remembered that there were people back at the station who were afraid of him. She felt again the thrum of the invisible thread connecting her and Moss, and though she didn't understand it, some of her tension melted. Suddenly she wanted to share everything, to sweep away all the secrets like cobwebs.

She drew the heartscale from her coat and handed it

to Moss. "This . . . this was my mother's," she said softly. "You were right—you can see things through it. I think what you saw before is the trail left by the ice dragons."

Moss's eyes grew wide. "Of course!"

"Then that means we can find Prince Gideon!" Nisha said. "That's a relief. I didn't want to say anything, but our chances weren't very good before. About one in two hundred and fifty, if we were lucky."

"Look through it again," Ember said to Moss. He did, tilting the scale toward the sky. "Look at me."

Moss did, and gasped. "You're all lit up!"

Ember watched nervously as Moss held up his own hand. He blinked, staring at it through the scale. "I don't understand."

"Do you see it?"

"Yes, but—" He turned the scale toward Nisha. "But that doesn't make any sense. You and I look different, but not Nisha."

"Let me see." Nisha snatched the scale from his hand. But she could see nothing that they described—not the dragons' trail through the sky, nor Ember and Moss's mysterious glow.

After examining himself through the scale again, Moss handed it back to Ember. He was even paler than usual. "I don't understand," he said again.

"I don't either," Ember said softly.

"I'm not a dragon," he said. "So what am I?"

Nisha threaded her arm through his. "You're Moss,"

she said. "And you don't have to look so grim. There's all sorts of things that could explain this."

"We could ask my father," Ember said, then stopped. She thought of the falcon's cage on the beach, the door she had closed to Chesterfield. "I mean, when we get back," she added quietly.

"That's right," Nisha said. "And until then, there's no use worrying. We should just be happy that we have a trail to follow."

Moss didn't look convinced, but his face had lost its sickly aspect.

"Are there any others like you?" he said.

Ember shook her head slowly. "I'm the only one."

"I think we should keep going," Nisha said. She gave Ember a pointed look, and Ember understood: Moss needed something else to think about. Ember realized that she did too. She felt overwhelmed. Nisha and Moss didn't hate her. Nisha sat in the sled, looking at Ember expectantly, as she always did. How was it possible that everything could feel so different, while still appearing the same?

Moss's face was very pale as he climbed onto the sled. Ember touched his arm as he went by, and smiled. After a short hesitation, he smiled back, and seemed to understand. They were misfits, but at least they were a *they*. Somehow, that made her feel lighter.

———

They traveled on through vast valleys and fields of snow

so light it scattered under the sled like sugar. But after a few miles, the sled gave a *crack*, and then a wobble. Ember called for the dogs to halt.

One of the narrow strips of wood that formed the base of the sled had separated from the others. It hung loose, causing the sled to drag. Worse, some of the other boards were cracked, and creaked ominously when Ember put her weight on them. The top rail had separated completely from the handlebar, and the nail was missing.

"It must have been damaged in the storm," Ember said. Panic washed over her. They couldn't very well walk to the South Pole.

Nisha examined the sled, chewing her lip. Then, wordlessly, she untied one of her ribbons and looped it around the loose piece of wood, tightening and knotting it until it was secure again.

"Good thinking," Moss said. "Just like when you fixed Professor Wentworth's wheelbarrow."

"So that's why you wear all those ribbons!" Ember said.

Nisha frowned. "I wear ribbons because I like ribbons. Still," she added with a grin. "They do come in handy sometimes."

They set off again. Every time a piece of the sled came loose, they would pause, and Nisha would secure it with a ribbon or two. Soon the sled began to resemble some sort of strange purple-furred creature, ribbons streaming as it trundled along.

The mountains sank into the distance, little more

than folds of darkness at the hem of the starry sky. Ember breathed in the frosty air, relishing the chill against her skin. In spite of everything, excitement stirred within her. She had used her fire to save Nisha, fire that had only ever destroyed what she cared about. She felt oddly light. The vast sweep of snow before her could have been the back of a cloud.

As the hours went by, she began to lose track of time— had they just eaten dinner, or breakfast? Was it time to sleep yet? It was worrying, because she knew that every passing hour only decreased their chances of finding the prince alive. Her eyes craved light. The stars were beautiful, as was the green of the aurora, but she wanted more. When they stopped, they huddled around the fire, gazing hungrily into the flames.

"What I wouldn't give for some hot chocolate!" Nisha sighed. "Do you think the prince has any in his supplies?"

"I don't think so," Ember said.

"That idiot," Nisha said. "How much farther, do you think?"

Ember looked through the scale. She was beginning to worry. The trail of light left by the dragons, while not susceptible to the wind, did not seem to be permanent. She now had to squint to see it, which meant two things: the dragons, traveling at a much quicker pace, were now far, far ahead—and the trail might not survive long enough for them to locate their destination.

"What's that?" Moss said suddenly. Ahead of them was

a pile of rocks on a low hill, silhouetted against the southern lights.

The dogs had seen it too. Finnorah gave a yip and jerked sharply to the right, drawing the other dogs with her. Ember had to pull them to a stop—they wouldn't go near the rocks, and seemed to want to charge off in the opposite direction.

"What's wrong?" she murmured to Finnorah after dismounting from the sled. The dog whined and nipped at Ember's coat.

Ember gazed at the rocks. They were an odd shape, piled in the middle of an empty expanse of undulating snow hills, and something about them made her shiver. She lifted the heartscale to her eye, and saw nothing.

She froze. Nothing. When she looked through the scale, the stones vanished like fog.

Slowly Ember strode toward them. "Stay there," she said to Nisha and Moss. Moss nodded, but Nisha let out a snort, and seconds later Ember heard her boots crunching after her.

"What is it?" she called.

"I'm not sure," Ember murmured. Behind her, Finnorah let out a long, low howl.

Ember trudged closer. She looked through the scale. Again, the rocks disappeared—through the glass, she saw only the flat top of the hill.

"What's so interesting about a pile of rocks?" Nisha complained.

Ember stopped. A terrible chill settled in her stomach. "Those aren't rocks."

They were bones.

The rib cage of a massive dragon loomed before her. It lay on its side, the bones of its tail curled around its body. Beyond it, visible through the white ribs, was a second skeleton, just as clean as the first. The wings, made of more delicate bones than the rest, seemed to have been broken by the elements, and lay in pieces beside the bodies.

Ember closed her eyes. She had hoped never to see another dead dragon in her life—and here were two of them. She held the scale up to her eye with shaking fingers, and watched the bones disappear, apart from a faint smudge. Given that the scale could pick out living dragons easily enough, its inability—or refusal—to show the bones struck Ember as ominous.

"This doesn't make any sense," Nisha said. She stood with her arms crossed, frowning.

"This must be the remains of another hunt." Ember took a step back. She wanted to go back to the sled and get far away from here. It wasn't just the dead dragons; the place had an eerie, watchful atmosphere. "Last year's, I guess. That storm must have blown away the snow that covered them."

"That's not what I mean," Nisha said. "This isn't how—"

The dogs began to howl in unison, sending ghostly clouds of breath into the sky.

"We should get back to the sled." Ember set off at a brisk walk, though in truth she wanted to run away as much as the dogs did. The breeze reminded her of fingers sliding along her neck.

But at that moment, the ground gave a shiver—and then the snow at the bottom of the hill, which Ember and Nisha had crossed seconds before, vanished.

Ember fell back with a cry. The snow crashed to the bottom of the crevasse that had appeared between them and the sled. Moss yelled at the dogs, which were now trying to run off with the sled.

"A snow bridge!" Nisha said. "We're lucky it didn't give way when we were standing on it!"

Ember's heart thudded in her ears. Snow bridges were one of the most dangerous things a traveler could encounter in Antarctica. What looked like solid ground was actually a layer of snow that could collapse at any time.

"Let's go around," Ember said. "Carefully."

They joined hands. It was difficult to tell where the crevasse ended and solid ground began—the snow was piled in drifts at the base of the hill. Ember knelt by the crevasse, trying to guess how deep it went. She could clear it, with her wings, but Nisha couldn't. Her bare hands crunched against the snow, Nisha was muttering things about velocity versus distance, and the dogs were snarling. But underneath those noises . . .

"Shhh," Ember said.

Nisha fell silent. Ember held herself very still.

Someone was humming. A quiet, melodious sound. Ember couldn't tell if the voice was male or female—it seemed an odd blending of the two, or perhaps there was more than one voice. The humming grew louder.

"What is that?" Nisha said, hearing it at last.

Ember recoiled. "It's coming from the crevasse."

She grabbed Nisha's hand, and they backed up, away from the crevasse, until Ember felt something sharp poke into her back. She yelled, leaping away from the dragon's bone.

"The bones," Nisha murmured. "They're wrong."

Ember barely heard her—she was too busy panicking. "What?"

"I tried to tell you before," Nisha said. "Those dragons shouldn't have decayed like that. Not in one year, not in a dozen years. It's just too cold here. But those bones . . . they look like they've been picked clean."

Ember blinked at her. Then, slowly, they turned back to the crevasse.

Something was rising from it. Something that, at first, resembled mist or smoke. Ember could see Moss through it, his eyes wide, standing on the other side of the crevasse. But then the wisps of smoke began to thicken, and Ember realized that they were mouths—hundreds of small, translucent mouths, opening and closing like jellyfish. And still that horrible humming continued—so sweet, and so soothing. It was a melody that could lull you to sleep, warm and faintly echoing, as if some of the voices were slightly out of time.

"Oh," Nisha whispered. "Oh no. It's—" She wasn't able to finish. She didn't need to. Ember had seen her aunt's sketch. She had heard the stories.

The grimlings.

"What do we do?" Ember realized she was gripping Nisha's hand hard enough to burn her if she wasn't careful, and she forced herself to let go.

Nisha swallowed. "Run?"

Moss was yelling at them. He gestured them back to the sled, but the crevasse between them seemed to be growing as more of the snow bridge fell away and the grimlings surged through it. It was now at least twenty yards long, and lengthening.

"Maybe they won't hurt us," Ember said. She tried to believe the words as she spoke them. "We don't know for sure that they killed those Scientists, right?"

"Right." Nisha's voice was faint. The dogs were going berserk. One of them had somehow freed itself from its harness, perhaps by gnawing it through, and it leaped at the grimlings. As soon as its muzzle touched them, they engulfed the dog with an echoing sigh and a flash of hundreds of luminescent teeth, and then it was simply . . . gone.

Not quite gone. The grimlings drew back, and the dog's skeleton tumbled to the snow, sightless eyes gaping.

As clean as the dragon bones behind them.

Ember's stomach convulsed. "Or—or maybe we do," she whispered.

The sight of the dog's gleaming skeleton was too much for Finnorah. With a heartwrenching howl, she ran, the rest of the pack at her heels and the sled flying behind them. Moss shouted for her to stop, but it was no use. The dogs—and all of their gear—faded into the night.

"Moss!" Nisha screamed.

The grimlings were circling him, drawing closer and closer. They didn't attack—it was almost as if they were *interested* in him. The humming rose and fell, little mouths darting out as if to sniff at Moss. He yelped, starting back.

"What were you saying about velocity?" Ember's voice was grim.

Nisha turned terrified eyes on her. "What?"

Ember drew a shaky breath. "I'll just have to estimate, then." She raised her hand, focusing on the wall of grimlings rising from the crevasse. She was tired, and it wasn't easy. But she felt the familiar fire burning under her skin, and concentrated—

The fire exploded, flame leaping from her fingertips and crashing into the grimlings. The humming jarred, a horrible, wrong sound. There was a hiss, as of ice melting in a pot, and a gap opened between the grimlings. Not very wide—but wide enough.

Ember grabbed Nisha's arm. "Run."

They ran for the gap, down the hill, their speed picking up as they went. Just before they hit the edge, Ember beat her wings, using the added propulsion to launch herself and Nisha over the crevasse. Nisha screamed, and she and Ember landed in a heap on the other side. They were through.

Moss helped them to their feet. "You shouldn't have done that," he said. "You've made them angry."

"Right, because they were in such a good mood before." Ember examined the horrible whirl of mouths, which had closed the gap she had created. "Why don't they attack you?"

Moss shook his head, and then one of the grimlings lunged at Nisha.

Ember blasted it back with a plume of flame. She shoved Nisha between her and Moss.

"We have to go after the sled," she yelled. The humming was almost deafening now, and so out of time that it was closer to the drone of bees than melody. She held out her hand again, flame spilling from her fingertips, trying to create another gap, a door they could squeeze through. But it seemed as if the grimlings had learned. The gap opened, grimlings melting in the fire, but as soon as it did, others swept in to take their place.

"We're going to die!" Nisha yelled. "They're going to devour us! We'll be a pile of bones in the middle of—"

Ember reached her hand out and covered Nisha's mouth.

"I think they're holding back because of you," she said to Moss. "They don't seem too fond of me and Nisha. Can you try to talk to them?"

Moss went pale. "I—I don't know how."

Another grimling lunged out. Its hideous teeth were translucent, like weather-beaten glass, but Ember had seen the damage they could do. She blasted another plume of flame at it—but this time, the fire sputtered and went out.

"Oh no," she whispered. The grimling retreated, teeth clacking. A wave of exhaustion passed over her—she had never felt so spent in her life. She tried again to summon the fire, but it was as if it slumbered inside her now, and she could not wake it.

She exchanged a look with Nisha. The other girl's eyes were panicked, but she set her jaw.

"We'll have to make a run for it," she said.

Moss took their hands. "I'll go first," he said. His hand was shaking so badly that Ember could barely grip it. "If you're right about me, maybe they'll let us through."

Ember swallowed. She tried not to think too hard about what Moss was volunteering to do, and what would happen to them if the grimlings did not, in fact, have any particular interest in him. What would happen to them all. She saw the dog dissolving again.

"All right," she said. "On three."

Fwoomp. Fwoomp. Fwoomp.

Ember froze. She had heard that sound before. It cut

through the grimlings' hum like a knife. She whipped around, scanning the darkness, but saw nothing.

Fwoomp. Fwoomp.

Slowly she looked up. All she saw were stars suspended in inky darkness. Then a patch of stars moved, wheeling in a lazy circle, and Ember realized.

She was looking at an ice dragon.

The moonlight glinted off its scales. The dragon let out a birdlike cry, and the grimlings went completely silent.

The dragon folded its wings and dove toward the ground, and Ember, Nisha, and Moss screamed in unison. It was coming right at them! The grimlings scattered, dissolving like smoke, but Ember's quick eyes saw them dart back to the crevasse they had risen from.

The dragon banked sharply, raising a cloud of ice crystals. Ember coughed as she inhaled a mouthful of them. She shoved the others behind her as the dragon landed, quiet as a breath, its eyes fixed on her.

EIGHTEEN
AQUAMARINE

A fire dragon's wings were typically translucent, ranging in hue from golden to molten orange, resembling those of a dragonfly in sunlight.
—*TAKAGI'S* COMPENDIUM OF EXOTIC CREATURES

G ode eventide, the dragon said. It did not move its mouth, but purred the words somewhere in its throat.

Ember felt as if she'd been struck.

"Did . . . did the dragon just speak?" Nisha asked faintly.

"I think so." Moss's voice was equally faint. "I don't know what it said. But it said something."

"It said hello," Ember murmured. She had heard the words, and though they were not in a language she recognized, she found that she understood them. She took a step forward.

Moss grabbed her. "Don't!"

Ember shook him off. She kept going, stopping only a yard or two from the dragon. It lowered its head so that its all-white eyes were at a level with Ember's. It was like gazing into a sentient cloud.

Litel childres, the dragon said. *Hware cumeth thu?* And something inside Ember translated: *Children, where did you come from?*

"From the research station," Ember said. To her astonishment, she found she was able to speak the same language as the dragon. The words felt strange in her mouth, curvy and lilting. "Well . . ." She paused, swallowing. "Technically, we came from the hunters' camp."

Tha sottas, the dragon snorted. Its voice inside Ember's head sounded female, though she could not have explained how she guessed this. *Those idiots.*

"We're not hunters," Ember rushed to clarify, frightened by the dragon's stillness and the white breath that curled from her nostrils. The dragon could turn her to ice in a heartbeat. Did she want to? Ember had no idea, which in a way was worse than if the dragon had actually done it.

What are you? the dragon said. *How do you speak my language?*

Ember hesitated. Her knees were shaking so hard they might have been trying to single-handedly—or single-leggedly—propel her backward. It was clear that, like the fire dragons, this ice dragon couldn't sense what she was. Would revealing the truth help her to trust them?

She turned, removing her scarf and pushing her uneven hair out of the way. She knew from the dragon's startled huff that her heartscale shone in the moonlight.

A dragon child, she murmured. *From the north. The lands beyond the sea. I have never met one of your kind.*

"Er, yes," Ember said. "So . . . as I'm like you, would you consider not eating us?"

The dragon snorted, tiny crystals of ice shooting out of her nostrils. It was a moment before Ember realized that the dragon was laughing.

We mostly eat seals, the dragon said. She stretched her back, a catlike movement. *Much tastier than humans. And we never harm children.*

Ember thought of Prince Gideon, kidnapped by a dragon. Clearly not all of them refrained from harming children. Were ice dragons like her, unable to lie? If she asked, and the dragon said yes, that wouldn't tell her anything. A smaller part of Ember wondered how the dragon knew seals were tastier than humans.

You are under a spell, the dragon said uncertainly. Ember nodded. *The magic hides your true form. We dislike magic.*

"Why?"

It goes against our code. Ember thought she heard an evasive note in the dragon's purr of a voice.

"Then you can do magic?" Ember said.

We can, but we do not.

Ember's thoughts flashed to the heartscale. "There was a strange light," she said. "Like a trail in the sky. We followed it here—"

That is not magic, the dragon said. *It was our footprints. Dragons*

- 261 -

leave them wherever they go—even you, dragon child.

A thousand questions filled Ember's head. "If that isn't magic, then—"

The dragon made a low sound that froze her tongue. *Why are you here, dragon child from the north?*

Ember swallowed. "We've come to rescue someone. My friend was stolen by a dragon several days ago." She flushed at her own words. She had just called the prince her friend, which must mean it was the truth. Yet he was also her enemy. She thought of how he had threatened her, and also his strange flashes of kindness—how he had saved her from falling and kept her secret from Lord Norfell, despite his hatred of dragons. She didn't understand how someone could be both a friend and an enemy, but she supposed it made sense that a person as disagreeable as Gideon had managed it.

The dragon regarded Ember with her strange eyes. While they looked all white at a distance, they were actually a mixture of grays and whites and silvers, swirling like the sea. Ember couldn't read them at all.

Tha smeeter childre, the dragon hissed. *The murderer child. You cannot have him. You should go back to your home, dragon child from the north.*

Ember blinked. "Then you know where he is?"

Yes.

"If you know where he is, take us to him," Nisha said, striding forward.

Ember was astonished. "You can understand her?"

"Not all of it," Nisha said. "It's not another language, you see. It's an ancient form of English—five or six centuries old, I'd estimate. Some of the words are the same. Others are a little twisty or strange, but often you can guess at them."

Ember gaped at her.

"My father collects old books," Nisha explained. "The older the better. The dragon talks like the stories he used to read to me and Aditi."

Ember turned back to the dragon. "You speak English!"

I speak the language of my ancient ancestors, the dragon said. *They were not from this land. We came to this place many centuries ago, after we were driven from our northern mountains by hunters. We wanted to find a place as far from humans as possible, where none had ever dwelled.*

"But . . ." Ember didn't understand. "But I'm from the north, and there were never ice dragons there. Only fire dragons, like me."

Once there were, dragon child, the dragon said. *Once there were dragons of all five elements, who dwelled in many parts of this world. Some separately, some coexisting. Dragons not only of fire and ice, but of forest and air and darkness. But over time, our numbers dwindled. More and more humans hunted us. Perhaps there are some who retreated to remote places, as we did. But most were lost. I am not surprised that fire dragons lingered longest—they can live almost anywhere. And humans always did fear them most.*

Nisha's brow was furrowed. "All this talking isn't going to help us find Prince Gideon. Tell her she has to take us to him."

Behind them, Moss drew in a breath. "I don't think making demands of a dragon is such a good idea," he said in a near whisper.

"Why not?" Nisha said. "Her people kidnapped a child. And now she wants to make polite conversation? I don't think so."

"Nisha—" Moss began.

"Strength respects strength," Nisha said. "That's what my mother always says. I think that if you're firm about it, she'll be more likely to listen."

What does the human child say? the dragon said. She sniffed at Nisha, as if that might help her understand.

Ember swallowed. "She says that you must take us to our friend, who your people stole from us," she said. Nisha folded her arms, and Ember took heart from her cool confidence. "We demand that you do so."

The dragon snorted. *You are not my blood kin, to make demands of me.*

"But you're in danger if you don't free him," Ember burst out. "He isn't just a boy—he's a prince, and his family is powerful. They'll never stop hunting you."

The dragon made a skeptical noise. She seemed to think. *I will consider your request, but only if you can offer currency in exchange.*

"Currency?" Ember repeated. "We—we don't have

any. But the prince does. I'm sure he has mountains of gold, or jewels, or whatever you—"

The dragon was snorting again. *I have no use for gold or jewels, dragon child.* She spread her graceful, glimmering wings. *I have saved you from the Hungry Ones. You are children, so I will forgive the life debt you owe me. Goodbye.*

"Wait!" Ember cried. "An ice dragon kidnapped Prince Gideon—for all we know he could be dead by now. And yet you claim that you don't hurt children. I think you're lying."

The dragon hissed. *I do not lie. I cannot.*

"Prove it." Her anger rose. She thought of Gideon's terrified face as the dragon breathed at his back. As horrible as he was, he hadn't deserved to be snatched away like that. Not that she was doing this for Gideon, she reminded herself, as an odd flush spread over her cheeks. She cared about saving the dragons, not him. "Prove that he's safe. Or we won't believe you."

The dragon's eyes swirled faster. It was clear she was agitated, and Ember felt a stab of hope. If the dragon was truly like her, and unable to lie, then that also meant she couldn't stand being called a liar. Ember hated it when someone didn't believe her—it gave her a prickly feeling behind her eyes that could linger for days. Once, one of the bakers at Chesterfield had accused her of stealing Eccles cakes from the kitchens, refusing to listen to her denials. She had spent the next week begging the young servant behind the theft to confess, while her sleep had been haunted by dreams of a giant cake chasing her through the university, spitting currants at her.

Very well, the dragon said. *I will take you to the City of Spires. Your friend is being kept there. But I cannot guarantee you will be allowed to see him—that will be up to the king.*

"The king?" Ember repeated nervously.

He is the king's guest, the dragon said. At the word "guest," which sounded almost the same in the dragon's English, Nisha let out a snort.

"His prisoner, you mean," she muttered. Ember touched her arm. They couldn't afford to make the dragon angry. Nisha caught Ember's look, and gave a slight nod.

"What's your name?" Ember asked. "Do you have names?"

Aquamarine, the dragon said. She seemed pleased that Ember had asked.

"That's lovely," Ember said, and the dragon preened. "I'm Ember. This is Nisha, and that's Moss."

The boy took a nervous step forward, and the dragon regarded him with her unreadable eyes.

You have a strange smell, child, was all she said.

"We should leave now," Ember said. She didn't know if the grimlings were gone for good, or if they were merely lurking, and she didn't want to find out. "Are you able to carry all of us?"

The dragon hesitated. *If I bring you to the king, will you think me honest?*

"Yes," Ember promised.

"Wait a minute," Nisha said. "'Did she say 'carry'? You want her to *carry* us?"

"Well, yes," Ember said. "What were you expecting?"

"I don't know." Nisha looked faint. "How about we just follow her in the sled?"

"The dogs are long gone," Ember said. She thought of Finnorah, so strong and steady at the head of her team. She didn't blame her for running—the dog had thought, understandably, that all hope for them was lost, and so had decided to save herself and the others. "They were heading in the direction of the camp. We don't have a chance of catching them."

"It would certainly be faster," Moss said. His face was even paler than usual.

Ember drew a deep breath. She gazed into the dragon's inhuman eyes and wondered if she was making a terrible mistake. Still, Aquamarine hadn't frozen them, or tried to eat them—she had, in fact, saved their lives. And with the trail visible through the heartscale starting to disintegrate, this might be their only hope of rescuing the prince.

The dragon sniffed at each of them. *Though you are small, I would prefer to carry only two.*

It took Ember a moment to realize what she meant. She nodded hesitantly.

The dragon reached out a hand—eerily humanlike, apart from the talons—and lifted Nisha by the back of her jacket. The girl gave a smothered scream, but to her credit, she didn't struggle. Moss closed his eyes as the dragon grasped him.

Stay close, dragon child, Aquamarine said, then lifted into the sky in a whirl of snow. Ember spread her own wings and followed.

They flew for hours, through inky skies scattered with starlight, over mountains of ice that seemed to float among the shadows. Ember's face felt half frozen, and her wings ached. She wasn't used to flying long distances—she was hardly used to flying at all. After an hour, she fell behind, and Aquamarine offered to carry her with her back foot.

The sky grew ever darker as they flew south, losing its purple glow. The stars burned like a million flickering candles. Ember wondered if Nisha and Moss were all right—the dragon's wing beats and the whoosh of the air meant they couldn't even hear each other if they shouted. Moss had at least uncovered his eyes, while Nisha seemed fascinated by the landscape unfurling beneath them; she kept craning her neck like an owl to see in all directions.

Ember gasped. Ahead of them loomed an enormous mountain range, jagged against the starry sky. Clouds curled beneath it, and snow painted its rocky slopes. The dragon was flying toward a towering glacier, which was tucked into the peak of one of the highest mountains. As they drew closer, they beheld strange shapes carved into the ice: doorways and turrets; spires that jutted like upside-down icicles; passages lined with ice pillars. It was a mad, chaotic thing, a random jumble of a city that nevertheless projected an air of purposefulness. Light spilled from open doorways and gleamed through ice walls, painting the glacier with greens and blues and silvers. Dragon silhouettes swooped over the city, fluttering in and out of the glacier like bees in a hive.

The dragon landed on a narrow ledge of ice. Before them loomed a towering doorway, large enough for at least two dragons to pass through. On either side was a statue, hewn from stone: one of a large dragon standing tall, chest puffed and mouth open; the other of a dragon with a meeker posture, tail curled around its body and a sly expression on its face. Ember wondered who they were. Did dragons have myths of heroes and villains, just as humans did?

"But—" Nisha pulled her scarf off her face. She seemed beside herself, and struggling for words. "But you can't have a city in a glacier! Glaciers move. It doesn't make sense."

Aquamarine cocked her head at Ember, who translated. After listening, the dragon said, *We rebuild constantly. Just yesterday, the entire fourth quarter collapsed. The king assigned workers to repair it—it is almost completely stable now. Would you like to see?*

"Er, that's all right," Ember said. "Was anyone hurt?"

The dragon laughed. *Ice does not harm us, dragon child.*

Ember translated all this for Nisha and Moss, who

didn't look comforted. "That's great," Nisha said. "Just great! So we're supposed to stroll in there, and if the roof falls in on us, oh well?"

Aquamarine seemed to understand, or perhaps she merely guessed. *I will not allow harm to come to you, children. I will take you to the palace by safe paths.*

And with that, she strode into the glacier, leaving Ember, Nisha, and Moss no choice but to follow.

"Are you all right?" Ember whispered to Moss as they walked in. He had been nearly silent since they had met Aquamarine. His expression, as he gazed at the glacial city, was a strange mixture of fear and anger.

"Yes," he said, in the sort of voice that meant "No, and I don't want to talk about it." He didn't meet her eyes.

Their breath rose in clouds as they entered the dragons' city. A long, high-ceilinged tunnel of ice stretched before them, which dipped and curved in strange places, built to be traveled by beings that could simply spread their wings and leap over obstacles. Aquamarine had to carry Nisha and Moss at several of these intervals. Other tunnels opened off the main one, just as grand and twisty. Candles set in pots of oil flamed in brackets along the walls, not bright enough to see comfortably by, throwing strange, reflected shadows in every direction.

"Who built this place?" Ember said.

We all build it, Aquamarine said. *We take shifts to repair what is lost as the glacier moves and changes. Each tunnel follows the ice—we* listen to what it wants, and shape our city accordingly. We do not impose our home upon it, as a human would.

Ember spread her wings and vaulted over a gaping chasm in the middle of the corridor. Aquamarine followed with Nisha and Moss. "I see."

"It would help if you had more lights," Nisha grumbled. She had stumbled for the third time, scraping her knees on the ice floor. Ember translated for the dragon, who snorted.

We do not need lights. The candles are for decoration.

The more candles they passed, the more Ember understood. The firelight illuminated strange, beautiful shapes in the ice, bringing out whorls and ridges that Ember had thought were carved there, but she now realized were natural patterns. It also brought out different shades of blue, from green to deepest indigo. Ember walked with her mouth half open, drinking it all in.

"It's beautiful," she murmured. Amid her fascination, she felt a surge of sorrow. She thought of this beautiful place emptying as hunters swept across Antarctica. She thought of the lights going out and the halls and corridors caving in, with no one there to repair them.

No. She set her jaw. She wouldn't allow that to happen. They would find Gideon and bring him safely back. His family would have no reason to seek revenge on Aquamarine or any of the others.

Aquamarine's spine straightened at Ember's praise, a

spring entering her step. Ember was beginning to realize that the dragon loved compliments. Which, she supposed, made sense in a world where everyone could only speak the truth.

They came to a vast, high-ceilinged room with the appearance of a banquet hall, lined with pillars carved from the ice. Not all the pillars were straight—some leaned to the side, or took an odd turn somewhere. At the center of the hall was—

"A carousel," Ember breathed.

The structure was enormous, a glittering thing hung with hairy green pennants that Ember took for woven seal skins, perhaps dyed with seaweed. In place of horses, there were strange creatures that reminded Ember of lions, though there was a fantastical quality about them, as if carved by someone with only the vaguest memory of what lions were. The entire structure was built of ice and stone. Some of the mounts were unfinished, roughly hewn lumps of ice that had been leaned against the wall.

We are building it for the festival of stars, Aquamarine said. *Our solstice celebration.*

Ember didn't have much time to stare at the ice carousel, for Aquamarine walked quickly, and she had to hurry to keep up. They passed several dragons in the hall, all of whom stopped and stared at the three of them.

Who are these human children, Aquamarine? one called.

Visitors, Aquamarine said. *They wish to retrieve the murderer* child. *Please ensure that the king is alerted to their presence.*

The dragons hissed at that, and Ember huddled closer to Aquamarine.

Don't worry, dragon child, she said. *None will harm you here.*

"I'll believe that once we're safely back at the Firefly, all our limbs intact," Nisha muttered when Ember translated. She squeezed her hand. "Right now, *you're* the only dragon I trust."

Ember flushed, but for once, she didn't try to pull away from Nisha's grip. They climbed up a long, steep slope, and again Aquamarine had to carry Nisha and Moss. At the top, the tunnel opened onto the night, and Ember gasped.

They stood at an exposed ridge near the very peak of the glacier. Before them stretched a wide avenue carved in the ice, leading to a huge knuckle of bare rock. Ice columns lined the avenue, and more statues framed a cavern that yawned out of the rock, lit by torches sputtering in the chill wind. The aurora was brighter than Ember had ever seen it, hovering over the mountain like a threat.

Ember swallowed, staring at that gaping darkness. "Is . . . is that—"

The palace of King Zaffre, Aquamarine said.

Nisha's hand tightened in hers. Moss's eyes widened. The wind played with his pale hair, and for the first time since Ember had known him, he shivered.

You must pay to see the king, Aquamarine said. *It is a requirement for all dragons from other courts.*

"There are other courts?" Ember said.

Other courts, other cities, Aquamarine said. *Other kings and queens, scattered across the continent. Though none are mightier than our king. The City of Spires is the greatest city in the land.*

Ember's head was spinning. The dragons' world was bigger than she had ever imagined. Kings and queens! "But we don't have any money."

That is not our currency, Aquamarine said. *You will pay with riddles.*

"Riddles?" Ember repeated, and Nisha said, more loudly, "Riddles?"

Yes. There are three of you, so you will answer three riddles. The dragon's tail swooshed over the snow.

"I don't understand," Ember said slowly. "How is that worth anything to you? Don't you already know the answers?"

No, Aquamarine said. She seemed puzzled by their confusion. *The king will give you unanswered riddles. Riddles are valuable, and so are the answers, sometimes. You may take as long as you like to solve them. If you do not solve them, I will be waiting here to take you back to your people. Bright skies, dragon child.*

She settled onto the snow, her eyelids fluttering. Her head drooped onto her front foot, and she appeared to sleep.

NINETEEN

ROSE GOLD'S RIDDLES

Many stories have little basis in fact. . . . The tale of Sir Maxwell
Clinghope, who slayed two dragons accused of burning down the
village of Netherwall in the fifteenth century, has been disproved by
archaeologists, who found that the fire was caused by a brawl
between two rival Stormancers. . . .

—*TAKAGI'S* COMPENDIUM OF EXOTIC CREATURES

"Well, this is completely mad," Nisha said. "Riddles! Aren't kings supposed to like gold?"

"You're good at riddles," Moss said in his quiet voice.

Nisha flushed, looking away from him. "Well, yes, I know."

"Let's just . . . see what happens," Ember said. "I'll go first, all right?"

She strode toward the cavern, though her heart beat frantically. After a pause, Nisha and Moss fell into step behind her, slipping and sliding over the icy slope.

Within there was darkness, and a sense of vast, empty space. Their steps echoed in the silence. Then two glowing white eyes loomed out of the shadows.

Children, the dragon murmured. Ember shuddered,

because the voice was ancient, deeper and darker than Aquamarine's. *The others warned me that you were coming.*

"Are . . . are you the king?" Ember said. She wished she could see the dragon, but in the darkness there was only the glimmer of talons, the whisper of a curved back.

No, the dragon said. *I am his steward, Rose Gold. I collect payment from visitors.*

Light flared, and Ember blinked. Moss had drawn a match from his pocket. From another, he unearthed two candles. He lit them and handed one to Nisha.

The dragon loomed over them. He was bigger than Aquamarine, and older, frailer—he shuffled slowly to a stone desk, as if his joints pained him. There were no chairs in the cavern, which was so enormous that its roof was lost in darkness. Stacked upon the dragon's desk were slabs of shale, roughly rectangular and heavily scratched. No, not scratched—engraved with tiny, looping letters. The walls of the cavern had numerous shelves cut into the stone, shelves upon shelves that stretched up into shadow, all stuffed with the same stone slabs. The dragon spread his wings and lifted heavily off the ground, riffling through the slabs on a shelf. He selected one and sank to the ground with a thump.

Ah, Rose Gold said. *That gets harder every year.*

"If you don't mind," Ember said, "could you explain why the king wants us to solve his riddles?"

Well, he has so many, the dragon said. *Naturally so—all kings are wealthy. People give him more every day, and being ancient and wise,* he solves most very quickly. But of course there are some he cannot solve. Difficult riddles, riddles so old their answers have long since been lost, are incredibly valuable. It's a gift, really, that he grants his guests the opportunity to help him.

"Wait a minute," Nisha said, once Ember had translated. "You're saying that we have to solve riddles that an ancient king couldn't figure out?"

You're welcome, Rose Gold said. Shall we begin? Without waiting for an answer, he lifted the stone tablet.

"Wait!" Ember said. "Do all visitors from other courts truly have to do this? How many actually see the king?"

I can't recall the last who won an audience, Rose Gold said. It does cut down on the number of visitors. The king is very busy.

"Right," Ember said. "Why don't we just—er—come up with some new riddles for him?"

Rose Gold paused. That is kind of you. I am sure there are many in this city who would take you up on the offer and provide you with services in return. But the king wants answers, not more riddles.

"All right," Ember said, after exchanging nervous looks with Moss and Nisha. The whole thing seemed completely mad, but she didn't know what else they could do but try. Perhaps the riddles would be easy. "What's the first one, then?"

The dragon selected a stone slab, tracing the scratches fondly with one claw. Then he read:

I am silent in my house,
Which is always moving,

Muttering, whispering.
I am strong and swift,
Yet if I leave, I will die.

Rose Gold put down the slab and let out a satisfied sigh. *One of my favorites. Bright skies, children.*

Ember and Nisha blinked at each other. Moss's face reminded Ember of the ruffled penguin's after it had fired off a lightning bolt. So much for her hope that the riddles would be easy.

"A house that moves?" Moss said. "What is that supposed to mean?"

"A ship?" Nisha said. "Sailors live on ships."

The dragon made a clicking sound, and Nisha hastened to add, "That's not my answer! Give us more time."

Of course, Rose Gold said. *You may take as long as you like. The last visitor went away, and came back five years later with the answer to her riddle.*

"Five years?" Ember repeated faintly.

It was a very good riddle.

Nisha was muttering to herself, her fingers pressed against her temples. "Can we hear it again?" Moss said.

Rose Gold recited the riddle again. Ember's thoughts were racing. She thought of ships, and carriages, and steam trains. The *Orpheus*, its deck crowded with sailors, which had been her home during the long journey to Antarctica. The salt spray against her face, the water dark and fathomless . . . from there, her mind leaped to the frozen river by the Firefly, its waters too cold and barren for fish. . . .

"Fish!" she said suddenly, interrupting Nisha's muttering. "Fish breathe water, so if they leave it, they die. The answer is fish in a river!"

Ah! Rose Gold said. *Well done, child, well done.* He turned the stone slab over, and scratched at it with his talon.

"Of course!" Nisha said, grinning. Moss clapped Ember on the shoulder.

The dragon retreated into the shadows, filing the stone slab away on another shelf.

"Don't get too excited," Ember warned. "We still have to answer two more."

Most visitors don't even answer one, Rose Gold said. He selected another stone slab from those scattered atop his desk. *Ah . . . this one is very fine. Very fine indeed. In fact, the king was just working on it. He would be ever so pleased if you found the answer.*

Ember grimaced. "Let's hear it, then."

Rose Gold read:

My home is forest, mountain, heath.
I wear bells that cannot sound,
And gloves that witches made.
I am weaker than the smallest child,
Yet with one finger, I have slain mighty warriors.

Ember, Nisha, and Moss were silent. Outside, the wind huffed over the ice city.

"Er," Nisha said. "All right." She rubbed at her temples again, her eyes narrowing in frustration. Ember realized, with a sinking feeling, that Nisha was stumped again, and was angry at herself about it. If Nisha, by far the cleverest among them, was stumped, what hope did they have?

"What wears gloves and bells?" Ember said, stumbling over the contrary clues. "And is weaker than a child?"

"Weak but strong," Nisha said. "It kills warriors, after all."

"Gloves that witches made . . . ," Ember repeated.

"It must be a metaphor for something," Nisha said distractedly. "Unless 'witches' means Stormancers."

"Scientists used to call them that," Ember said. "Centuries ago. It was an insult—do you think that's it?"

Nisha began to pace. She kept up a steady stream of muttering. Ember interrupted now and again with her own ideas. Moss kept mostly silent—his attention seemed far away. Each guess they gave the dragon was wrong.

"How many do we get?" Ember said.

Ten, the dragon said.

Ember frowned. "Ten guesses?"

Ten years, the dragon said. That is the maximum. Mind you, most people give up before then.

Ember swallowed.

No shame in not knowing, children, the dragon said. This

particular riddle has been with us since before the Great Exodus, when our people first came to this place. We lived in the mountains then. Green in summer, snowbound in winter. It was a beautiful place, the stories say.

The old dragon's eyes were misty. Nisha glowered at him. "Thank you, but I'm not sure a history lesson is helpful."

Moss's eyes widened. "Foxgloves!"

Ember and Nisha stared at him. He hadn't spoken once in the last twenty minutes. Moss rushed on. "They're shaped like bells. Another name for them is 'witches' gloves'—that's because they're poisonous. They could kill anyone. But children pick them, so they're also weak, I guess."

"What about the last line?" Ember said.

"Well, the Latin name for foxglove is 'digitalis,'" Moss said. "That means 'like a finger.'"

There was a long silence.

Most impressive, Rose Gold said finally. There was something close to reverence in his voice.

"I'll say," Nisha said. She was staring at Moss as if she'd never seen him before. "I never would have figured that out!"

"Professor Maylie has lots of books about flowers," Moss said. He was mumbling now as everyone stared at him. "I've never seen any foxgloves myself. But I—I like to read about them."

Ember shook her head. She recalled how quick she had

been to leave Nisha and Moss behind after the prince had been stolen. But where would she be now without them? She smiled at Moss, and he gave her a small, flustered smile back.

She turned back to Rose Gold. "What's the final riddle? It is the final one? If we answer it, we can see the king?"

Oh, yes, Rose Gold said. Just one riddle left . . . one little riddle. Ah, here we are. He bent to remove a slab from one of the lowest shelves in the cave. And then he read:

I have two arms, two legs,
One neck, one eye,
Three hands,
And twelve hundred heads.

TWENTY

THE PRISONER

The fire dragon was well known in antiquity. The Roman emperor Nero attempted to domesticate the beasts, hoping to put them to use in battle. This ill-advised endeavor led to the Great Fire of Rome in AD 64, after which further efforts were abandoned.

—*TAKAGI'S* COMPENDIUM OF EXOTIC CREATURES

E mber waited, but Rose Gold was silent.

"Well?" she said impatiently. "What's the rest?"

That is all, the dragon said. *Bright skies.*

Ember swallowed. The other riddles had been difficult, but this one . . . it made no sense at all.

"Two arms and two legs," Nisha murmured. "A person, then."

"What sort of person has twelve hundred heads?" Ember said. "Maybe it's a hydra."

"Aren't hydras snakes?" Nisha said.

Moss chewed his lip. "It must be some sort of monster."

Most likely, the dragon agreed. *This riddle has been in the king's library for centuries. No one has been able to solve it. We suspect it refers to a creature that has long since gone extinct.*

"But—" Ember sputtered. "But how are we supposed to know the answer, then?"

How indeed? Rose Gold said. *It is vexing in the most delightful way, isn't it?*

Ember folded her arms. "That's not fair."

The best riddles generally aren't.

Moss made an exasperated sound. "Now I know why he can't remember the last visitor who got to see the king."

"Three hands," Nisha muttered.

"You might as well give up," Moss said. "It's pointless. They won't let us see him."

"Could we try a different riddle?" Ember asked Rose Gold.

No, the dragon said calmly.

"Come on," Nisha said. "We can get this. Just like the last one. Let's just go over it again."

So they did. Nisha muttered and paced, going back and forth so many times that Ember worried she would wear a groove in the stone floor. Moss stood in the shadows, pale and quiet as a wisp, his gaze bleak. Ember tried to recall every encyclopedia she had ever read, going through them one by one. She drummed her fingers against the stone, then tapped her foot, then joined Nisha in her pacing. Nothing helped.

"Nisha," Moss said finally. At least an hour had passed, and Nisha's muttering had grown hoarse. Moss's candles had gone out, so Ember summoned fire into the palm of her hand, which sputtered fitfully. "I don't think—"

Nisha stamped her foot. "We are *not* giving up!"

"But . . . I don't think it's possible," Moss said. "We can't find the answer if the answer doesn't exist anymore."

The frustration Ember had been suppressing surged like a wave. Moss was right. They had come all this way for nothing. Everything they had been through—the magical storm, the grimlings, the long, dark hours on the sled—it had all been pointless, because of one stupid riddle. The king wouldn't see them, which meant they would never have a chance to plead for the prince's release. He would remain the dragons' captive until his father came and razed their glittering city to the ground.

She stormed out of the cave without a word. She didn't know where she was going. The icy wind spiraled about her as she stepped out into the starlight, and the fire she carried went out. She didn't bother to relight it—she just kept walking.

Nisha and Moss caught up to her eventually. Nisha grabbed her arm and spun her around.

"You can't just storm off like that," Nisha said.

Ember shook off her hand. She wanted to be alone, to think, to fume. "Why not?"

"Because we're in this together." Nisha's voice was stubborn. "We either succeed together, or we fail together."

Ember threw up her hands. "What does it matter? They'll never let us see the king. We have no way to get Prince Gideon back."

"There must be more than one way into the palace," Moss said. "Maybe we can sneak in somewhere else."

"More than one way," Nisha repeated. She turned back to the palace, her expression growing distant.

Ember watched her. She had seen that look, usually just before Nisha reeled off the answer to an impossible math problem. "What is it? Do you know another way in?"

"No," Nisha murmured. "More than one way in . . ." She looked up and announced, suddenly and imperiously, "Follow me."

"Nisha?" Moss said.

She ignored him. "Light, please."

Ember blinked. "What?"

Nisha made an exasperated sound. "Maybe dragons can see in the dark, but humans can't."

"Oh." Ember held out her hand, summoning another flame. Nisha grabbed Ember's other hand, and one of Moss's, and dragged them back to the cave.

Rose Gold looked up in surprise when they entered— Nisha was stomping so determinedly that she reminded Ember of Aunt Myra. *Children, is everything—*

"I know the answer," Nisha interrupted. "A garlic farmer."

Everyone stared at her.

"It explains the three hands," she said. "One of the hands could be a spade. And the twelve hundred heads—heads of garlic, you know? Two arms and two legs—"

And one eye, Rose Gold said. *I am sorry, child, but that doesn't work.*

Ember's heart sank. She opened her mouth to tell Nisha that it had been a good try, but they were going to have to figure out another way to the prince, as unlikely as that was. But to her surprise, Nisha was smiling.

"You didn't let me finish," she said. "'Garlic farmer' *does* work—if it's a one-eyed garlic farmer."

Rose Gold was silent. Then he let out a snort.

A good effort, he said. *But I do not believe that is the answer, child.*

"But it is *an* answer," Nisha said. Her face was flushed with triumph, her eyes gleaming. "Riddles can have more than one, can't they?"

The dragon's tail swished slowly back and forth. *I—*

"Nisha's right," Moss said. A slow smile spread across his face. "You said we had to answer each riddle. Well, we have."

Rose Gold was quiet for a long time. Ember waited for him to apologize again, to remind them that they still had another ten years, minus a few hours, to come up with the answer.

I suppose you're right, he said.

Ember couldn't believe it. "We are? So . . . we can speak to the king?"

The dragon lifted his tail and pointed into the darkness,

where Ember could just make out the hollow of a passage leading into the mountain.

That way, the dragon said.

They clung to each other as they walked. Ember's head was spinning—she half expected Rose Gold to come chasing after them, to say that he'd changed his mind. Nisha was beside herself with triumph, giggling in the darkness and muttering, "We did it!" over and over again. It was infectious—Ember found herself laughing along with her. Even Moss was grinning.

To Ember's relief, after winding around and around, the passage ended in another towering cavern lit with a flickering glow. She could see the edge of it, light spilling over the threshold.

"Where do you think the dragon king is?" Nisha murmured. "And where is he keeping the prince?" Her voice echoed strangely, and Ember wished she could draw the echoes back. The place was too still, too quiet. She tried not to dwell on the fact that they were deep inside a mountain with a massive weight of rock above them.

"I don't know," Ember said. "I suppose we should just keep going."

"Maybe he's out," Moss said. "If so, and if we can find the prince, we can make a break for it."

Something rustled in the cavern at the end of the

passage. Ember's steps slowed, and her thoughts ran immediately to grimlings. But surely not here? She drew a shaky breath.

They entered the cavern, which was enormous, even larger than the reception room. Pillars of rock curved from the roof and walls like twisted arms, and smaller rooms or passages beckoned from the shadows. The room was bright—or bright compared to everywhere else. Dozens of stone oil lamps had been placed in natural crevices and upon rock shelves. A peat fire burned in a fireplace cut into the stone wall. Nisha rushed over to it, warming her hands.

"Oh, that's much better," she sighed.

Ember made to follow her, but all of a sudden, a messy green shape hurtled out of the shadows, colliding with her with a *thump*.

Ember went sprawling across the ground, and the shape landed on top of her. Ember caught a flash of green cape and furious tawny eyes before the figure slammed her shoulder into the ground, pinning her in place. It was Gideon!

Ember struggled. The prince was off-balance, and she rolled him onto his back. His head struck a stone, and he let out a vicious curse. He reached for one of her wings, likely to twist it as he'd done during their scuffle back at camp.

"No you don't!" Ember grabbed a handful of brown-gold curls and yanked them as hard as she could. The prince cried out, then slammed his elbow into her stomach.

Ember, gasping, felt herself rolled onto her back. Gideon had gained the upper hand and was pressing her into the stone floor.

"You're on their side," the prince snarled. "You are! Admit it. You planned this, you monster! Is it ransom you want? Is that it?"

Ember wheezed. She knew she should hit him, or perhaps burn him—both were appealing options—but she could barely focus on anything beyond her stomach. Hands closed around Gideon's shoulders, and then Nisha and Moss were hauling him off her and shoving him hard against the wall.

"You . . . you . . ." Nisha didn't seem able to find the words to adequately describe Prince Gideon. She kicked him in the knee.

The prince howled. "Nisha!" Moss exclaimed. Then he seemed to reconsider. He drew his foot back and slammed it into Gideon's other knee.

"Stop," Ember said. Nisha paused midkick, glaring. She and Moss kept the prince pinned to the wall.

Ember drew herself slowly to her feet, holding her stomach. The prince glared at her. At some point during their scuffle, her hand or elbow must have struck him, for his lower lip was bleeding. His hair stuck up and his fine clothes were in disarray. Ember had never seen him look less princelike, and it made her smile.

"That's right, laugh," Gideon spat. "I'm sure it's funny to a creature like you to see the Crown Prince of Antarctica held captive."

"I didn't come here to laugh at you, you dolt," Ember said. "I came to rescue you."

"Not that you deserve it," Nisha growled.

"Rescue me?" The prince stared at her in cold disbelief. "How ridiculous. You *wanted* something like this to happen. You probably lured those dragons to our camp and told them to kidnap me. You're a liar as well as a monster. When I get back to my palace, I will hire a dozen Stormancers to transform you back into your true shape. Then I will see you locked in a cage for the rest of your life."

Moss's hand curled into a fist. Nisha's cheeks reddened. "Why, you—"

Ember held up a hand, and they both stilled, watching her mutinously. She came forward, very slowly, until she was standing only a breath away from Gideon. He was barely two inches taller than her, and she hardly had to look up to meet his eyes.

"You listen to me," she said quietly. "The three of us risked our lives to follow you here. We only survived because another dragon—one of those monsters you hate so much—brought us to this place. I don't know why they kidnapped you instead of killing you, but I guess everyone makes mistakes. And in case you were wondering: I'm not here for you. I'm here for them. I would love to watch them turn you into a giant icicle, or throw you off the side of this mountain, but if they do, Queen Victoria will tell your father to hunt them all down. So you can shut up and let us save your sorry neck, or you can spend the rest of your life—which may be very short—with 'I'M A DOLT' burned into your forehead."

She summoned a flame into her palm, and the prince jumped. He stared at her for a long moment.

"Why should I believe a word of this?" he said finally. "You tried to sabotage the hunt."

Nisha groaned. "Yes, and I'd do it again," Ember said. "I told you—I'm not here for you."

She glared at him fiercely. Gideon looked as if he was the one who'd been punched in the stomach. His face was pale, his eyes underscored with dark circles.

"I won't come with you," he said. "Go. Leave me here."

Ember gaped. The prince shook off Nisha and Moss and paced away from them.

"Are you—" she began.

"You heard me." He stopped by the fire, leaning a hand against it. "Go. I . . . I understand that you came here to rescue me. But I have no intention of going with you." He spat over his shoulder, "You can burn me if you like. I won't change my mind."

"You insufferable snob," Nisha snapped. "Are you really too proud to accept our help? You'd rather stay here and risk the dragons freezing you to death when they get sick of looking at you?"

The prince said nothing. He continued to stare into the fire. His back was straight, but the hand that leaned against the wall shook. Nisha opened her mouth again, but Ember shook her head, and she fell silent.

Ember went to stand beside the prince. "Here," she said roughly, holding out a handkerchief from her pocket.

The prince frowned at it. But then his manners kicked in, and he said, in his irritatingly polished way, "Thank you." He took it and pressed it to his lip.

Ember examined him. His expression was as disagreeable as always. But his eyes were red-rimmed, as if from crying. "The dragons didn't hurt you, did they?"

"They didn't do anything to me," he said. "They—they fed me. It was stewed seal, and it was repulsive, but it was food. They took me for walks around their . . . city. No one hurt me. No one made me do anything. They kept using the word 'gesta,' which I assume means guest, in their primitive language."

Ember bit her lip to keep from snapping at him. Her gaze drifted to his neck. "They took the heartscale, though."

"Yes." He stared into the fire, his voice low with anger.

"Surely you don't blame them?" Ember said. "You killed one of them. They're not just going to let you parade about with a trophy around your neck."

Gideon was silent. Ember waited, watching his face,

which swirled with emotion that she couldn't read.

"My father told me to wear it," he said. His voice was so quiet even Ember had to strain to hear. "He told me that if I killed a dragon, I should wear the heartscale at all times. He didn't tell me why—I just assumed he was worried that one of the hunters would steal it. He made me promise I'd do it, so I did."

"I don't . . ." Ember stopped. What he was saying sank in, and Ember's jaw dropped in horror.

"You think—you think your father wanted the dragons to harm you?" she asked.

"I think the heartscale made me a target," the prince said. His hand clenched into a fist, then relaxed. "And I think he knew that."

Ember couldn't comprehend it. It was impossible that any father would do such a thing—wasn't it? "But why?"

"He's been angry with my grandmother." The prince's voice was distant and flat, lacking the usual arrogance. "He's tried to convince her to let him turn the entire continent into a hunting ground, so that he could bring in as many hunters as he likes and get a cut of all the winterglass they collect. But she keeps saying no, we have to listen to the Scientists, and the Scientists want to stop hunting altogether. He goes on and on about it. About all the money he's losing every day because his mother is too softhearted to see reason." Gideon slid to the floor. He folded his legs and stared into the fire. "I've suspected this since they took me. I just . . . kept trying to convince myself I was wrong."

"It makes sense," Nisha said. She wore the same abstracted look she did when mulling over a complex trigonometry equation. "Your father thought that if you were killed, or badly hurt, Queen Victoria would be so angry that she'd listen to him. It's a logical plan. Horrible," she added quickly, as Ember stared at her. "But logical."

"Yes," the prince murmured. "If I had been killed by a dragon, Queen Victoria would have let my father destroy them all. She loves me. Sometimes it seems like she cares more about me than she does about my father. We've always gotten along."

Ember thought that Queen Victoria must be rather unpleasant, if this was true, but she kept it to herself.

"He can't have known the dragons would kidnap you, though," Moss said.

"No." Gideon gazed at the fire without seeming to see it. "I don't know why they did that. When they snatched me away from the camp, I was certain they were just taking me to a private spot to eat me. But . . ."

Despite her aching stomach, Ember felt a stab of sympathy as she imagined the terror Gideon must have felt. Nisha, though, didn't look inclined to feel sorry for him.

"But you haven't been eaten," she said bluntly. "And, well, if your father did that, he's clearly more horrible than you—which is saying something. But I still don't see why you won't let us rescue you."

The prince didn't reply. He just kept staring into the fire.

Nisha turned to Ember. "What do you think?" she said. "I say we take him with us whether he wants to go or not. I liked your idea about his forehead."

Ember let out her breath. "Why won't you come with us?"

"He doesn't have any reason to," Moss said quietly.

Gideon looked at him. Ember wondered if it was the first time he had ever acknowledged Moss's existence.

"You don't have a home to go back to," Moss said. "I know how that feels."

"You know nothing about me," Gideon said, his voice low. "None of you do."

Ember and Moss exchanged helpless looks. Ember was just thinking about how much less enjoyable it would be to threaten this quiet, morose version of the prince when there came the sound of huge talons clicking against ice.

Niwa freonda! purred a voice from the corridor. *New friends! You are welcome indeed.*

Nisha let out a shriek, and Moss stumbled backward. An ice dragon poured into the room, its every step as smooth as the pulse of water in a stream. Ember didn't even need to guess—she knew this was the dragon king, just by looking at him. It wasn't only that his scales gleamed like lamplit silver, or that his horns curled from his head like enormous sabers, or that he was the fattest dragon Ember had ever seen. It was that he commanded attention in a way no other dragon had—even his shadow seemed larger, darker, than those of the other dragons. Ember stood her ground, her heart thundering.

So you are the lovely children who solved my riddles. King Zaffre let out an enormous sigh. *Thank you. You have no idea how they have tormented me all these years. Like an itch I couldn't scratch. Have you ever spent months wrestling with a particularly troublesome riddle?*

Ember's traitorous knees were acting up again. "I . . . I can't say that I have."

Ah, but I forget, the king said. *Humans don't trade in riddles, do they?*

"No," Ember said. "We use money. Gold. Coins."

Of course, of course. Useless things. Such a strange system.

"You don't seem to enjoy your riddles much," Ember pointed out.

The king stared at her. *They are challenging, it's true,* he said. *But the feeling when you solve one—ah! There is nothing that rivals it.*

Ember swallowed. "I . . . I'm glad we could help."

Yes, the dragon king purred. *I hope Rose Gold wasn't too unpleasant. He can be terribly thoughtless in receiving visitors—he is so preoccupied with his accounts. And it has been a long time since our kind has had dealings with humans—I'm afraid that we don't quite know what to do with you.*

"Er, that's all right," she said. She found this last statement a bit ominous but chose not to dwell on it.

What can I do for you, children? he said.

"Well, actually, we're here because of him," Ember said, motioning to Gideon. He hadn't stirred from the floor when the dragon entered, or even started—as if he was used to the dragon king's presence. "Unfortunately."

Ah, yes. The dragon king examined the prince. *This one is very unpleasant.*

"We know," Ember said. She braced herself. "We—we came to retrieve him. To take him home."

Oh, the king said. *All right. Would you like some supper before you go?*

Ember blinked. And blinked again.

"What?" she said finally.

Supper. I'm afraid all we have is seal blubber—unless, of course, your taste runs to lichen, though your friend here didn't seem to care for it. But, if I may tempt you, this has been an exceptionally good year for coastal rock lichens—

"No, I mean, you'd let us take him?" Ember said. "Just like that?"

Of course. He is not a prisoner.

"Er . . . you did kidnap him, though," Ember said.

The king inclined his head. *A fair point. But we had no intention of holding him for long. We kidnapped him to help him.*

"How?" Ember couldn't get past her disbelief. "And why? He killed a dragon in cold blood."

We do not punish children for their crimes, the king said. *We hoped to teach him how he had erred by showing him that we are not his enemies, and by treating him kindly. This is how we deal with our own children when they take the wrong path.*

Ember sneaked a glance at the prince, who had gone back to gazing sullenly into the fire. "I'm not sure it worked."

Perhaps not, the dragon said. *But we had another motive: the heartscale he wore. It was imperative for us to retrieve it before more evil was unleashed.*

"What is he saying?" Nisha said. She had come to Ember's side, nearly hopping up and down with impatience. Ember translated for the others, leaving out her comments about the prince. "What do you mean by 'evil'?" she asked the dragon.

The Hungry Ones, of course. He paused. *Do your people not know of this?*

Ember shook her head. Then she started. "Wait. I remember my aunt saying that the grimlings—the Hungry Ones—tend to appear in places where dragons had been killed."

Sometimes. King Zaffre's glowing eyes swirled. *The Hungry Ones are a result of a terrible crime—but that crime is not killing a dragon. It is removing the heartscale from the dragon's kin. You see, the heartscale holds a dragon's spirit—a spirit that can remain there for many years before passing on to the Farthest Skies. If the heartscale stays with the dragon's kin, the spirit sleeps quietly. But if it does not, if it is removed by a stranger, that spirit becomes angry. It latches on to the place where it was killed and becomes a wicked ghost, forgetting everything but its fury. It is a terrible fate from which there is no returning. This is why the theft of a heartscale is seen as the most grievous of all crimes.*

Ember's head spun. She was filled with a sickening horror at the thought of what the prince had done. "Then that poor dragon . . ."

Fortunately, we arrived before any damage was done, King Zaffre said. The dragon who kidnapped your prince was his victim's kin. The dragon's spirit had not yet become corrupted. But it was close. Another hour, and we might have lost her.

Ember's hand went to the heartscale around her neck. "Is all this true for fire dragons, too?"

I do not know, the king said. Perhaps, perhaps not. Perhaps something else is unleashed from the theft of a fire dragon's heartscale. He peered at the one Ember wore. Where did you get that?

"It was my mother's," she said, her mouth dry. "My father—my human father—found it shortly after she was killed. He kept it for me until I was old enough to have it."

By the natural laws that govern our kind, then, your mother's spirit was safe, the king said. She will have known her heartscale was intended for you. Spirits are wise. Had your father kept it for his own selfish reasons, it would have been different. Or perhaps not—perhaps, as I said, there is a different law governing the spirits of your kind.

Ember let out a shaky breath. She translated what the king had said for Nisha and Moss, who both looked very grave.

"I'm sure she's all right," Nisha said softly. "After all, she guided us here, didn't she? She helped us."

Ember swallowed. Turning back to the king, she said, "I'm sorry for what the prince did."

As am I, the dragon said. It is a terrible crime to allow children to commit evil deeds. Were he a dragon, his kin would be harshly punished.

Ember looked at Gideon and decided not to translate this. "Then—then we have your permission to take him home?"

Of course, King Zaffre said. *Though my heart pains me to think that he may commit such a crime again. I hope that he has learned.*

Ember nodded, though she had her doubts on that front. Was it possible for someone like the prince to learn from his mistakes? She wasn't certain he was even capable of admitting he had made any—when Ember had translated what the dragon king had said about heartscales, he had shown little reaction, apart from a tightening of his jaw.

"We didn't actually come for the prince," Ember said. "I mean, we didn't only come for him. We came to help you—his people will be angry that he was kidnapped. They may bring more hunters here in revenge."

I see, the dragon king said. *We are ready to defend ourselves.*

Ember thought of the weaponry Prince Cronus had at his disposal—not only men and bows, but ships and cannons that could find the dragons wherever they fed and render the entire coast unsafe. She thought of how easily the hunters had shot down the dragon that the prince had killed. And she thought of the captive fire dragons, wounded and chained and broken, mere trophies to be awarded to the highest bidder. She couldn't let the ice dragons share their fate.

"You don't understand," Ember said. "Prince Cronus is powerful. You're all in danger from him—you must be more careful about avoiding humans. And perhaps if you used magic—"

The dragon king let out a hiss. *We have nothing to do with magic.*

Ember frowned. "What do you mean? Aquamarine said that you could do magic, but you chose not to. If the lives of your people were at stake, I don't understand why—"

Choice is a powerful thing, fire child, the king said. *We choose not to do a great many things that go against nature. Magic is one of them. Magic twists the world, forces it into shapes it was not meant to hold. Only evil can come of such a violation of the natural order.*

Ember couldn't hide her shock. "But . . . but that's ridiculous. It's true that magic can be used for evil, but it can also be used for good. My father is a Stormancer, and he would never—"

We have no dealings with Stormancers. The king's voice, once so warm and pleasant, now held a chill. *We do not speak of them. It is against our code.*

Ember was frustrated. "But—"

A tremendous boom erupted in the distance, followed by three shorter, sharper booms. Ember's hands flew to her ears. The sound was so loud it shook the room and sent an icicle crashing to the floor. Nisha fell against the prince, who reached out to steady her.

"What is that?" Ember yelled, for the booms, after a short pause, were continuing. They formed a pattern, something that reminded her of Morse code, but it had a more musical quality. Another icicle shattered against the floor, so close that it showered her in ice shards.

The dragon king cocked his head as the booms continued. After a moment, he closed his glowing eyes.

The terrible sound finally stopped, though its echoes lingered, chasing each other through the glacier. Ember warily lowered her hands.

The dragon king opened his eyes. There was a heaviness to him that had not been there before, as if he carried a weight on his back. *One of our scouts has returned. She brings dark news. Ships filled with hunters who came to our shores, and a terrible slaughter. So many innocents . . .*

"No," Ember breathed. "Where? How many dragons were killed?"

But King Zaffre was already turning. *I must go, children. You may stay here, if you like, until I return. Or you may ask Aquamarine to return you to your Scientists. I am sorry to cut our meeting short.*

"Wait!" Ember cried. Unthinkingly, she seized hold of the dragon king's enormous tail as he slipped out the door. The king froze and slowly turned to look at her over his shoulder.

"I . . . I'm sorry," Ember said. She released the tail, wondering if she'd just violated another part of the dragons' code. "But you have to take us with you. This is all because Prince Gideon was taken—it must be. If we can show them that he's all right, maybe they'll call off this attack."

Even as she said it, she felt a stab of doubt. If Gideon was right, and Prince Cronus had expected that his son would be injured or worse by the ice dragons, would seeing him alive convince him to call off whatever attack he had organized? Yet she had to try.

She gripped her mother's heartscale. The dragon king's gaze slid from her to the heartscale, and he seemed to ponder.

Very well, he said. *But I must warn you: I fly fast.*

TWENTY-ONE

THE KILLING GROUNDS

*Fire dragons had no common language, and possessed a limited
array of calls compared to most animal species. This inability
to communicate effectively with their own kind is likely indicative
of a primitive level of intelligence. . . .*

—*TAKAGI'S* COMPENDIUM OF EXOTIC CREATURES

"S top, stop!" Ember cried. "I see someone down there!"

The dragon king didn't seem to hear her. They
had soared over the continent like a storm, glaciers and
mountains and snowfields whipping past in an impossible
kaleidoscope. As they moved north, the sky brightened and
the stars dimmed, until finally the sun peeked over the
horizon, and Ember almost gasped with relief. True to his
word, King Zaffre was much faster than Aquamarine, who
had traveled at a snail's pace in comparison.

But he was also unpleasantly erratic—he often rode the
air currents, which eddied and dropped without warning,
and Ember's stomach soon felt as if it had been twisted
inside out, then put through a wringer for good measure.

Gideon had been sick at least twice. He rode across from her, dangling from the dragon's left front foot, his hood drawn miserably over his face. They had almost reached the coast now—Ember could make out a shimmer of blue in the distance. She wondered where exactly they were— the terrain was unfamiliar.

Ember poked at the dragon king's claws, which held tight to the back of her jacket. Finally, he looked down. As he did, the air current they were riding subsided, sending them tumbling through the sky. Ember screamed, and the figure she had spotted looked up, her bright blue hood falling back.

Ember gasped. "That's my aunt! Please, take us down!"

King Zaffre tilted his spiky ear toward her, and she repeated her request. After rumbling something in his throat that Ember couldn't hear, he folded his wings and dived.

It was the most terrifying thing Ember had ever experienced in her life. After free-falling for what felt like an eternity, the dragon king spread his wings to circle sharply out of the dive. The snow beneath them exploded, sending a white cloud into the air. The dragon king wheeled around the small figure of Aunt Myra, who seemed to be yelling something, gradually slowing until he was able to deposit the four of them on the ground. Ember slid and stumbled and rolled, finally coming to rest on her back, her wings tangled around her.

She groaned and did not get up. "I think I left my stomach up there."

"The prince certainly did," Nisha said, tossing a glower over her shoulder. "Again." She stood above Ember, brushing snow from her coat, clearly having recovered more quickly from the terrifying dive.

"Ember!" Aunt Myra was at her side in an instant, and her ruddy face and yellow curls were so comforting and familiar that Ember almost wanted to cry. "What on earth—I have never in my life—is that Prince Gideon?— *You stay right where you are!*"

This last statement was directed at the dragon king, who had alighted with sparrowlike delicacy on a boulder. Aunt Myra whipped a telescope out of her jacket and brandished it between them like a club. "Don't move! You keep away from her!"

"It's all right," Ember said. She forced herself to sit up, though her stomach lurched. "He's helping us."

Aunt Myra didn't lower the telescope. Her gaze darted from Ember to the enormous dragon snuffling at his wings, blowing off the ice that had accumulated as they flew. "He's *what?*"

Ember did her best to explain, but queasiness made her stumble—her stomach still hadn't made its way to the ground. Nisha picked up the story, recounting the hunt and the journey to the dragons' city in breathless, harrowing terms. Moss murmured a comment every now and then.

The prince sat in silence, his face turned away from them. His brown-gold hair was even more disheveled from the flight—it stuck out in every possible direction, like a blackberry bush.

"Wait a moment," Aunt Myra said, holding up her hand. She had asked only one or two questions, processing Nisha's tale with surprising quickness. Ember braced herself. She knew that Aunt Myra would rage at her for sneaking off and joining the hunt, and punish her in some way, perhaps by locking her in her room or ordering her to clean the chimneys. (Ember had never been punished for anything, and had formed her perception of what it involved from fairy tales.) Ember tried frantically to think of some sort of defense against the onslaught, but could come up with nothing—she had disobeyed both her aunt and her father. What defense would Aunt Myra accept?

Aunt Myra said, "You're saying that Prince Cronus has a fleet of ships anchored offshore? I don't understand—he wouldn't have had time to organize an attack of that size since Prince Gideon was abducted."

Ember was dumbfounded. "Aren't you angry with me?"

"It doesn't seem as if there's much time for that," Aunt Myra said, her voice grim. "Besides, I suspect your father will be plenty angry enough for both of us." Then she did something unexpected—she wrapped Ember in a hug. "Don't you do that ever again," she said in a quavering voice.

"I–I won't," Ember said, though there was little chance

she'd be joining another dragon hunt any time soon. She felt as if she'd been turned upside down again, as she had during the descent with King Zaffre.

"What are you doing way out here?" Nisha said.

"It isn't way out. We're only a few miles from the Firefly," Aunt Myra said. Ember started—the king had been flying even faster than she'd thought. "I was just heading back from the Consternation Hills. The other Scientists are still there." She motioned to the dogsled in the distance— Ember hadn't noticed it, in the tumult of their arrival. The dogs were crouched low, their gazes trained on the dragon, who calmly ignored them all as he attended to his wings.

Ember pictured the Firefly, its windows glowing cozily against the darkness, the Scientists settled in their armchairs, arguing with each other or pacing about the library. She felt a stab of yearning that surprised her. Had she actually started to see the station as home?

Children, the dragon king purred. *We must go.*

Ember nodded. To her aunt, she said, "We have to find Prince Cronus and show him that Gideon is safe. Right now, he has an excuse to slaughter as many dragons as he likes, and Queen Victoria isn't going to mind. We have to take that excuse away from him."

Her aunt nodded slowly. "Your best bet is to land close to the harbor and let the prince travel the rest of the way on foot. One of the sailors there can send word to his father's ship. I'll come with you."

Ember turned to the dragon king. "Can you carry all of us?"

No, he said. *It is stretching my limits to take you four children.*

Aunt Myra's brow furrowed. "My word! It almost sounds like he's speaking English! Do you suppose he would allow me to document—"

"I'm sure we can ask later," Ember said quickly. "Right now, we have to go."

"Yes, quite. Well, that 'no' was clear enough, even with His Highness's strange accent. I will meet you at the harbor." She whistled to the dogs.

Ember was relieved—and somewhat astonished—that Aunt Myra had agreed with her plan so quickly. But then, she remembered, Aunt Myra had always been like that, thundering about the station, flitting from this project to that project, giving decisive orders. It seemed to be how she was made. "Thank you," Ember said quietly.

Aunt Myra gave her a slight smile. "You can thank me once we're back at the Firefly, going over all this with a mug of tea." She glanced at the dragon. "Or perhaps something a bit stronger."

King Zaffre lifted them into the air again. They soared along the coast, then swung slightly south as the dragon followed whatever instinct guided him. They slowed, and the wind's roar quieted.

They are close, King Zaffre said, banking. *They—ah!*

Ember looked down. At first, she couldn't understand

what she was seeing. When she did, her stomach lurched, and she felt a ringing in her ears.

Below them was a field of death.

Dragons, possibly as many as two dozen, lay motionless on the snow. Their scales had been removed, and they barely looked like dragons anymore, as if something inside them had been taken when the hunters had stolen their magnificent armor. Ember closed her eyes, but still she saw them, as if the gruesome scene had been burned into her eyelids.

This is not a sight for children. The dragon king's voice was low, and Ember sensed a grief behind it that was beyond her ability to understand. He wheeled, gaining speed as he did. A few moments more brought them to a cluster of low hills, and here the dragon king landed. His glowing eyes had dimmed, his elegant neck bent, as if he had gained a hundred years in a single moment.

The humans' harbor is a mile that way, he said. *You must go. Take your prince.*

Ember couldn't speak. Finally she managed to choke out, "I'm sorry."

"It's so horrible," Nisha said. She brushed away tears.

Their heartscales have been stolen, the dragon king said. *It is very bad. Not only for us, but for any humans nearby.*

"What if we get them back?" Ember said. Her anger and sorrow were crystallizing into red-hot determination. They had to do something. They had to make this better.

I'm afraid that it is likely too late, the dragon king said. I must go. I must advise my people to stay close to the City of Spires, and to send word to other cities that the coast is no longer safe.

"But—but can't you do something?" Nisha burst out. "How about freezing Prince Cronus or his men?"

We do not like to kill, human child, the dragon king said. A note of disapproval entered his voice. Unless it is unavoidable. It goes against our code. Killing is the business of your kind. Even if I were to lead an attack against those ships that lurk out in the sea, it would not end well for us. Dragons have never been a match for humans—it is why we left our northern home. His gaze moved to the heartscale Ember wore, and he added, sadness deepening his voice, It is a lesson you know well, fire child.

With that, he spread his huge wings and lifted off into the sky.

Ember turned to Gideon. "Your father has his own ship, doesn't he? I'll bet you know what it looks like." Deliberately, she folded her arms. "You'll take us to it."

Something like panic crossed the prince's face, quickly concealed under a disdainful expression. "Suppose I don't want to."

"Suppose you want your teeth rearranged," Nisha said. "Don't you feel sorry about what your men did to those dragons?"

Briefly, Gideon looked as if he was about to be sick again. "They're not my men. And why should I care if a few beasts are slaughtered?"

Nisha made a disgusted sound. Moss said, "There's no use talking to him." Gideon pulled his hood up and turned away, no doubt to resume his sulking.

Ember would surely have punched him, or followed through on her threat to his forehead, if she hadn't seen a glimmer of tears in his eyes when they landed. Had it just been the wind stirred by the dragon's descent? Ember didn't know, but some instinct pushed her to swallow her fury at the prince, and instead say to Nisha and Moss in a casual voice, "You're right—there's no use talking to him."

Nisha opened her mouth to argue, but Ember fixed her with a "trust me" stare. "We'll just have to figure something else out," Ember went on. "Come on." She set off, Nisha and Moss falling into step behind her. "I wouldn't want to linger here, anyway. With all those stolen heart-scales, there's sure to be a horde of hungry grimlings circling these hills any minute."

Ember smothered a dark smile as, after a few heart-beats, the prince's boots began crunching through the snow behind them.

TWENTY-TWO

FIRE AND ICE

Upon tropical islands, fire dragons were abundant, especially in areas of heavy rainfall and flowering vegetation, with glades open to the sun, and where a variety of small animals offered easy prey.

—*TAKAGI'S* COMPENDIUM OF EXOTIC CREATURES

The harbor was a hive of activity.

Sailors rushed up and down the dock, their heavy boots thudding, dragging wagons loaded with supplies from the warehouses that lined the bay. Gas lanterns suspended from wooden poles shone at odd intervals, for the light was already fading, the sun sinking into another long twilight. Anchored in the bay were a dozen submarines and demiships, mighty and bristling with cannons, the wind playing through their flags. Ember, squinting, saw several empire flags, but she could not make out any with Cronus's coat of arms. Dozens of small boats rowed across the waves, either heavily loaded and making for one of the ships, or empty and returning for additional supplies. There was no sign of Aunt Myra anywhere.

"What should we do?" Moss said.

"Let's steal a kiteship!" Nisha exclaimed, a gleam in her eyes that Ember was beginning to associate with trouble.

"I think we should figure out where we're going first," Ember said. She turned to Gideon, who was leaning against the warehouse with an insouciance that Ember doubted was genuine, particularly after being sick so many times. "Well? Is your father's ship here? Do you see any of his men?"

The prince only glared at her.

"You can hardly expect him to be excited about seeing his father again." It was Moss, his voice quiet. "He did try to have him killed."

"Look at it this way," Nisha said to the prince. "The sooner we return you to your father, the sooner you can go back to ordering people around and strutting about like a ninny. You'd like that."

Ember sighed. She said to Moss, under her breath, "We could just wait until somebody notices him."

Indeed, Gideon's golden hair and expensive clothes were already attracting attention from the grubby sailors passing by. One did a comical double take, then rushed off in the opposite direction.

"What about the heartscales?" Moss said. "We need to give them back to the dragons."

Ember nodded slowly. Her left wing gave an odd sort of twitch, but she ignored it. "If they're anywhere, they'll be on Prince Cronus's ship."

"Or in the palace," Moss said.

"We might have a better chance of getting into the palace than we do of getting onto the prince's ship," Ember said.

"Less, I'd wager," said a darkly amused voice behind them.

Ember's left wing was twitching frantically now. She turned and met the eyes of the tall, red-haired man gazing down at them.

"Less," Lord Norfell repeated, "because I'm about to escort you to His Highness's ship. He will be ever so pleased to see that his son is alive and well."

Ember felt the ground sway beneath her. She saw Lord Norfell crouched beside her back at camp, his dagger slashing through the darkness. . . .

Lord Norfell laughed, a laugh that held no malice, but an almost childlike delight. "You've proven yourself far more challenging quarry than most, Miss St. George. You almost escaped me. Well done." It was a genuine compliment, and it filled Ember with sick dread.

"You!" The prince surged forward. "You kept at me about wearing that heartscale. Did you know something would happen to me if I did? *Answer me.*"

Ember fell back a step before that imperious glare, but Lord Norfell only spread his graceful hands. "Your Highness, I haven't the slightest idea what you mean. I am your humble servant."

"If you're his servant, who are those men with you?" Nisha said. Her hand was on Ember's arm, having pushed her slightly behind her.

Ember, who had been focusing only on Lord Norfell, realized that three men stood at his side. They were all well dressed, but too lightly, shivering in their London wools.

"Prince Cronus's men, of course," Lord Norfell said smoothly. "He's been keeping a lookout for your return, Miss St. George. The rest of the hunt thought that you and your friends had been kidnapped along with the prince. But you are a slippery creature, as I conveyed to His Highness. How very interesting that you were able to secure the prince's release. I look forward to hearing your account."

Ember thought back to her sighting of Prince Cronus in the harbor, how it had seemed Lord Norfell had his ear. "You're—you're working with him, aren't you?"

Lord Norfell seemed amused by this. "Working with? He's the queen's son. I owe him my loyalty. I am, perhaps, more motivated in my service than most. Prince Cronus seeks to expand the Winterglass Hunt. I will do what it takes to aid him in that highly entertaining endeavor. He knows this, and will reward me accordingly, as any generous ruler would."

Ember felt sick. "Where are the other hunters?"

"Oh, they set off on a rescue attempt after the prince was abducted," Lord Norfell said. "I expect they're still out there in the wilderness, chasing ghosts. I volunteered to return to Port Gloaming to send the news about his son's abduction to Prince Cronus—who, as luck would have it, had already sent for a significant number of ships. Sometimes fortune smiles on us, does it not?"

Lord Norfell nodded at the men standing behind him. "Mustn't tarry, gentlemen. Prince Cronus will wish to be reunited with his son as soon as possible. And of course, he's very eager to meet the rest of you." His gaze lingered on Ember.

"Wait," Gideon said suddenly. He shot Ember a look she couldn't interpret. "She remains here. Send her back to the Scientists. I . . . I don't want that creature anywhere near me."

Ember's knees went wobbly with relief. The thought of going anywhere with Lord Norfell made her feel as if the darkness of the port was closing in on her.

Lord Norfell cocked an eyebrow at the prince. "I'm afraid I must disappoint you, Your Highness. For your father has expressed great interest in meeting Miss St. George. Happily, I doubt that you shall have to tolerate her for long." He snapped his fingers at Cronus's servants, and they hustled the four of them onto the dock and into a small rowboat. One of the men casually removed a pistol from his coat and held it at his side, watching them.

Ember trembled as the boat was rowed out into the bay. It had to take a slow, roundabout route to avoid all the ice. Moss sat beside her, white. Nisha was on the other side, still clutching Ember's arm. Her gaze darted from

Lord Norfell to the man with the gun to the towering ships they passed, and Ember knew she was trying to work out an equation that she could solve, something that would get them out of their predicament. Gideon sat across from them. Ember could feel his eyes on her, but she didn't look up. She was frozen, unable to think, let alone move. Again and again, she saw Lord Norfell's dagger slashing toward her.

At one point, as the boat rocked to and fro, Ember's pocket gave a jerk. It was Montgomery—the doorknob must have woken up. Tears welled in Ember's eyes as she thought of her father's cozy office. Would she ever see it, or him, again? She placed her hand over the doorknob, and it stilled.

A massive ship loomed into view, hidden from the harbor by an iceberg. It flew Prince Cronus's flag, as well as Queen Victoria's. The rowboat was hoisted up the side, then Lord Norfell clambered out and disappeared. Prince Cronus's servants remained, their hands resting casually on the pistols at their belts. A few moments passed, and then the rowboat was lifted the remaining distance, and Ember, Nisha, Moss, and Gideon were hustled onto the deck of the ship.

The deck was deserted. Ember blinked in astonishment. The flags flapping in the wind seemed overloud. Then she heard a muffled splash, and a shout. A rowboat, crowded with men, pushed off from the ship and headed toward the shore.

Someone had ordered most of the crew to leave.

Ember's heart thudded. Lord Norfell reappeared, ascending the stairs from belowdecks. Beside him was a golden-haired man in a fur cloak pinned with an enormous fireglass brooch.

"Oh, good," Prince Cronus said. His gaze settled on Ember, bringing with it a sense of cold and emptiness. "You found it."

All the breath left Ember's body. Lord Norfell bowed. "My lord."

"Well, Gideon," Prince Cronus went on, his posh voice dry with distaste. "You've succeeded in impressing me at last. Unfortunately, it's in the most vexing way possible."

Gideon had gone so pale at the sight of his father that Ember wondered if he would faint. He said in a trembling voice, "You—you planned it, didn't you? You wanted the dragons to take me."

"Of course not, you stupid boy," Prince Cronus said with an awful calm. "I planned for them to kill you, or at least ensure you weren't returned to me in one piece. Your grandmother is already inclined to listen to the Scientists who argue we've judged dragons too harshly, and this isn't going to help. What sort of vicious beast kidnaps a child and then releases him without a scratch?" He gave Gideon a long, appraising look. "You are determined to be an inconvenience to me. You take after your mother in that way."

Gideon was still as stone. Ember wondered how much

of his father's true character he had guessed at before the hunt, and if he had simply refused to believe it. As much as she despised Gideon, she felt a wrench of sympathy.

Prince Cronus turned to Lord Norfell. "How many in the harbor recognized him?"

"Oh, few enough," Lord Norfell said. "As for those who did . . . their silence can be easily bought."

"What are you talking about?" Nisha demanded. She showed no nervousness whatsoever in Prince Cronus's presence, tearing her elbow out of the servant's grip. "You will release us at once. We didn't consent to be brought here. I don't care if you are a prince—you can't just hold people captive against their will!"

Prince Cronus didn't even glance at her. "Who are the others?"

"No one, Your Highness," Lord Norfell said. "Scientists' children."

"Then why are you bothering me with them?" the prince snapped. "Toss them overboard."

"No!" Ember screamed. One of the men grabbed her roughly. The other two gripped Nisha and Moss and dragged them toward the railing. The gray sea was laced with ice and snow—even brief exposure would be deadly.

Gideon's eyes were glassy. Briefly, as if drawn by some instinct, his gaze swung to Ember's.

"Do something," she mouthed, her eyes pleading. The men had hauled Nisha and Moss over to the railing. They were having more difficulty with Moss, who, watching Nisha being lifted into the air, was now snarling and struggling like a wildcat. Gideon was the only one not being restrained. But his expression was wild with panic, almost uncomprehending.

A horrible, inhuman snarl cut through the air. To Ember's astonishment, it had come from Moss—the man holding him almost dropped him. Nisha, punching and kicking fiercely, was halfway over the railing. Moss slammed his elbow into the man behind him, then turned to the one holding Nisha. Then—

He changed.

It happened faster than a blink. Moss's outline dissolved, and in his place crouched a small ice dragon, its eyes glowing, its scales like starlight.

Ember's heart stopped.

The dragon breathed a cloud of ice at the man restraining Nisha, and he stumbled backward, gasping and shaking, with icicles in his hair. Then it was over—the cloud lifted, and Moss reappeared, collapsing onto the deck.

Total silence.

"Well, well," Prince Cronus said, astonishment displacing some of the arrogance in his expression. "We have more than one beast in our midst, it seems."

Ember couldn't comprehend it. She could barely even breathe. She stared at Moss, who was staring at nothing, his face white with shock. It was clear that what had just happened was as incomprehensible to him as it was to them.

Prince Cronus turned to Lord Norfell. "I thought you were proficient in detecting spells, Norfell. Yet you told me that you had discovered only one dragon child."

"I don't understand this, Your Highness." Lord Norfell's eyes traveled over Moss. "The boy is not under a spell. I can sense no trace of magic on him whatsoever."

"How do you explain it, then?"

"I . . . I cannot, Your Highness." Lord Norfell bowed his head. "Please allow me time to . . . examine the creature."

"The girl too." Prince Cronus gestured, and his servant hauled Nisha away from the railing. "She may be hiding a secret of her own."

"Of course, Your Highness." Lord Norfell gazed at Nisha. His eyes held a terrible fascination. "Of course."

"This one, though." Prince Cronus gestured to Ember without looking at her. "You are certain the spell concealing her true form can be broken in the way you have described?"

"Completely, Your Highness." And Lord Norfell unslung his bow and lifted an arrow to it. "Allow me."

Everything stopped. Ember saw the knife in the darkness, now an arrow, tipped in dragonbone. She was going to die.

"Wait," a voice said.

Gideon strode forward. Relief blossomed in Ember's

heart. His steps were jerky, but his expression, as he turned to Ember, was cold.

"Let me," he said. Ember's relief turned to ash.

"You?" Prince Cronus's brow furrowed.

"This beast has been nothing but trouble since I met her," Gideon spat. "She tried to sabotage the hunt. I hate the sight of her."

Amusement flitted across Prince Cronus's face, along with a glimmer of pride. Ember didn't think for one second that he was proud of Gideon—more likely, he was pleased that his men could see that he'd raised a son as cold-blooded as himself.

Prince Cronus shrugged and motioned for Lord Norfell to hand over the bow and quiver. "I see no reason why you shouldn't do the honors, Gideon. You have a successful kill under your belt—why not make it a pair?"

Gideon faced her, the bow clutched in his hands. Ember's mouth opened and closed. *They're going to kill you too,* she wanted to say. Gideon wasn't supposed to be alive—he would surely only remain so until Prince Cronus and Lord Norfell devised a way to make it look as if the dragons had killed him. But she was frozen in place, unable to speak. In her pocket, Montgomery gave an odd jerk, like a heartbeat.

She met Gideon's tawny eyes, and saw in them a hint of despair. That was the moment Ember was certain she was doomed. Even the prince's kind streak, buried under arrogance and malice, was resigned to killing her. She gazed at him pleadingly, but a hard mask settled over his face.

Gideon lifted the bow, and Ember's breath froze. His hands shook, but his jaw was set as he drew back the arrow and fired—

On Lord Norfell.

The man screamed, sagging onto the deck, his hands gripping his leg. In a rapid, practiced motion, Gideon drew another arrow from the quiver and trained the bow on the three servants, who wore identical expressions of shock. At the same time, he shouldered Ember toward the stairs and shouted, "Run!"

Ember ran, her legs like jellyfish, her heart a stampeding horse. Past Prince Cronus, who leaped for her—too slowly. Montgomery rattled around in her pocket, as if it too wanted to escape.

A mad idea struck her. She had no time to ponder whether it would work—a shot rang out, and she spread her wings and soared down the stairs. The bullet ricocheted off the railing.

"I'm sorry about Puff," Ember said through panting breaths as she hit the floor. "But if you just do this one thing for me, Montgomery, I swear that I will have you gilded and fixed onto a door of oak and stained glass and all sorts of marvelous things—"

She ran for the first door she saw. It was ajar, revealing a cabin that she guessed belonged to the captain, given its size. Without bothering to check if anyone was inside, Ember slammed it shut, then wrenched the doorknob off. Someone said, "Hoy there!" from the other side of the door, but Ember was already twisting Montgomery into place, her quick fingers working faster than she had thought she was capable of, though her hands were shaking and slick with sweat.

The man yanked on the doorknob from the other side, but Ember sent a flame licking through the crack between door and floor, and he sprang back with a yelp. Heavy boots thundered down the stairs after her, and men were yelling. Another shot rang out, which went wide. Would it work? Would the room be empty now? She had no idea. She could only hope.

She turned the doorknob.

Instantly, the sailor's pounding was replaced by a heavy sort of silence. A watchful, waiting silence—

"Step away from the door," Prince Cronus said.

Slowly Ember turned, her hand still gripping the doorknob. Prince Cronus stood at the bottom of the stairs, pointing an arrow at her chest. A servant stood behind him, also with his gun aimed.

"Thought you'd make a break for it, did you?" he sneered. "Leaving your friends captive, while saving your own skin? I can't say I'm surprised. There is no honor among beasts."

Ember said nothing. She felt as if the door was breathing at her back, in and out.

Prince Cronus flicked the bow, a bored gesture. "Come here."

Ember stepped forward, holding tight to Montgomery, allowing the door to swing open.

Cronus's smile faltered. "What . . ."

Heat spilled into the ship, heat that rolled over Ember like a gentle wave. Prince Cronus raised his arm over his face, cursing. Then came a powerful *whoosh*, and the sound of chains snapping and wood exploding into flame—

A fire dragon thrust its head into the ship and let out a heartrending scream.

Ember barely had time to leap out of the way as the dragon crashed through the door, sending scraps of wood flying. Prince Cronus yelled, firing his arrow wildly, but before he could draw again, the dragon opened its mouth and blasted the entire hall with flame.

Prince Cronus and the servant leaped behind the staircase just in time, but everything around them was burning. The dragon sniffed the air, its nostrils catching the cold breeze. It screamed again, then stampeded up the stairs, splitting half the steps in the process. Another dragon followed closely behind, and then a third. The staircase collapsed, and the fourth dragon had to fly itself out, shattering the edge of the deck in the process.

The last dragon was smaller than the others. Ugly welts covered its back, and there was an iron ring around one of its feet, from which dangled a bit of chain. It glanced over its shoulder and spied Ember crouched on the floor. It gave a start, trilling low in its throat, and Ember felt a thrill as she realized that it recognized her—it remembered her! More shots and screams rang out on deck, and the young dragon leaped into the air, past the broken staircase and out into the night.

Ember wrenched Montgomery off the door. Then she spread her wings and followed the dragons. Fire roared and smoke hung thick in the air.

The deck of the ship was a wasteland. Scorch marks were everywhere, the railing was broken in multiple places, and the flags were burning. Ember leaped aside as one fluttered toward her like a falling star.

"Ember!" Nisha cried. Ember gasped with relief. There, crouched by the mast, were Nisha, Moss, and Gideon. She rushed toward them.

"What happened?" Nisha cried, grabbing her arms. "We thought you were done for, and then we heard the dragons, and then they burst out onto the deck, and then they screamed at us, and then Moss turned into a dragon again and screamed right back at them, and then they grabbed the prince's servants and tossed them into the sea, and then they flew away, and I just can't—"

"We have to go," Ember said. "Now." As if to underscore the word, the ship gave an agonized groan and listed to its side.

To her surprise, Gideon seemed to have the coolest head. "You lower one of the rowboats, then fly down to join us."

Ember nodded, and they ran for the boat. The three of them leaped inside, and Ember began to lower it. The ship gave another groan, but Ember ignored it. A few more feet. A few more—

A reassuring splash from below. Ember released the ropes and sprang onto the rail.

A hand closed around her ankle. Slowly Ember turned and met the eyes of Lord Norfell.

He lay in a half sprawl, staring up at her. He must have crawled across the deck—a dark trail followed him. His skin was the color of flour.

"Help me," he wheezed.

Ember froze. The ship creaked, listing deeper. A breeze sighed over the deck, and flames erupted through the broken stairwell, licking at the wood planks.

"Ember?" called Nisha's voice from the darkness below. Oars slapped against the water.

"Please," Lord Norfell said. He squinted, as if he was having difficulty focusing.

Ember's hand went to her mother's heartscale. It would have been so easy to shake free of Lord Norfell's grip, to leap into the sky and leave him to his fate. She thought of how alone she had felt as that dagger swung toward her.

Only she hadn't truly been alone. She had her father, and Nisha and Moss. Lord Norfell had no one. How could he, being what he was?

The deck groaned. At any moment, the ship would tip onto its side and sink. Lord Norfell slid back onto the deck. There was no mischief in his eyes now, no sly amusement. Only pain and an animal sort of fear.

Afterward, Ember would be unable to explain why she did it. She could only say that she had seen something stir in Lord Norfell's gaze, something that had stopped her from turning away. She grasped at his collar and dragged him over the railing, which was not an easy task. Tucking her arms under his, she launched herself into the darkness, sinking rapidly even as she flapped her wings as hard as she could.

Fortunately, the rowboat hadn't gone far. Ember and Lord Norfell landed in the prow with a thud.

"Ember, what . . ." Nisha's voice trailed off as she beheld Lord Norfell's unconscious form. "What did you bring him for?"

Ember only shook her head wearily. She sagged onto a seat beside Gideon, who, unsurprisingly, was minding the tiller, leaving the hard rowing to Nisha and Moss.

"Are you all right?" the prince asked a little warily.

Ember wasn't sure how to answer. She was having difficulty comprehending what had just happened. "Possibly. You?"

"Possibly." Gideon looked away. His eyes were red, and his green coat was slightly charred. He pointed up into the sky. "Look."

Ember started. The clouds were lit by bursts of red and orange. At first she thought it was the aurora, but no— it was the fire dragons, wheeling through the air as they tasted sky and freedom at last. After a few moments, one of them gave a cry, and they flew north, farther and farther, until the light they breathed shrank to the size of stars.

TWENTY-THREE

ALL THE COLORS
IN THE RAINBOW

*Contrary to popular belief, fire dragons were not lizards, nor were
they cold-blooded. Despite their reptilian appearance, their speed, stealth,
and biology made them more likely members of the Aves (bird) family.*

—*TAKAGI'S* COMPENDIUM OF EXOTIC CREATURES

Ember stirred. She was warm and cozy, and had no
desire to open her eyes. Outside her window, all was
quiet—it must be a holiday at Chesterfield. She rolled over,
intending to go back to sleep until her father called her.

A fluffy paw batted at her face. "Eat!"

Ember groaned. As if encouraged, Puff settled onto her
chest and snuffled against Ember's chin with her cold, wet
nose. "Now!"

"You cheeky devil," came a familiar voice. "Can't you
let her sleep, after all she's been through?"

Ember's eyes flew open, and she beheld her room at
the Firefly.

"Good morning!" Aunt Myra said. She sat in a chair
beside Ember's bed, her heeled boots propped on the edge,

reading a book. "Sorry about that—you wouldn't know it, but this little monster has had two breakfasts already. I thought it might keep her quiet, but now I suspect she sees me as an easy mark."

Puff jumped onto Myra's lap. "Now!"

"You'd think Lionel would have warned me that you had a talking cat," Aunt Myra said with a sigh. "Gave me a start when I carried you in here. Let me tell you, the last thing you want to encounter at night is a creature under the bed wailing death threats at you."

"Sorry," Ember said, grimacing. She couldn't remember Aunt Myra carrying her back to her room. The last memories she had were of helping Moss and Nisha row to shore, though her vision swam and her body ached with weariness, then of the boat crunching against the rocky beach. The harbor had been in chaos, the sky still lit by the flames of Prince Cronus's sinking ship. She had spotted her aunt in the distance on the beach, and then she seemed to remember falling, and green arms reaching out to grab her. She felt a surge of panic.

"Are the others—"

"They're fine," Aunt Myra said, settling back in her chair. Puff seated herself antagonistically on Myra's open book and began to wash her paw. "Nisha and Moss are still asleep. I offered Prince Gideon a room here, but he just stormed off to the castle with his steward."

Ember shook her head. "What happened to Prince Cronus?"

Aunt Myra looked grim. "His ship foundered. There were no survivors—apart from Lord Norfell. He's being treated by one of the sailors' doctors down at Port Gloaming. You'll be happy to know most sailors' doctors view painkillers as an unnecessary indulgence."

Ember bit her lip. "Would you have saved him?"

"No," Myra said calmly. "After what he did to my niece? Nisha told me what happened. I would have left him to rot at the bottom of the sea. But I don't question your decision, Ember. It was yours to make."

Ember couldn't meet her aunt's eyes. "I'm sorry."

Myra looked surprised. "For what?"

"For what? For joining the hunt! For sneaking away, for not telling you—"

"Oh, Ember." Aunt Myra let out a long breath. "I'm the one who should apologize. We didn't have the easiest of introductions, did we? I'm disappointed that you would risk your life like that—but I feel I'm to blame. I gave you very little reason to trust me."

"I'm still sorry."

"Well," her aunt said gruffly. She didn't seem to know what to say after this, so Ember asked, "What about the hunt?"

"Gideon's called it off. He sent a search party this morning to track down the hunters—they're still out there, you know, looking for him. As for what will happen in the future, that's anyone's guess. Gideon is the Prince of Antarctica now, and that decision rests with him."

Ember's stomach churned as she remembered the dead dragons. By now, it would be too late to find their heart-scales and return them to the dragon king. "Did Nisha also tell you about the heartscales?"

"As it turned out," Aunt Myra said, her mouth twitching, "she didn't have to. I ran into a gang of Prince Cronus's hunters when I was on my way to the harbor to meet you. Oh, they were crowing about those poor dead dragons, they were. Told me that all the winterglass had been taken to the castle to be inventoried. So I thought I'd pay a visit."

Ember stared. "Surely the prince's servants wouldn't let you into the castle."

"They certainly didn't." Aunt Myra patted Puff, which earned her a warning hiss. "But you know, I went to jail once for housebreaking, and twice for theft, and I'm happy to say I completely deserved it."

"You mean—" Ember's breath caught. "You stole the heartscales?"

"Can you steal something that's already stolen?" Aunt Myra said. "Well, in any event, yes, I took them into my possession. Then I sent them south with a team of Scientists, to that city you described. If I understood what you said correctly, the spirits of those dragons won't act up provided they know we're returning them to their families?"

Ember's eyes welled with tears. She couldn't speak.

"It doesn't undo the wrong that was done," Aunt Myra said softly. "But perhaps it's something."

"What . . . ," Ember began. "*How* did you—"

"How did I break into a fortified castle, staffed by several dozen trained royal guards, and get myself out again in less than an hour?" Aunt Myra grinned. "Because I've done it before. Windsor Castle, no less. Wasn't even caught that time. I'll have to tell you the story one day, when your father's not around—it's a real corker. Suffice it to say, I know these royal castles inside and out."

Ember shook her head, marveling.

"What, you think your father's the only one able to walk through walls?" she said. "My methods may not be as flashy, but they get the job done, and all without turning anybody blue. There has never been a thief like me." Her gaze grew distant and longing. "Those days are over, but I haven't forgotten."

Footsteps sounded in the hall. The door swung open, and Lionel St. George strode in.

Or, rather, parts of him did. A foot, an arm, and the hem of his black cloak. The arm seemed to be holding a tea tray, though it was difficult to tell, as the hand itself was invisible.

"Blast," his voice said from the vicinity of where his head should have been. "I thought I used enough invisibility powder, but I'm afraid, Myra, that I may have given several of your assistants a fright."

Aunt Myra let out an irritated sigh. "Of course you did. This sort of thing is why I never invited you to any of the Scientist parties back in London, Lionel."

Ember's father dusted his hair, and more parts of him appeared in a disconcertingly random order. Finally he stood before them, red-faced and smiling sheepishly.

Ember gave a cry. She made to leap out of bed, but her father motioned her back.

"I don't think so," he said, settling on the edge of her bed and taking her hand. "After what you've been through, I want you to remain in bed for the rest of the day. I would like you to heed me in this, Ember."

Ember looked away from the disappointment in his eyes. She had hoped her father would shout, or at least get angry. Anger was easy; anger was like fire, which burned hot but eventually went out. Disappointment, on the other hand, had a cold, lingering quality that made her wish she could sink into the carpet and live there like a dust mite. "Yes, Father."

He let out a long sigh. "Ember, do you have any idea how worried I was?"

"I'm sorry," she whispered.

Her father ran his hand through his hair, dislodging more invisibility powder (a good thing, for one of his elbows was still missing). "I'm not truly upset with you, my dear. I understand that it would have been a terrible burden to ask you to abandon those dragons. More, perhaps, than either I or your aunt could imagine. I just wish . . . well, I wish I could have been of more help."

"You did help," Ember said in a small voice. "It was Montgomery who saved us all, in the end."

He gave her a tired smile. "Well, it's good to know some of my spells turn out."

"Wait," Ember said. "How did you get here?"

"I'm not here." Lionel tapped his mouth with one finger. "And if I was, I could only stay a short time. If the police find out I've traveled outside the country, I will most certainly be locked up. Can't get off on a technicality, either—the judge specifically included travel via interdimensional portals in the conditions of his verdict, the smug stuffed shirt."

Aunt Myra rolled her eyes. They looked so alike, sitting beside each other, even down to their posture—the only differences were her father's height and Aunt Myra's lionlike mane of hair. "I found that doorknob of yours in your pocket, Ember," she said. "It wasn't a difficult leap to guess that was how you and your father had been communicating. In fact, he used to experiment on doorknobs as a teenager—none too successfully, I might add. I recall one time when I opened the door to the root cellar and nearly walked into this awful red maze. . . ."

"You didn't—" Ember stopped, remembering that her father had asked her to keep Montgomery a secret from Aunt Myra. He was gazing out the windows as if suddenly fascinated by the falling snow.

Aunt Myra folded her arms. "Really, Lionel. I thought we had agreed to be honest with each other. What about that rambling speech you gave when you visited me in prison, about trust and starting over?"

"I am all for honesty when honesty is warranted, Myra,

but I should remind you that the last time we spoke, you stole my pocket watch."

She snorted. "You should be thanking me for that. Blasted thing made the day start over again when I wound it. Only I was invisible, and watching myself . . . from *inside the watch*."

"It was a prototype."

"A prototype of what? An insanity spell?"

"As I've said before, I don't need you to comment on my spellwork."

"I find it amusing that you like to go on about how I need someone to protect me from my bad instincts," Aunt Myra said, rolling her eyes to the ceiling, "while you need someone to protect you from your bad ideas."

"Bad ideas? Was it a bad idea to get you out of that wretched prison, then, as soon as I was able?"

Myra turned pink. "You know I've promised a dozen times to pay you back for—"

"I don't want you to pay me back," Lionel said with a withering look. "I couldn't care less about the money. If your pride would allow you to accept my help once in a while, you'd realize that. That's why you've spent the last few years avoiding me, isn't it?"

Aunt Myra was blushing furiously now. "I was avoiding *you*?"

Ember, suspecting the two of them could go on all day like this, interjected, "Father, what about Moss? He can turn into an ice dragon. I don't understand it—Lord

Norfell couldn't detect any magic on him."

He turned his attention back to her. "Moss? Ah yes, the boy. In fact, I've already examined him. Magically, I mean. It's true that he is under no spell. But that isn't to say he's without magic."

"Then he's a Stormancer?"

"Oh no," her father said. "No, he possesses a kind of magic I've never sensed before. One that has nothing to do with lightning or stormspeech. I can only assume that ice dragons possess some sort of innate shape-shifting ability, perhaps connected to the nature of their element. They can assume human form at will."

"At will?" Ember stared. "Ice dragons can take human form? Whenever they want to?"

"Yes. It's not a skill possessed by fire dragons, that's clear. But who knows, perhaps they too have their own magic that has gone undiscovered. . . ."

"So Moss is a dragon." Ember was awed. To think there was someone else like her in the world! She could hardly comprehend it.

"Believe it or not, he is half dragon," her father said. "I used a spell I invented to transform human shadows into corporeal beings, and he—"

"You cast a spell on a child?" Aunt Myra said in a scandalized tone.

"On his shadow," Lionel said defensively. "The boy was perfectly safe."

"What if his shadow had run away?" Aunt Myra

demanded. "I thought shadow magic was against the law! They say all kinds of things can happen to a person missing their shadow."

"Well, it didn't run away, and the spell was easily undone," Lionel said, looking harassed. He shifted into an awkward position in his chair, likely to conceal his own lack of shadow. "And not all laws are sensible, Myra—you'd be surprised how rare it is for elected officials to know the first thing about magic. Anyway, no matter how I twisted the spell about, I was only able to transform half the shadow—the left half, for some reason. I assume it's because the boy is only half human."

"So one of his parents was human," Ember said slowly. "And the other was . . . a dragon disguised as a human?"

Her father leaned back, tenting his fingers. "Perhaps in the past, when they lived closer to our world, it was common for ice dragons to take human form and walk among us. Perhaps there are more children like Moss—human in appearance but with dragon blood in their veins. He can understand their language, apparently, just like you can."

Ember's jaw dropped. She remembered Moss's strange mood after they had met Aquamarine. She had thought she was translating for both of them—but Moss had understood all along? "He never said anything!"

"I expect it gave him quite a turn."

"But who were his parents?"

"That I don't know. Nor do I understand why he wasn't recognized."

Ember thought back. "The dragons told us there are other cities in Antarctica, with other kings and queens. He could be from one of those."

"Hmm," Lionel said. "I'd like to have a conversation with those dragons. These sorts of natural magics are fascinating. I have a great number of questions. . . ."

"Good luck," Ember said glumly. "The ice dragons hate Stormancers, and they won't talk about magic. It goes against their code."

"Does it? Interesting." Her father's expression assumed the abstracted look he wore when he was at one of his magical experiments. Seeing it, her aunt gave a sigh.

Ember tried to sort through it all. Just yesterday, she had lived in a world where she was one of a kind. That had always been a bad thing, a lonely thing, and she had often dreamed of having a dragon friend. Now that she had one, though, she felt strange. As if the world had been turned inside out like a Magician's pocket, spilling curiosities in all directions. She had always known where she fit in the old world, for better or for worse, and now she didn't. Then she thought of Moss, and how frightened he must be, and the strangeness softened into sympathy.

She felt an odd prickle at the back of her neck. She turned to the window and found a penguin staring in at them.

"Ah! How charming," her father said. He tapped on the glass, as if they were at an aquarium. The penguin simply sat there, staring in its calm, penguinish way.

"It's as if he came to check on you," Aunt Myra said.

"Er," Ember began, "there's something I—"

"Eat!"

Puff abandoned Aunt Myra's lap and stalked over to the penguin. Though it was bigger than her, she seemed to recognize it as a bird, and thus part of the food category.

"Puff," Ember warned, but the cat ignored her, and charged at the glass. The penguin raised its wing—

Zap!

Puff gave a startled yowl and skittered under the bed. The lightning bolt flashed across the window like a cloud of fire. Lionel St. George gave a shout, and Aunt Myra threw up her hands. When the fire cleared, the penguin was lying on its back several yards away.

"Bad cat!" Ember said as Puff hissed and spat. "Look what you did!"

Fortunately, the penguin recovered. It drew itself to its feet and ruffled its feathers, as if it had merely taken a nap. Then, with the air of an absentminded visitor recalling an errand, it placidly tottered off.

Aunt Myra fixed her brother with an appalled look. "Really, Lionel! You've been here, what, two hours? What-ever possessed you to enchant a penguin?"

Lionel St. George's mouth hung open. "Myra, I—"

"It wasn't him," Ember cut in. "I . . . I can explain."

And she did. But when she finished, her aunt simply fixed her father with another appalled look.

"They're all right," Ember added quickly. "I mean, the magic doesn't harm them."

"Good!" Lionel exclaimed, though he still looked a bit green under Aunt Myra's daggerlike gaze. "Very good. I'll, ah . . . I'll go for a stroll later, see if I can recover the magic they've absorbed."

"See if you can?" Aunt Myra said. "We'll see if you can outrun my Scientists when they find out what you've done to those birds."

"You could just leave them like that," Ember said, suppressing laughter as Aunt Myra's face went redder and redder. "I think they like it."

"Er . . . probably best not to," her father said.

Aunt Myra muttered something under her breath that sounded like "Typical." She poured a cup of tea from the pot on the dresser and pressed it into Ember's hand. "We'll let you rest now, Ember. Drink this, and sleep."

"But I'm—" *Not tired*, she wanted to say, but her honesty stopped her. In fact, she *was* tired—not the bone-deep weariness of last night, but still more exhausted than she had ever felt before.

"After traveling all the way to the South Pole, then flying a dragon back to the harbor to sink Prince Cronus's ship, I should say you're in need of a bit more rest," her father said mildly.

Aunt Myra shook her head. "She's your daughter all right, through and through."

"But . . ." Ember didn't want her father to leave. Seeing her expression, he patted her arm.

"I'll stay here until you fall asleep," he said.

Ember sipped her tea. Puff settled on her lap, purring. Her aunt declared, with a sidelong scowl at her brother, that she was going to make sure that Moss was still in one piece, and thundered off.

"Like a herd of wild horses, Mother always said," her father muttered as her footsteps faded. "Anyway! This is a marvelous place, isn't it? Do you know there is not a single species of insect on the entire continent?"

He leaned forward. "There is one thing I'm curious about, my dear. How on earth did you fix the spell?"

Ember choked on her tea.

"Oh my!" Lionel snatched the teacup away from her, then rushed to retrieve a cloth. "Steady on, there . . ."

Ember coughed and hacked. When finally she had regained control of herself, she said brokenly, "How I what the *what*?"

Her father handed her a glass of water. "I'm sorry, Ember—I just assumed you were responsible for it . . . or perhaps the ice dragons, somehow . . ."

"Are you saying," Ember said slowly, "that I'm not going to burst into flames anymore?"

Her father nodded. "The spell—well, it always had a visible flaw. Visible to me, that is, given that I'm the one who cast it. It was sort of like dozens of tiny tears—places where the edges of the spell wore thin. The tears allowed your natural flame to seep through, a flame that is as integral to who you are as your heart or your thoughts. But it seems that flaw is gone."

"How?" Ember murmured. Her head spun. Did this mean . . . could she go back to Chesterfield? Could other people be safe around her?

"That's the question," he said.

Ember distractedly summoned a shimmer of heat into her palm and ran it over her sleeve, which was damp with tea. Her father watched her, his brow furrowed.

"You seem to have gained more control over your powers," he said thoughtfully.

"Oh. I guess so." Ember shook her hand, and the flame disappeared. "I've had to use them a lot these last few days."

"Hmm." Her father's abstracted look was back. "That must be it. Fascinating."

Ember stared. "It is?"

"I can think of no other explanation," her father said. "Perhaps the problem was not the spell itself, but the buildup of energy beneath it. Using your powers regularly released that pressure. We shall have to test this theory further, of course. But I would recommend you continue using your powers as often as possible."

She lay back on her pillow, wincing as Puff kneaded her leg. "Does this mean I don't have to stay here?"

"You never had to stay here," he said. "But this certainly means that you can safely return to Chesterfield with me. If you like. I understand, of course, if you would prefer to remain with your aunt for a time . . . you did always love

Science, and she is certainly better equipped to provide an education in that field than I. It's your decision, of course."

Her father's voice was carefully even, though he hadn't been able to hide the note of hope when he had spoken of her returning to Chesterfield.

Ember gazed out the window into the snowy dark. The sky was a dusky rose mixed with golds and violets— all the colors, it seemed, of the rainbow. She had thought she would have to remain here forever, and that had made even a place as beautiful as Antarctica feel like a cage. She didn't know how she felt now that the bars had vanished.

"Rest now," her father said. He tucked her blankets in. "Later, there will be more time for talk."

Ember did sleep, then—a deep, dark sleep, haunted by glowing eyes and a glacier shaped like Chesterfield University, filled with ice dragons strutting about in spectacles and tweed jackets.

Whump.

Ember started awake with a yell. Someone had leaped on top of her, dislodging a yowling Puff from her legs.

"Oh, don't be so dramatic," Nisha said. "You've slept enough."

Puff crouched on her haunches, hissing like a round, furry snake. Her second-least-favorite thing, after strangers, was being disturbed when she was sleeping. "Away!" she yelled at Nisha.

"Oh, it's the widdle kitty!" Nisha scooped Puff up and squeezed her to her chest. "Moss said you had a talking cat. She's so cute!"

Puff froze. Never in her life had she been squeezed to a human's chest, and it seemed to have stunned her. Ember leaned back fearfully, certain that Nisha was about to lose an eye.

"We had a cat when I was little," Nisha said. She plunked Puff down on her lap, stroking her. "Aditi accidentally let him outside, and he was hit by a carriage—oh, she cried for days about it." She glanced over her shoulder. "Moss! Will you stop sulking and get in here?"

There was a sigh from the corridor, and Moss drifted into the room.

"That's better," Nisha said. "Honestly, you don't think Ember will be afraid of you, do you? That would be weird."

"Are you . . . are you both all right?" Ember said, while surreptitiously examining Moss's shadow to ensure it wasn't missing its head or something.

Moss gave a shrug. He sat awkwardly on the desk chair, looking as if he wanted to fade into the wall. Of course, he usually looked like that.

"Do you know that Baxter stopped us in the dining room and invited us to a game of lookabout?" Nisha said. "I think he just wanted to ask us about the hunt, but still. It was the first pleasant thing I've heard him say." She motioned to Moss. "He hasn't been able to turn into a dragon again. He doesn't know how he did it before. It may be something he can only do when his life's in danger, your father said. He's a very nice man, isn't he? I mean, he's extremely odd. But apart from that . . ."

Ember examined Moss. Though he looked clean and well-fed, there were dark circles under his eyes. "Are you sure you're all right?"

"I don't know what I am." He was quiet for a moment. "I always felt like I was part of this place. Now I understand why."

Ember didn't know what to say. Moss was both like and unlike her. A dragon and not a dragon, his past shrouded in mystery. She couldn't begin to understand how that felt. But if she could help him, be there for him as no dragon had ever been there for her, she would.

"I'm just afraid I'll wake up like that," he said abruptly. "Or that the next time I'm angry, I'll change again. I—I don't want to hurt anyone."

Ember touched his cold hand. Perhaps she could understand what he felt after all.

"Would you like to visit me in London?" she said. "I could show you around Chesterfield's botanical gardens."

Moss's expression brightened. "I . . . That would be fantastic."

"You can both come," Ember said, turning to Nisha. "If your parents will let you."

Nisha grimaced. She was still petting Puff, who, to Ember's astonishment, had settled into a wary sort of sphinx on Nisha's lap. "They'll let me. We had a talk. I mean, after my parents stopped yelling. When I told them why I ran off, my mother started crying." She paused, looking away. "I shouldn't have left without telling them. You know, Aditi, she . . . she got sick so fast. She wasn't even able to say goodbye. I just keep thinking, if I had died out there . . ."

Ember squeezed her hand. "I wouldn't have let you."

She nodded slightly. "I know. I had fun. Even when I was terrified! I haven't had fun like that since Aditi was alive. It was like having her back, in a way." Her smile grew sad. "You know, I didn't want to tell you this, in case you thought it was creepy. But you—you remind me of her."

Moss burst out, "I hope you're not going to leave forever, Ember."

"Yes, that would be perfectly awful," Nisha said. "I mean, I'm sure you'll have plenty to do in London. But . . . it would be nice if you didn't have to leave at all."

Ember smiled, reaching out to scratch Puff's chin. She didn't know what to say, because she didn't know what the future held. But she did know that, suddenly, she had two homes, where before she had only had pieces of one.

TWENTY-FOUR
THE PRINCE'S GIFT

*Ice dragons, perhaps uniquely among their kind, are capable of speech.
This astonishing discovery, first documented by Myra and Ember
St. George of the British Antarctic Laboratory and Research Station, has
led to unprecedented efforts by zoologists and draconologists to study
these elusive beasts, as well as the creation of a special conservation zone
at the South Pole.*

—*TAKAGI'S* COMPENDIUM OF EXOTIC CREATURES,
Second Edition

E mber hovered nervously on the threshold as the enormous palace gates swung open. One of the guards motioned for her to enter, and she took a slow step forward. If the guards hadn't been frowning at her, she suspected she would have run away.

It had been almost a week since the sinking of Prince Cronus's ship, and Ember hadn't seen Gideon once. He had kept to his castle, as she had kept to the Firefly, apart from her daily excursions with Aunt Myra to gather soil samples. Part of her had been hoping she could avoid seeing Gideon altogether.

But that morning, to her surprise, he had sent for her.

Inside the castle, Ember turned around and around,

awed. She stood at the end of a long, grand gallery, the floor covered with polished marble. The marble was decorated with leaves and hundreds of small, ugly fairies. Ember tried to avoid stepping on their beady little eyes—it was disconcerting to be glared at by things you had to walk over. Lining the gallery were marble columns, and at the end was a sweeping marble staircase. She could have been standing in a country estate back in England. What was she doing here?

There came a muffled *yip*, and a dog trotted toward Ember—Finnorah!

Ember crouched down to rub the dog's snout. She licked Ember's face excitedly. "Hello, girl. Made it back, did you?"

"She came straight home," a voice said. "It was the wisest thing to do, given that she thought us all dead."

Gideon strode out from one of the rooms lining the gallery. He wore an ordinary white sweater, and was without his green coat and sword. For once, he looked like a boy, and not a prince.

"Welcome to Gloaming Castle," he said, giving her a distrustful look that mostly undermined his politeness. Ember wondered if he would always look at her as if she was about to bite him.

She folded her arms. "It's lovely. But I'd rather not be locked up in it, thank you. I hope that's not why you brought me here."

"What? Oh." The prince flushed. "No, I'm . . . I'm not going to lock you up. I haven't told any of the hunters about you either. Or anyone else."

Ember wondered if she was supposed to take this as an apology. "Nice of you."

The gazed at each other in wary silence.

"You're leaving, then?" Gideon said.

"Yes. Tomorrow. But I'll be back to visit." Ember still wasn't entirely sure how she felt about this. On the one hand, she was overjoyed to be going back home to Chesterfield. But she would miss Nisha and Moss, and her aunt. She would visit using Montgomery (minding the fabric of the world, of course), but that wasn't the same. At least she would be spending Christmas with both her father and Aunt Myra. When her father had visited yesterday, he and his sister had only argued twice, which Ember suspected was some sort of record.

"Why?"

Ember frowned. "Why will I visit? Well, my aunt is here, and—"

"No, why are you leaving?" Gideon said. "I thought you liked it here."

Ember examined him. He stood with his arms crossed, wearing his usual arrogant frown. But there was something awkward underneath it, as if he was wearing a costume that didn't quite fit anymore.

"London is my home," she said.

He shrugged, as if he hadn't truly cared in the first place, but had only asked to be polite. "I'm going to London soon too," he said. "My grandmother invited me to stay while all this . . . gets sorted out."

Ember knew he meant his father's death, and pretended not to notice how his voice faltered.

"Will you stay for long?"

"No." Gideon gazed out the window at the gently falling snow. "As much as I enjoy my grandmother's company, I . . . I always miss this place when I'm away. Besides, there's so much to do here. My father didn't do a very good job managing the territory—Port Gloaming is falling apart, and the Scientists have been after him about building a proper road for years . . . It's going to be different now, though." He blinked, as if remembering she was there. "I have something to show you. Come."

Ember didn't much appreciate being addressed like one of his dogs, but the prince was already striding away, oblivious. Finnorah trotted at his heels, seeming reluctant to let him out of her sight.

He led her up the grand staircase, then along a hall with gold-leaf wallpaper and oil portraits of frowning aristocrats. Every room they passed had a fireplace, most of them lit, warming empty spaces. Though Ember marveled at the luxury, the castle intimidated her. It was too large, too empty. She was glad she didn't have to live there.

"Here," Gideon said, several staircases and passages

later, after Ember had become thoroughly lost. He drew a key from his pocket and unlocked the door to a little room with a window overlooking the ice-choked sea. It was lined with shelves and wooden crates, and smelled faintly musty.

Gideon strode to a shelf and drew out another key. He unlocked a small crate, then handed it to Ember.

"Open it," he said.

She drew back the lid. Silver light sparkled, dazzling her. She started—she was gazing at three heartscales.

"My father is responsible for those," Gideon said quietly.

Ember closed the box. She disliked looking at the heartscales—they felt cold and lifeless in a way her mother's didn't. "I think it's too late to save them."

"I know."

"Well, what do you want me to do with them?"

"That's for you to decide. They belong to the dragons," the prince said.

Ember frowned. "To the ice dragons. I'm not an ice dragon."

Gideon gave her a blank look that suggested the distinction eluded him.

Ember sighed inwardly. "Shouldn't you give them to King Zaffre yourself?"

"No." The prince's voice turned cold. "I will have no more dealings with those creatures. I've put a stop to the

Winterglass Hunt, but that doesn't mean I plan on giving them gifts."

"Or an apology, of course," Ember muttered.

"I didn't quite catch that," Gideon said with a glare.

"Oh, never mind." Ember smiled innocently. "Your Highness."

Gideon gave her a dark look that Ember might have found intimidating once. Now, though, she just wanted to roll her eyes.

"So you won't be hunting ice dragons anymore," she said. "What about those fire dragons that escaped? I hope you don't think they're to blame for what happened on that ship."

Gideon's face darkened further. Ember felt bad for mentioning that night, which surely the prince had no interest in dwelling on, but she needed an answer.

"A Spanish vessel spotted the beasts off the coast of Argentina several days ago," he said. "There's plenty of wilderness in that part of the world, much of it impassable. I doubt any hunter could track them. If they're wise, they'll stay well away from humans. Not," he added in a pointed tone, "that I expect much wisdom from fire dragons."

Ember opened her mouth. But the prince was striding away again, and she could only trail behind, stewing. He led her back to the grand hall, bowed his head stiffly, and stalked off. Finnorah followed, though she at least had the decency to cast a look over her shoulder. Ember was left alone with the box, staring after him. She wondered why he had bothered to summon her to the castle—if all he wanted was to give her the heartscales, he could have simply sent them to the Firefly. And now he had stormed off without even a proper goodbye.

She made an irritated sound. Well. She was glad to be rid of Gideon, anyway. She repeated this until the twinge of disappointment faded.

Ember breathed a deep sigh as she left the castle and strode down the snowy headland. In the distance, the Firefly shone bright as its namesake. The stars gleamed over a frozen land, a strange wilderness where ice dragons hunted and prowled, or recited riddles in their city of ice. Her breath rose in glittering clouds as she stood still, taking it all in.

Before her was a world of adventure, vast and frightening and wondrous, and she had a home in it, and people who waited for her return.

Ember spread her wings and leaped into the sky.

A NOTE ON
THE WORLD

This book takes place in the late Victorian era, sometime in the 1880s, in a world both like and unlike
ours. To give just a few examples, the British Empire,
while massive, never included Antarctica, nor did people
use canals and "kiteships" to get around London. In some
cases, decades were rearranged to suit the story; Robert
Scott, one of the explorers Ember learns about in school,
actually came to the continent in the early 1900s, during
the Heroic Age of Antarctic exploration. Unfortunately, the
hunting of endangered species was just as popular in our
world, though dragons aren't usually the targets.

The Firefly is inspired by a real, modern-day Antarctic
research station: Halley VI, which is operated by the British Antarctic Survey. It too is made of detachable modules
on hydraulic stilts that can be moved easily, which is useful if your research station is located on a sheet of ice that
has a tendency to melt and crack open. Like the Firefly, it's
by the Weddell Sea, and it also looks a bit like a caterpillar. Halley VI, though, wasn't built with the help of magic
(probably).

The ice dragons Ember encounters speak Middle
English, which was an actual language spoken in England

from about the eleventh to the fifteenth century. Any and all errors are naturally due to the fact that this is a dragon version of Middle English, which would have diverged from the human language sometime during this period.

Two of Rose Gold's riddles, "fish in a stream" and "one-eyed garlic farmer," are taken and (loosely) translated from the Exeter Book, a collection of poetry composed by a lot of different people that was written down in the tenth century. Not all of the riddles translate well into today's English. One of them describes a bird that hatches from barnacles, which is where people used to think some geese came from. Needless to say, few nowadays would be able to figure that riddle out.

Nisha's answer is, in fact, the correct one.